PATRICIA MacDONALD's

suspenseful tales have captivated readers across America, as well as in France, where she is a #1 bestselling author. Her previous novels include the Edgar Award–nominated *The Unforgiven*. She currently resides with her husband and daughter in New Jersey, where she is working on her next novel.

PATRICIA MacDONALD
SISTERS

W⊕RLDWIDE®

TORONTO • NEW YORK • LONDON
AMSTERDAM • PARIS • SYDNEY • HAMBURG
STOCKHOLM • ATHENS • TOKYO • MILAN
MADRID • WARSAW • BUDAPEST • AUCKLAND

Recycling programs
for this product may
not exist in your area.

ISBN-13: 978-0-373-18960-1

SISTERS

Copyright © 2012 by Patricia Bourgeau

A Worldwide Library Suspense/October 2014

First published by Severn House Publishers Ltd.

SISTERS

To the newlyweds Marie-Madeleine Rigopoulos
and Yannis Basho.

Happiness, always.

ONE

THE CAR PULLED up and parked at the curb in front of the red-brick Queen Anne-style house which Alex Woods had always called home. She gazed out of the passenger-side window at the bare branches of the trees surrounding the house, the shutters that framed the darkened windows. All the other houses on the block were festooned with strings of lights or had Christmas candles in the windows. Her house sat like a black hole in the middle of the twinkling, cheery block. It was late afternoon and the December sky was a pewter-gray. Mounds of gray-edged, crusty snow speckled the yard. Alex sighed.

'You know, Alex, you don't have to stay here,' said the driver of the car, her Uncle Brian. 'You can stay with us. Aunt Jean and I would love to have you. So would your cousins.'

'I know,' said Alex. She had stayed at her aunt and uncle's house when her parents died in the car accident late in spring. Frightened by the very thought of losing both parents in one terrible moment, Alex's two young cousins had treated her with cautious respect. Now, six months later, she imagined that her loss was ancient history to the two younger boys. They were busy thinking about what Santa might bring. Alex was just another relative, a grown-up whom they hardly knew. 'That's really nice of you. And I know you mean it sincerely. But I can't put this off. I have to face it.'

'At least let me come in with you,' said Brian. 'This is going to be tough.'

Alex shook her head. 'No, I'm OK. I'll be OK.'

Brian Reilly frowned. 'Your mother would want me to look after you.'

Brian was younger than Alex's late mother by six years, but he had the same ginger hair, pale eyelashes and shy smile. Alex had heard countless stories of what a wild young man Uncle Brian had been but now, his hair thinning, his wedding ring settled into a permanent groove on his finger, it was hard to imagine. She could still remember Brian, handsome and nervous in his tuxedo, when she was a flower girl at his wedding to Jean. These days he coached Little League and went to church on Sundays. 'You have looked after me, Uncle Brian,' she said. 'I couldn't have managed these last months without you and Aunt Jean. All that paperwork for the estate. I couldn't have coped with it, long distance. I really appreciate everything you've done. I mean it. And it's not as if you won't see me. I'll be at your house for Christmas.'

Brian frowned. 'I can't help but worry. I know you're not a little kid anymore, but when I look at you I still remember the day you were born. Your mom and dad were so happy that day.'

Avoiding his tender gaze, Alex squeezed his hand briefly. 'I had wonderful parents,' she said, and her voice quavered.

Brian gazed at the house, tears welling in his gray eyes. 'I think about them all the time, you know,' he said quietly. 'I miss them so much. Your mom and dad. Of course I loved my big sister, but I loved Doug too. He was a great guy. They were both...'

Alex nodded, but didn't try to speak.

'They'd be so proud of you. How strong you've been. It

must have been almost impossible for you to concentrate after the accident,' he said.

'It was,' said Alex. 'I thought I might quit.'

'I don't know how you did it. Finishing your studies after something like that.'

Alex had been completing the coursework for her masters degree in arts administration, out in Seattle, when the accident occurred. After a lot of internal debate, she decided to stay at school that summer so she could finish up in December. She was afraid if she came back east before she was done with her studies, she might fall into a depression and never get back to them. 'That's what kept me going,' she said. 'I knew they would want me to finish.'

'You did good,' he said.

'Thanks,' said Alex. Then she sighed. 'Well, I guess I better…'

'Yeah, right,' said Brian.

Alex took a deep breath and opened the car door. 'Thanks for picking me up at the airport, Uncle Brian.'

'When is your stuff arriving?' he asked.

Alex frowned. 'About a week,' she said. 'That's what the shipping company told me. I didn't have that much stuff anyway. I left a lot of it in the apartment for my roommates. Students. None of us had any money.'

Brian nodded. 'Well, the house is all cleaned up. And the car works fine. I turned it over the other day, just to be sure. Aunt Jean got you a few supplies at the supermarket. All the utilities are still on so you won't freeze in there, or be sitting in the dark.'

'That's good,' Alex said, trying to smile.

Brian glanced at the bleak house that had once been his older sister's home. 'I wish you wouldn't stay here, Alex. It's too hard. I know you have to clean it out if you want to put it on the market, but you could come over and work on it during the day, and stay with us at night. We're only forty minutes away.'

Alex shook her head. 'That's so nice of you. But I'm going to be looking for a job in the city. It just makes more sense to live here where it's only twenty minutes away. Besides, I grew up in this house,' she said, forcing herself to sound brave. 'It's filled with happy memories for me.'

'If you're sure,' he said doubtfully. 'Look, let me at least come in with you.'

'No, really. It's not necessary. I'm all right.'

'Well, I'll just wait here until you're inside,' he insisted. Alex did not protest. She got out of the car without looking at her uncle, pulled her bag from the backseat and waved at the car window. He watched her as she picked her way through the patches of snow up to the doorway. She took out her old keys and unlocked the front door. It opened into the dark vestibule. It still smelled like home. She stepped inside.

Standing in that hallway, as she had so many times before, she waited. She waited for her dad, carrying a mug of tea, wearing his half-glasses and his LL Bean flannel shirt to look out from the kitchen door, smile and say gently, 'Hey, kiddo.' She listened for her mother's voice to float down the stairs calling out: 'Honey, is that you? Are you home?'

It was silent. For the rest of her life, it would always be silent. She would never hear those ordinary words, those voices again. It's me, Mom, she thought. I'm home.

THOSE FIRST FEW hours were the most painful. Uncle Brian had been as good as his word. Every system worked. She was able to turn on every light to banish the feeling of overwhelming darkness. But she moved among the familiar rooms like a stranger, seeing each one of them through the lens of her loss. Each one was difficult to walk into. Whether it was putting her clothes away in the closet, or opening a cabinet to get a glass, every action felt like a painful first. It wasn't as if she had never been alone in the house before. Being an only child, she had often had the house to herself. As a kid, she had sometimes imagined painting the rooms a different color, changing the decor to suit her own teenaged tastes. Well, now it was hers to do with as she pleased. She owned this house now. She shared it with no one. She would live in it alone. Every move she made reminded her of that shattering fact. She wondered if it would have been easier to walk into these rooms with a brother or a sister by her side. Yes, she thought. Without a doubt, it would have been easier. Someone else who knew. Someone else who felt the same loss.

No point in thinking of that, she told herself. She hadn't minded being an only child. Her father, an only child himself, never saw any problem with it. Her mother fretted aloud sometimes, especially when she was having a hard time fitting in at school, wishing they had been able to give her a sibling. Alex never paid much attention to that fretting. She had her dogs and her cats, always, and friends, neighbors. It was fine. She never could understand what her mother was worrying about.

Now, she knew. Not that she would change it. That was like one of those exercises in trying to change the past. If you could change one thing in the past, it might change every subsequent thing. You might regret the differences. There was no point in thinking about it. She told herself all these things, eating alone at the kitchen table, locking the doors and going to bed alone in her old room. Maybe if she had a husband. Or children. But she had made other choices, focusing on school and planning a career. She had no way of knowing that her family would be wiped out in an instant. No one would ever imagine such a fate for themselves.

In the succeeding days, as she settled into the house, her phone buzzed constantly with messages of encouragement from friends back in Seattle.

The job of cleaning out the house seemed impossible and she briefly considered leaving everything in place and just walking away. Her parents' belongings seemed to confront her with fresh pain every time she opened a drawer or a door. She knew what her mother would tell her to do. Clean it out. Give their belongings to those who really needed them. Alex picked up empty boxes from the liquor store and began to pack up clothes and shoes for the Salvation Army. Each day she woke up and was startled and depressed anew. In her father's office she looked with a heavy heart at his shelves of books which lined the walls. Who would want them? People didn't collect books anymore, unless they were valuable. How was she to know which was which? She made a note to call her father's colleagues at the Revolutionary War Museum in Boston, where he had been curator, and ask. Meanwhile, she thought, they could just stay there. They weren't hurting anything.

Her first weekend at home she was invited to the annual neighborhood Christmas party. At first she said no, but her parents' old friends and neighbors pleaded with her to come. The night of the party she dawdled until it was almost too late, but finally ran across the street, coatless, avoiding the mounds of snow, and arrived, shivering, at the front door of this year's hostess.

'Alex!' cried Laney Thompson as she enveloped Alex in a tight, reassuring hug. 'I'm so glad you came. Oh, look who came to see you!'

Alex felt something brush against her legs. She looked down and saw her parents' calico cat, Castro, rubbing lightly against her.

Immediately her eyes filled with tears. She knew that Laney had taken the cat after their death. She had been grateful for Laney's offer, since she was living in Seattle at the time and her apartment building forbade pets. But seeing the cat again brought back sweet, painful memories.

Alex crouched down and rubbed Castro around the ruff of his neck. 'Hi, buddy,' she whispered. 'Remember me? How ya doin'?'

'He's doing fine,' said Laney. 'He's made himself right at home. But if you want him back…'

'No, no,' said Alex. 'That's OK. He seems happy here.'

'Well, if you change your mind, you know you can just tell me,' said Laney. 'Now, stop fiddling with that cat and come say hello. There's a lot of people here who want to see you.'

Alex quickly wiped her eyes, stood up and took a deep breath. Laney squeezed her hand for courage, and then led Alex through the cheerful, crowded house which smelled of pine boughs and cinnamon. She placed a punch glass in Alex's hand, and stayed beside her as neighbors came to kiss her and make her welcome.

'Do you remember Seth?' Laney asked as a tall man wearing a tweed jacket over a black T-shirt approached them. He had wavy, uncombed dark brown hair and dark eyes behind black-rimmed glasses. 'He teaches out at the University of Chicago.'

Alex nodded, although it had been years since she had even spoken to Seth Paige or his older sister, Janet. They had both been out of high school by the time Alex got there. She had seen them at neighborhood parties over the years. Janet, now a mother of two, had come, with her father, to her parents' funeral. 'Sure, how are you, Seth?' Alex asked.

'I'm fine,' he said. 'I wanted to tell you how sorry I was about your parents. I couldn't make it back from Chicago for the funeral, but Janet and my dad told me about it.'

'Thank you,' said Alex, stiffening. She didn't want to talk about her parents' death. It was one of the reasons why she had tried to avoid the party. 'Home for Christmas?' she asked brightly.

'My dad had surgery and he needed someone to look after him. It was semester break and Janet has to spend Christmas with her in-laws in Virginia so…I was elected.'

'Is he OK?' Alex asked. 'Your dad?'

'Getting better,' said Seth, nodding. 'So, are you back to stay?' he asked.

Alex shrugged. 'I'm going to look for a job in Boston. I just got my masters in arts administration.'

'You're looking for a museum job?'

'Museums, galleries…'

'Like your dad, eh? You know, your dad helped me out a lot when I was working on my dissertation,' Seth said. 'He was a walking encyclopedia when it came to the American Revolution. And a great guy as well.'

Alex felt the tears welling up and nodded. 'Yes, well, thanks. It was nice to see you again.' She smiled blindly and turned away from him, pretending to look at the food table. When he began to talk to someone else, she set her punch glass down on the table and headed for the front door. On her way out, she thanked Laney, dismissing her protests that she should stay. She hurried back across the street and into the safety of the house. It's the holiday, she told herself, as she turned out the front porch lights. It makes everything harder.

SHE HAD BEEN home for one week when the phone rang and the caller, a woman, asked to speak to Alex Woods. 'This is she,' said Alex.

'I'm calling from John Killebrew's office. Mr Killebrew was your parents' attorney.'

'Yes, I know,' said Alex. 'I met with him when I was home for their funeral.'

'Mr Killebrew would like you to come into the office. He has something to discuss with you.'

Alex felt vaguely guilty and wondered if there were legal matters which she had left unattended. It had been so difficult these last two semesters at school, summer and fall to try and focus on her work and make decisions about her parents' estate as well. She had not inherited a lot besides the house, but there were several bank accounts and insurance, as well as a few outstanding debts. As her parents' executor, Uncle Brian had handled most of it. But he had been scrupulous about asking her opinion in every matter. 'All right,' she said.

'Shall we say tomorrow at ten?' the secretary asked brightly.

Alex looked around at the piles of belongings still unsorted, the half-empty boxes on the dining room table. 'OK. Ten o'clock,' she said.

JOHN KILLEBREW'S OFFICE was in a Victorian house in the center of Chichester, the town where Alex grew up. She had often passed that house lugging her books on her way to the high school, never dreaming that in less than ten years she would be entering that office, orphaned, and trying to cope with the myriad financial and legal matters that attended the sudden loss of both her parents.

Thanks to Uncle Brian, much of it had been handled over the last six months. She had come to this office twice to sign a lot of legal documents when she was back here for the funeral, and Uncle Brian had taken care of the rest. There were probably only some details to discuss. She walked up to the bespectacled, middle-aged receptionist in the hushed office, which resembled an English gentlemen's club. 'I'm Alex Woods,' she said.

The receptionist smiled at her kindly. 'I know who you are,' she said. 'He told me to send you in when you arrived. Go right ahead. It's the door at the end of the hall.'

'I know where it is,' said Alex. 'Thanks.'

'I'll let him know you're here.'

THE GRAY-HAIRED attorney arose from his chair and came around to shake Alex's hand. 'Have a seat,' he said, indicating a maroon leather chair in front of his desk. Alex sat down.

'How's it going?'

Alex shrugged. 'I'm trying to clean out the house. It's a difficult process.'

'I'm sure it is,' said the attorney.

'I didn't know whether you might want my uncle to be here,' said Alex. 'With him being the executor of my parents' estate.'

'No, no,' said Killebrew, shaking his head somberly. 'There's no need for that. This isn't actually…about the estate.'

Alex frowned at him. 'It isn't?'

'No, Alex.' He folded his arms over his chest and frowned. 'I have something to give you.' He reached across his desk, picked up an envelope and handed it to her.

Alex immediately recognized the neat, bookkeeper's handwriting. 'From…my mother,' she said.

John Killebrew nodded.

Alex was flustered. 'Should I read it now?'

'I think it might be a good idea,' he said. 'You may have some questions.'

Alex tore open the envelope with trembling hands and pulled out the sheet of paper. She began to read.

My darling girl,
If you are reading this, that means I am gone. I asked Mr Killebrew to keep this for me, in the event that I predeceased your father, and give it directly to you. I hope you will not think worse of me because of what I'm going to tell you. I feel sure that you will understand.

A long time ago, when I was still a teenager, I got pregnant. As you know, being a Catholic, abortion was really out of the question for me. Instead of going to college, I went away to a home for unwed mothers, had the baby and gave her up for adoption. I was told that she went to a good family. Second semester I enrolled at the university as planned. I got my degree, met your dad, and you know the rest.

After you were born, there were complications and it turned out that I couldn't have any more children. I always regretted not being able to give you a brother or sister, and have been tormented by the knowledge that you actually have a sister whom you know nothing about. I'm afraid I can't tell you anything about her, because it was a closed adoption. I often hoped that she would seek me out but, so far, she has not done so.

I don't know what, if anything, you might want to do about this, but I didn't want to leave this earth without letting you know that, somewhere, you have a sister.

Darling, if you want to try to find her, you have my blessing. If you decide to tell your father about the contents of this letter, that's up to you. It must be your decision. I have chosen to keep it a secret all these years. He probably would have understood, just as I know that you will, but it was a secret I kept

*to myself. Still, I think that you have a right to know
that your sister exists. I'm sure that you will do what's
best. I love you more than anything,*
Mom

Alex read the letter again. Her heart was thudding and
her hands were icy. Finally she looked up at the attorney.
'Do you know about what this says?' she asked.

John Killebrew nodded. 'Yes, your mother confided in
me, and she trusted me to use my judgment. She wanted,
at least initially, for this information to stay between you
and her.'

'She never told my father,' Alex said.

'That's correct. As it turned out, your father, obviously,
did not survive her.'

'No,' said Alex.

'I hope you understand why I chose not to give this to
you immediately after your parents' death. It seemed as if
you had enough to cope with at the time.'

Alex stared down at the letter in her hands and nodded.
'I appreciate that.'

'I don't know what you want to do about this…' he said.

Alex shook her head. 'I don't either.'

'Think it over,' he said. 'There's no hurry to decide.'

'Why didn't she tell me?' Alex cried.

'I don't know. I'm sure she had her reasons.'

'I feel…blindsided.' Alex's voice sounded surly to her
ears.

'I'm sure you do, right now. But this could turn out to
be a great consolation to you, Alex. A sister you never
knew you had.'

'I don't want some sister I never knew,' Alex replied angrily, tears springing to her eyes. 'I want my parents back.'

John Killebrew watched her silently, knowing better than to remind her of the futility of that wish.

Alex brushed her tears away impatiently, and took a deep breath. 'I'm sorry, Mr Killebrew. It's not your fault. Look, if I did decide to try and find this…woman…'

'I won't lie to you. There are obstacles. In a closed adoption, only the adoptee is allowed to instigate a search for the birth family. But if you decide that you want to find your sister you can petition the court to have the records released, and see what the judge decides. We can help you with that.'

'I don't know,' Alex said. She sat numbly in the chair, the letter dangling from her fingertips.

'It's a lot to absorb all at once,' said the attorney. 'Go home and think it over.'

As if I had any choice, she wanted to say. Instead she said, 'I will.'

TWO

FOR THREE DAYS, Alex found her thoughts gravitating to the sister she had never met. It was easier to ruminate about whether or not to search for this long-lost sister than to face directly the prospect of this first Christmas alone. As she hunted in the attic for wrapping paper, or tried, with sorry results, to replicate her mother's toffee, Alex felt assaulted by the expectations of the season. She didn't want to do any of it. She wanted to spend Christmas alone in a dark room, with a blanket over her head. But she knew that her aunt and uncle would never allow it. In their good-hearted way they were determined to include her, to remind her that she still had a family, even if she felt as if she didn't. And she knew what her parents would want her to do. They would want her to try.

She avoided midnight Mass on Christmas Eve, and wore her robe and pajamas until Christmas afternoon. She fielded phone calls and texts and, at around two o'clock, was dismayed to hear a knock at the front door. She opened it a few inches and looked out, frowning. Seth Paige stood on the front step, holding a Christmas cookie tin and a bottle of wine.

He smiled, and then frowned as he realized she was in a robe and pajamas. He looked upset at the sight of her.

'Merry Christmas,' said Alex.

'Are you…are you spending Christmas alone?' he asked.

'No,' said Alex, pushing her hair out of her face. 'I just…um…I just haven't gotten dressed yet. What's up?'

'I brought you some Christmas cheer,' he said, hoisting the wine bottle. 'And some of these cookies. Janet went on a baking binge before she left town.'

Alex opened the door a little wider and accepted the wine and the cookies. 'Do you want to come in?' she asked in a discouraging tone.

Seth hesitated. 'Yes,' he said. 'Just for a minute.'

Alex let him in and tightened the sash on her robe. She led him past the stack of boxes in the hallway into the living room. She sat down on the edge of a sofa cushion, the wine tucked in the crook of her arm, the cookie tin perched on her lap.

Seth sat down in a chair opposite her and rubbed his large hands together. 'I wanted to come by because I felt bad about the other night. I was afraid that you might have left the party because of some stupid thing I said about your dad.'

Alex shook her head. 'No, no. I wasn't in a party mood,' she said. 'Actually, it was nice, what you said about Dad.'

'Are you spending most of your time alone here?' he asked, unable to keep the reproof out of his voice.

Alex sighed and looked around at the disorder. 'Well, I'm trying to clean the house out. It's really kind of solitary work, you might say.'

'Tough going through everything,' he said. He pushed his glasses automatically back up on his nose.

'Yes,' she said. 'I don't know what to do with half the stuff. Their clothes… I think my mom saved every piece of Tupperware… All my dad's books… Would you be interested in any of those? I hate to throw them away.'

'I'll come and take a look. Absolutely,' he said, nodding.

'Do you want to look now?' she asked.

'No, another time. It's Christmas.'

Alex nodded, slightly embarrassed. 'Right.'

Seth hesitated. 'I know how it is,' he said. 'I remember the Christmas my mother died. I was only twelve, but I'll never forget it. I mean, everything about her death sucked, but that Christmas really stands out in my mind.'

Alex smiled and felt herself uncoil slightly. He really did know. She could not even remember Mrs Paige, but women in the neighborhood used to cluck about how tough it must be for Mr Paige to raise his kids alone. 'You're right,' she said. 'It's not good.'

'I just want to be sure that you're not going to sit here by yourself for the rest of the day,' he said. 'You can always come down and join me and my dad. He's still pretty much confined to a chair, but there's food, some decorations and the requisite loop of Christmas songs.'

Alex smiled. 'Thanks. That's really nice. But I'm going to my aunt and uncle's for Christmas dinner.'

'You're sure?' he said.

'Scout's honor,' said Alex, awkwardly raising two fingers.

'In fact, I should probably get dressed.' She stood up. 'But thank you for the cookies and the wine. That was thoughtful.'

'No problem,' said Seth. He stood up and headed to the front door. Alex shuffled along in his wake in her slippers. 'I know it doesn't feel this way,' he said, turning to her, leaning down unexpectedly and kissing her cheek. 'But merry Christmas, Alex.'

Alex had a jumble of impressions of his soft black hair brushing her face, the sharp edge of his glasses, his masculine scent, his bristly cheek. She wondered, anxiously, if she had brushed her teeth. Before she could respond he was quietly closing the front door behind him.

After Seth left, Alex placed his Christmas offerings in the kitchen. That was so nice of him, she thought. Then she trudged upstairs and managed to find a dark green sweater in her closet, a long, narrow black skirt and black boots to wear to her uncle's house. In her parents' bedroom she found a star pendant on a long chain on her mother's bureau which Alex had given her mother for Christmas several years ago. Alex looped it around her neck and the pendant sparkled against her dark sweater. She patted the star tenderly and left it on.

In her own room she combed her hair and applied make-up to alleviate the paleness of her skin, the circles under her eyes. She didn't want to look like a Grinch. Her nephews, Aiden and Finn, would be excited about this happiest of days. She understood that. She had always loved Christmas as a child. Even if this was the worst Christmas of her life, she wasn't going to deliberately spoil theirs. It was time to go.

THE REILLYS' HOUSE was brightly lit, fragrant with the scent of roasting turkey, and buzzing with excitement. Most of the excitement was generated by Aiden and Finn, as well as the younger members of Jean's family who were in attendance. But Alex saw the sadness in her uncle's eyes when he embraced her.

'I'm glad you came,' he said.

Alex nodded. 'We always come here for Christmas,' she said bravely.

Brian cleared his throat. 'And you will always be welcome here,' he said. 'All your life. Don't forget that.'

'Brian. Can you pour the eggnog?' Jean called out.

Alex pushed him away. 'Go on. Go. I'll be fine.'

And, in the end, she was all right. Jean's family members were both solicitous and full of goodwill. The kids were boisterous, the dinner was delicious—as always—and Alex made a point of helping out where she could.

It was not until evening, when the house was quieting
down and most of the guests were gone, that Alex felt the
melancholy descending again. She sat down in the family
room in an armchair beside the tree and gazed at the glit-
tering ornaments and lights.

Her heart felt as dark as the night sky outside. She
wished she had not promised to stay over. They had wanted
her to come and stay on Christmas Eve, but that was out of
the question. She dreaded the whole idea of her little cousins rising at the crack of dawn on Christmas morning and
demanding that she get out of bed and join in the merri-
ment. But she had agreed to spend the night on Christmas
Day and not drive home after eggnog and champagne. It
had seemed a dreadful prospect, to make the long drive
back in the dark to that empty house. Now she was seriously rethinking her decision and wishing she could leave.

Brian came into the room and sat down heavily on the
far end of the sofa. 'Wow, those boys are practically in orbit.
Especially Finn. Too much Christmas.'

Alex smiled and kept her gaze focused on the tree, blinking back tears. 'It was a very nice Christmas,' she said.

'Oh, Alex,' he said sadly. 'I'm sorry. I know this is so
painful for you.'

She could see that he was preparing to talk about the
losses of this Christmas. She felt almost panicky at the
thought. She was tired of the holiday, tired of being strong,
and afraid she might dissolve into tears. She wanted to
avoid his kindness. 'I wanted to talk to you about something,' she said.

'Anything,' he replied.

'I got a strange…Christmas present this week,' she said.

He looked both disappointed and relieved. 'What was
that?'

Alex drew in a breath. 'Well, I got a call from Mom and

Dad's attorney, Mr Killebrew. He had a letter which Mom left for me in the event of her death.'

Brian raised his eyebrows. 'Really? What did it say?'

'I wondered if you already knew about this,' Alex said.

Brian frowned. 'I don't think so. About what?'

'Mom wanted to tell me that, as it turns out, I'm not an only child.'

Brian looked at her in amazement. 'Excuse me?'

Alex took a deep breath. 'It seems that she got pregnant as a teenager and…had a baby. A baby which she gave up for adoption.'

Brian gaped at her in disbelief. 'What? No. That's not possible.'

'I guess you didn't know about it,' said Alex.

'No. This is a mistake. That can't be…'

'Well, I don't think she was making it up,' said Alex.

Brian frowned and shook his head. 'No, no, of course not. But I…I would have known.'

'Known what?' Jean asked as she came into the family room and collapsed onto the sofa beside her husband. 'Lord, I'm beat. Those boys of ours definitely had a big Christmas,' she said cheerfully.

'It was a lovely Christmas,' said Alex.

Jean, a small, birdlike woman with big eyes and short, spiky hair, leaned over and patted Alex's knee. 'You are a trooper, Alex,' she said. 'You were trying to make it easier for all of us.'

Alex smiled wanly. She loved her uncle's wife, a woman who was always calm, no matter the situation. Jean's sturdy practicality had helped Alex get through the last few months.

'No, really, it was a fine day.'

Jean took a deep breath as Brian began to absently knead her shoulder. She looked from Brian to Alex and back again. 'I have a feeling I interrupted something. What were you two talking about anyway?'

Brian face was knotted with concern. He sighed, and seemed to be choosing his words carefully. 'It seems…Alex just told me that Cathy left a letter with her attorney. Apparently she had a baby and gave it up for adoption when she was a teenager.'

'Get out,' said Jean. 'Catherine? You're kidding me.'

Brian shook his head.

'Wow,' said Jean.

'I know,' said Alex.

'Well, she was always a very devout Catholic. I can't imagine her doing anything else if she got pregnant,' Jean admitted thoughtfully.

'That's just it. She was never pregnant,' Brian protested, running a hand through his thinning hair. 'I would have remembered that.'

'Apparently it happened when she was supposed to be headed off to college. She had the baby in a home somewhere for unwed mothers,' said Alex.

Jean waggled a hand at him dismissively. 'Darling, you were what…twelve or thirteen? I'm sure you didn't have a clue what was going on in Cathy's life in those days.'

Brian shrugged, acknowledging the truth of his wife's observation. 'I guess, maybe not…'

'No maybe about it.' Jean turned to Alex. 'What else did she say? Was it a boy or a girl?'

'A girl,' Alex said.

Jean did some mental calculations. 'She'd probably be… what…in her early thirties by now?'

'I suppose,' said Alex.

'Do you know what happened to her? Was Cathy in touch with this girl?'

Alex shook her head. 'She said that she hoped the girl would try to contact her, but I guess she never did.'

Jean sat back and shook her head. 'I can't believe this. I never would have guessed this of your mom.'

'Me neither,' said Alex.

'Who was the father?' Jean asked. 'Did she say?'

'No. Nothing. That's all she said.'

Jean looked at her husband quizzically.

'What?' Brian asked.

'Well, who would it have been?' Jean asked.

'What? What are you talking about?'

'The father. Who would the father have been? Do you remember her boyfriends?'

'This would have been her senior year in high school,' said Alex.

'In high school? No. Cathy didn't have boyfriends. She was very…studious. She was always volunteering for good causes or babysitting,' said Brian.

'No dates?' said Jean. 'I can't believe that.'

I can, Alex thought. Her mother had always reassured her that a lack of dates in high school did not doom a girl to a single life. Out in the world, her mother told her, everything would be different.

'Would you have even noticed if she had a boyfriend at that age?' Jean asked.

'She did not have a boyfriend,' Brian insisted. Then, he hesitated. 'Unless…'

'Unless what?' Alex asked.

'Well, there was one guy, but I didn't think they were… you know…involved…'

'Who was it?' Jean asked, sitting upright and staring at her husband.

Brian spoke slowly. 'Cathy used to tutor kids in math. Not little kids. Kids her own age. She started helping this

one guy who got left back. Neal was his name. Neal Parafin. He was a mess. Always in trouble. Always getting
suspended from school and being picked up by the police.
You know. A delinquent. He had grown up in foster care.
The nuns asked Cathy to help him. And Cathy could never
say no to a stray.

'Anyway, he'd come over for tutoring and my mother
would invite him to stay for dinner once in a while. He
didn't talk much. Very quiet and moody. He had this long
hair, I remember. And he was scrawny. Dark circles under
his eyes. He looked unhealthy. When I think about it now,
he was a very wary kind of kid. But you could see he was
very attached to Cathy. My parents were worried about it.
I used to hear them talking.'

Alex was imagining her mother as she had seen her in
high school yearbook photos. Young and serious, her frizzy,
strawberry-blonde hair pulled back from her sweet, round
face in a ponytail, trying to help this boy who was such
an outcast. That sounded like her mother. She had never
stopped being involved with at-risk kids through the schools
or charitable organizations.

'So, what happened?' Jean demanded.

Brian exhaled and shook his head. 'Well, it was getting
toward the end of summer—she was ready to go off to college and Neal became angry. I mean, he was always moody
but…he got much worse. It turned out that he wanted her to
run away with him. I found this out later. After it happened.'

'After what happened?' Alex asked cautiously.

Brian spoke slowly. 'One hot night in August, Neal
showed up in his car. He wanted her to go for a drive. He
had this real beater car, but it was like his one possession
and he was so proud of it. If you criticized the car she would
always stick up for him and say how it was the best he could
afford and not to be a jerk about it.'

'Meaning you,' said Jean.

Brian nodded. 'True. Well, that night she got in the car and they were parked in our driveway. They didn't go anywhere though. I guess they were talking. And then we heard the noise. We all heard the noise—it sounded like firecrackers going off in the driveway. My dad started yelling. We all ran to the door. Out in the driveway, Cathy was hysterical. She was standing beside the car door, shaking and screaming. I'll never forget it. She was wearing this pink and yellow dress. It was all covered with these dark blotches. It was blood. I didn't realize right away what I was seeing. Neal was slumped over the wheel.'

Jean's eyes widened. 'He shot himself?'

Brian nodded somberly. 'Apparently he had a gun. My dad called the police. It seems like they were there in a few minutes. My parents wouldn't let me out of the house. They wouldn't let me look. They didn't want me to see him up close.'

'Oh my God,' said Alex.

'It was awful,' said Brian.

'No kidding,' said Jean.

'My mother never told me that story,' said Alex.

'She never talked about it,' said Brian. 'Over the years I mentioned it a time or two and she just changed the subject.'

Jean nodded thoughtfully. 'Wow. And now you're thinking that boy, Neal, might have been the father of her baby.'

Brian held his hands open wide. 'I don't know. I didn't think they were involved in that way. I knew he was upset about her leaving, but I didn't know anything about a pregnancy or a baby. As far as I knew, Cathy went off to college as planned. At least…'

'That's what you thought,' said Jean.

Alex felt sick to her stomach. 'Do you think she was in love with him?'

Brian shrugged. 'With Neal? I never thought so. I thought she just felt sorry for him. My dad said he should have known that helping Neal would bring Cathy trouble. My mother would try to make him hush, but he would carry on about it, saying he never should have let that kid into the house in the first place.'

'What did my mother say?' Alex asked.

Brian shook his head sadly. 'I only heard her talk about it once, the night it happened. The police were questioning her in the living room. She still had blood all over her sundress and she was wearing this heavy sweatshirt over it because she was shivering even though it was a hot night. Her face was as white as a ghost and streaked with tears. I was upstairs on the landing. I wasn't supposed to be listening but I did anyway. The officer asked her if they'd had some kind of lovers' quarrel or something. Cathy said no, it wasn't that. They asked her if she knew why he had done it, then. Why did he kill himself? I always remember what she said. She said that he couldn't bear to be left behind again.'

THREE

THAT CHRISTMAS NIGHT, in the Reillys' narrow guest-room bed, Alex slept restlessly and dreamed that an agitated young man whom she didn't know was trying to force her to take a package from him. The package was wrapped in brown paper and he told her that she needed to deliver it. 'I don't know who it's for,' she protested, but he insisted that she did. She was looking down at the wrinkled paper which was wrapped around the package and was trying to read the address, but could not decipher the words written there. When she woke up, with a start, she was filled with sadness.

On the drive home from her uncle's house, she made up her mind. In the days before Christmas it had seemed like a terrible conundrum to her, but now, suddenly, it seemed simple and clear. She was going to do it. She was going to find her sister.

She knew that Mr Killebrew's office would be closed for the holiday, but on the following Monday morning she called the attorney's office and told the receptionist that she needed to speak to him.

Mr Killebrew came on the line. 'Alex,' he said gently. 'How was Christmas? Did you get through it all right?'

'Somehow,' said Alex. 'Listen, I've been thinking about it and I've decided that I want to find my sister.'

'OK,' said the attorney slowly.

'You said you could help?'

'Well, the adoption laws in this state are quite specific,'

said Killebrew. 'As I said before, in a closed adoption only the adoptee can instigate a search. Parents who want to find the children they gave up for adoption can register their information in case the adoptee tries to find them, but they are not entitled to the adoptee's information. That goes for family members too. If the adoptee doesn't come looking for them, the members of the birth family don't really have any right to the adoptee's information.'

'So I can't search for her, even if I want to?'

'No. Not exactly,' said Mr Killebrew. 'We can petition the court to have the records released, but normally that is only going to happen in cases where the family of origin has an urgent need to know. For example, if there were medical reasons they might allow it.'

'That doesn't apply here,' said Alex glumly. 'There's no other recourse?'

'As you know, a lot has changed because of the Internet. For one thing, it's a lot more difficult to suppress information than it used to be. Privacy is little more than a quaint concept these days.'

'That's for sure,' said Alex. 'So you think I can find her online?'

'She may have registered on one of those websites that were set up for just this purpose,' he said. 'She may visit the site, every now and then, looking for members of her birth family.'

'And if she hasn't?' Alex asked. 'Is that it?'

'Not necessarily. Our firm employs an investigator who can, very often, bypass certain channels to find the information you're seeking.'

'I'm not sure I understand,' said Alex.

'Let's just say he is able to cut certain corners that we can't.'

'Oh, I see.'

'Why don't you just leave this to me, and I'll get back to you.'

Alex thought about it for a moment. 'All right. That seems…reasonable. I'm not sure yet what I'm going to do, so I'm not asking for anyone to contact…her. I just want the information.'

'Of course. Understood,' said Mr Killebrew.

'OK, well, I'll wait to hear from you.'

'It won't be long,' the lawyer said.

IN FACT, ALEX received a call from the attorney's office just two days later. The receptionist asked if she could come in that very afternoon. Her heart thudding, Alex said, 'Absolutely.'

When she arrived, Mr Killebrew was waiting, a grim look on his face.

'So, you have news for me,' Alex said expectantly, sitting down opposite him.

Mr Killebrew nodded and reached for a folder on his desktop.

Something in his expression made Alex feel suddenly apprehensive. She thought of the terrible story her uncle had told her about Neal, the young man who might have been Catherine Reilly's lover so long ago. It seemed as if nothing but sorrow had come from that ill-starred relationship. She pressed her lips together, not wanting to let her anxiety show.

The attorney cleared his throat. 'We have, indeed, located your sister. Her name is Dory. Dory Colson.'

Dory Colson. Alex repeated the name to herself. Somehow, the name made it real. To her surprise, she found herself fighting back tears.

Killebrew continued. 'Dory is thirty-two years old. Unmarried. No children. She was adopted by the Colson family as an infant and grew up in Boston.'

'Wow,' said Alex.

The attorney looked at her. 'What?'

'So close? I never knew she existed, but we've lived our lives separated by only a few miles.'

'Yes,' he said gravely. 'Are you…? Do you want to hear more?'

'Sure. It's just…it's a little overwhelming. Suddenly I have a sister. Her name is Dory. It's a lot to take in.'

Killebrew frowned. 'There's more,' he muttered.

'Did the detective speak to her? Does she know about me?'

'No,' said the attorney. 'She knows nothing about this.'

Alex wished that he would just hand the file over to her. She felt as if he was keeping something from her which was rightly hers. She wanted to read it herself. She didn't need a go-between anymore. 'Well, is her current information in that file? I mean, can I contact her now?'

Mr Killebrew placed his hands on top of the file. 'You can. If you wish.'

Alex recoiled at his tone. 'What do you mean…if I wish?'

Killebrew sighed. 'You may decide you don't want to.'

'I suppose that's possible,' said Alex stiffly. 'But that's really up to me.'

'It is,' he said. 'It is up to you.'

'May I have the file, please?' Alex held out her hand.

Killebrew hesitated, keeping his hands on the file as if he were trying to prevent it from blowing away.

'Is there a problem?'

'You've had such a tough year, Alex. I really wanted to be able to give you some good news,' he said.

'Well, you already have. I wanted to find my sister, and

now, thanks to you and your detective, I will be able to do just that.'

The attorney frowned. 'Alex, I hate to have to tell you this.'

Alex felt a chill. 'Tell me what?' she asked.

'There's no easy way to say this. Your sister, Dory Colson, is in prison.'

Alex stared at him. For a minute she could not believe her ears. 'In prison? You're joking.'

'It's not something I would kid about,' said the attorney.

'Prison?' Alex repeated helplessly. 'Why?'

'Dory Colson is in the state prison at Framingham. She's two years into her sentence. She is doing twenty years.'

'Oh my God!' Alex cried. 'For what?'

Killebrew hesitated. 'For murder. She's in prison for murder.'

'Murder?' Alex repeated the word as if she could barely comprehend it.

'I'm afraid so,' he said.

'But…I don't understand… What…'

'I'm sorry to be the bearer of this news. I know this is not what you were hoping to hear.'

'Who did she kill?' Alex asked.

Mr Killebrew met her gaze stolidly. 'Her sister,' he said.

There was a long silence in the room as Alex tried to absorb what she had just heard. 'I'm her sister,' she said at last.

'She had another sister,' said Killebrew. 'Her name was Lauren. Three years ago, Lauren was stabbed to death in the family home. Dory pleaded guilty to her murder.'

Alex recoiled. 'Oh my God,' she said again.

Killebrew looked at her levelly. 'I'm sorry. I know it's a shock.'

Alex shook her head. 'Are you sure about this?'

'Absolutely,' said Killebrew. 'Our investigator double-checked everything. I knew this was going to come as a blow.'

'Why?' asked Alex. 'Do you know why?'

'Why she killed her? No. I don't.'

'I can't believe this,' Alex murmured. She thought of her mother's letter, urging her to find this woman. A murderer.

Killebrew frowned. 'If you were to decide to drop the whole thing now, no one would blame you. And Dory would be none the wiser. She doesn't even know you're looking for her.'

'Yes, I understand,' said Alex distractedly.

'I know this is not what your mom had in mind when she wrote you that letter.'

Alex nodded. He was right about her mother's intentions.

'Is her address in there? In case I do want to contact her?'

'It's all in the folder. There's an address at the prison where you can write to her. No emails. She has no computer access. Or you could call her.'

Alex could not picture that phone call. What words would she use? 'Can I see the folder?'

Killebrew pushed it across the desk. 'You can have it. It's yours.'

Alex opened it, looking at the paperwork within. Then she closed it again. She hesitated before putting it into her bag.

'I'm so sorry about this,' said Killebrew.

Alex felt numb. 'It's not your fault. You just did what I asked you to do.' She got up from the chair. 'Thank you so much, Mr Killebrew. I appreciate it.'

'Do you know what you're going to do?'

Alex shook her head. 'I don't. I'm very confused right now. To tell you the truth, I didn't think it mattered that much to me. But right now, I feel…devastáted.'

'Alex, if you decide to go further with this, be careful. I can tell you from experience that people in prison are always looking for sympathy and will take advantage of your good will. She's a dangerous criminal…' he said.

Alex nodded. 'I'll be careful,' she said in a small voice. She shook his extended hand and hurried down the stairs, leaving the office with as much dignity as she could muster. She crossed the street to her car and unlocked the door with trembling hands. She kept her composure until she was alone behind the wheel. Then she began to shake.

Alex fumbled with her keys and turned on the ignition so she could get some heat. Outside the short, cold day was dimming and the street lamps were beginning to glow. She wanted to just go home, but she was shaking too hard to drive just yet.

All her losses came flooding back to her. She felt tortured when she thought of her mother, offering her this information from beyond the grave, thinking, when she lovingly wrote that letter, that she was providing Alex with a treasure. Some treasure, Alex thought.

You don't have to do this, she reminded herself. This is not your problem. Like Mr Killebrew said, Dory doesn't even know that you are looking for her. You can take this folder and put it in the trash. You can forget you ever even knew about her. You don't owe this woman a thing.

Alex took a deep breath. She turned on the car and pulled out of the parking space. Sometimes, she told herself, you need to leave well alone.

FOUR

THE FIRST THING she did when she got home was to put on her most comfortable sweats and make herself a cup of tea. She crawled into her father's armchair with a book and tried to read. Her eyes scanned the printed lines but she had no idea of what she was reading. Her thoughts kept returning to what she had learned from the attorney. No matter how Alex tried to banish the thoughts from her head, it was impossible. She felt as if she had opened Pandora's Box, and now she could not force the questions she had unleashed back into it. The questions rose and buzzed around her.

After half an hour she went over to her computer, sat down and, hating herself for her weakness, Googled Dory Colson.

With several clicks of a key she was looking at front page headlines and indistinct photos of a woman with her face a blur, her hands manacled, being hustled into a police car. Promising herself that each article she read would be the last, Alex continued on until late at night, reading everything she could find about the crime. She learned that Lauren and Dory Colson had been very close in age. According to the breathless reports in the paper, the Colsons adopted Dory after years of trying to have a baby, and then Mrs Colson, as so often happens, immediately became pregnant. At the time of her death, Lauren had been an up-and-coming country music singer who lived in Branson, Missouri, and was about to embark on a national tour. She had come back to Boston to have surgery and to recuperate from the procedure at her family's home in the South End.

Apparently Dory, who still lived at home, began to suspect that her new boyfriend, a doctor named Rick Howland, was showing an interest in Lauren, although both the boyfriend and Lauren denied any involvement. There were some photos of Lauren, blonde and lissome, dressed in leather, jeans and chiffon. People who knew the family said that Dory had long been bitter about Lauren's success. Tension between the sisters escalated. On the day of the murder, a deliveryman from the dry cleaner said that he heard the sisters arguing. Hours later, Dory called the police and said that she had found Lauren dead in the house. She was arrested that evening and charged with the murder. Within a few weeks she had pleaded guilty, and was sentenced to twenty years in prison.

Alex sat for a long time, staring at the blinking cursor. All right, she told herself. You did what your mother asked and now you know. Put the folder in a drawer and move on with your life. But despite the soundness of that decision, Alex could almost hear her mother's voice, wondering how this could have happened to her child. It's not my problem, Alex wanted to cry out. I'm not responsible for what happened to Dory!

'Leave me alone,' she whispered to the empty room.

THE NEXT DAY Alex took the train to Boston. She was excited to have been summoned for an interview at the prestigious Orenstein Gallery on Boston's Newbury Street. But she had mixed feelings about presenting herself for a job. She felt vulnerable and definitely not at her best. She dressed carefully for the interview and covered the dark circles under her eyes with make-up. And, she thought, as she waited for the train to the Back Bay, it was a relief to be out of the house.

Louis Orenstein, a bronzed, balding man in his early fifties dressed in a bespoke silk suit, had a reputation for having discovered some of the premier artists of the day, especially in modern sculpture, which was Alex's favorite art form. Louis needed an assistant and grilled Alex carefully about her credentials for almost an hour. When she left Orenstein said he would be in touch, and Alex was cautiously optimistic that she had made a good impression.

After the interview was over, she went to a coffee shop on Boylston Street and bought herself a cappuccino. She sat, staring out at the pedestrians passing by, trying to think about job prospects, but her thoughts continually gravitated back to Dory Colson.

In the course of her search on the computer the night before, she had easily located the Colsons' address in Boston. The South End was not far from the Back Bay where Alex was now sitting. She knew that she should let it alone, but the idea of seeing that house where this mysterious sister had lived, grown up, and committed murder drew her like a magnet. She finished her coffee, left the coffee bar and looked in the direction of the train station. Then, telling herself that she just wanted to walk by the house, she started to walk toward the South End instead.

THE SOUTH END of Boston was nothing if not newly chic. The Colsons lived on a quiet, tree-lined street, not far from the bustling shops, bistros and theaters which now gave vivid life to the once rundown Tremont Street. Alex had memorized the address. She arrived in front of the building and looked up at it. It was old brownstone with concrete pilasters and a wooden front door which was polished to a shine. Perhaps, at one time, it had been one of the nicer houses on the block. Now it looked distinctly less prosperous than its gentrified neighbors.

She thought about walking up to the front door, knocking and identifying herself. After all, she thought, Dory is your blood relative. But now that she was here she felt an uneasy certainty that she would not be welcome. As she stood at the foot of the steps, debating with herself, a bicycle skidded to a stop beside her. A handsome, bearded man, his chestnut hair pulled back into a ponytail, got off the bike. He was probably nearly forty, but he was dressed like a student in jeans and a down vest.

'Excuse me,' he said as he picked up the bike and waited for Alex to move out of his way. She stepped aside, and he began to carry the bike up the steps. Just before he got to the top he turned and frowned at her. 'Can I help you?' he said.

Alex hesitated. 'I was…looking for the Colsons' house.'

'You found it. They live on the first floor,' he said. He frowned at her. 'Are you a friend of theirs?' he asked suspiciously.

'Not exactly.'

'Reporter?' he demanded.

'No,' she said. 'No. Not at all. It's…I'm a relative,' she said.

His frown cleared. 'Oh, well come on in then.'

The man carried the bike to the top of the steps and looked back at her. Alex wanted to flee. Instead she climbed the steps behind him.

'I'm Chris, by the way,' he said. 'Chris Ennis. My wife and daughter and I live upstairs. I have to carry this bike inside and leave it in the hallway or some druggie will steal it. Here, go on in.' He pushed open the front door and stood back to let her pass.

Alex walked up the steps and into the dark vestibule. She saw the door to the apartment on her right and stairs leading up to the second floor. She peered at the nameplate beside the bell.

'That's the Colsons',' said Chris as he unwound a plastic-covered chain and began to fasten his bike to the newel post. 'Go ahead and ring it. Elaine might be home. She's the secretary at the Catholic church. Her schedule is flexible.'

Alex hesitated, and then rang the bell as Chris snapped the lock shut on his bike and removed a brown paper bag reading Free World Food from the basket.

There was only silence inside the apartment. Alex was secretly relieved. She had not intended to go so far.

'No answer?' he asked pleasantly.

'No. I should have called.'

'Do you want to wait?' he asked. 'Come on upstairs and I'll make you some herbal tea. You can meet my daughter.'

She knew she should leave immediately, but curiosity gripped her. This man seemed quite familiar with the Colsons' schedule. Maybe he knew Dory—knew something about her life. 'Oh, that's really nice,' said Alex.

'It's no problem,' said Chris, starting up the stairs.

Alex followed him. 'Have you lived here a long time?' she asked.

'Oh, yeah. Forever,' said Chris. 'Joy and I moved in with some other kids when we were still students. Garth and Elaine were already here. They weren't too thrilled at first to have a bunch of students living upstairs. Now we're an old married couple, and we've all lived in this building so long we're like family.' He unlocked the door to his apartment and went inside.

It was like stepping back to the Age of Aquarius. Indian bedspreads covered crumbling plaster, and there was a huge peace sign on one of the doors. The shelves were lined with books and the furniture was old and somewhat shabby. An orange cat was splayed out on the floor and did not even flinch when Alex stepped over him. Potted plants hung in the windows from macramé hangers. Alex heard the sound of an earnest, thin voice singing along to a guitar accompaniment.

'Hey, honey,' Chris called out as he put the paper bag on the counter and began removing vegetables and tubs of organic rice and tofu. 'That's my daughter. She'll never hear me,' he said. 'She's lost in her music.'

Alex sat down at the kitchen counter. There was a papier-mâché picture frame in the shape of a sun on the wall. Inside it was a photo of Chris—much younger—next to a beautiful young woman with a beaded, feathered headband around her long, black hair and a beauty mark near her mouth.

Chris turned and saw her looking at it. 'That's Joy,' he said proudly. 'That's my wife.'

'She's beautiful,' said Alex.

'She is,' he said, smiling. 'So, I've never seen you around here. Are you from Boston?'

'Actually, I'm here from Seattle,' said Alex.

'And you're related to the Colsons?'

Alex had no intention of revealing her exact relationship.

'Distantly,' she said. 'I've never actually met them. Lauren was a country music singer, wasn't she?'

'Country music. Go figure. A girl from Boston. 'Course, Garth was from out west somewhere. Who are you related to? Garth or Elaine?'

Alex made a stab in the dark. 'Um. My mother was a cousin of...Elaine's. She told me about what happened with Lauren and her sister.'

Chris shook his head. 'Yeah. That was a shock. I always thought Dory was a gentle soul. You can know a person for years and have no idea. I mean, that she would even be capable of doing something like that.'

'Apparently she was jealous of her sister,' said Alex.

'Well, who wouldn't be? Lauren was going places. Everything revolved around her when they were kids. Elaine used to home school Lauren, while Dory went to the public school. It was just for convenience's sake. I mean, Lauren always had a music lesson or an audition. But still, I think Dory resented it.' Chris suddenly stopped what he was doing and frowned at her. 'Are you sure you're not a reporter?' he asked.

'No,' Alex protested, feeling instantly guilty.

The singing abruptly stopped. There was the sound of a door opening down the hall and a slim, ethereal-looking teenage girl with long, wavy chestnut hair and a short voile dress came into the room. She was probably seventeen, but looked younger. 'Dad?' she said. Then she saw Alex and frowned. 'Who's this?'

'Hi, babe,' he said cheerfully. 'Got your homework done?'

'Who is she?' the girl asked.

Chris frowned. 'I forgot. What did you say your name was?'

'Alex.'

'Alex, this is my daughter, Therese.'

'Hi, Therese. Was that you singing?' Alex asked.

'And playing guitar,' Chris said proudly. 'She writes her own songs.'

'Wow, you're very talented,' said Alex.

'Alex is related to the Colsons,' said Chris.

'Lauren was gonna sing one of my songs on her next album,' said Therese sadly. 'But then…'

'Lauren was Therese's idol. And she said maybe,' Chris reminded her, pulling two mugs down from the cabinet.

'She promised,' Therese insisted. 'What are you doing anyway?'

'I'm making some tea.'

'Mom said you'd take me to practice,' the girl complained.

'Oh, that's right. OK, babe. I'm sorry.' Chris turned to Alex. 'I forgot. I'm going to have to go.'

'No problem,' said Alex, standing up and feeling relieved. 'I should be going anyway.'

'Do you want me to tell them you were here?' he asked.

'That's all right. I'll give them a call. Thanks so much for your hospitality.'

'No problem,' said Chris, walking to the door. 'Try ringing the bell again on your way out. Maybe Elaine's back. Therese, get your gear.'

'I will,' said Alex. But when she reached the bottom of the steps and heard him close the door to the apartment above, she passed by the Colsons' door without stopping.

On the ride home from the city she thought about what she had done. She felt as if she was compelled by an out-of-control kind of curiosity, even though common sense told her it could be a mistake. In her effort to find out about her sister, she had actually gone to the Colsons' apartment, having found a way to get inside the building. Be honest with yourself, she thought. This is not going to go away. It just isn't.

That evening after she had emptied a few drawers, forced herself to eat something nourishing, and watched a mindless reality show on TV, she knew that she was avoiding the inevitable. She went to her father's desk and sat down. She picked up a pen from the silver cup by her own framed photo and pulled some heavy vellum paper out of the desk drawer. For a long time her pen hovered over the blank page. Finally she lowered the pen to the paper. 'Dear Dory,' she began to write. 'You don't know me...'

FIVE

THE MUSEUM OF Fine Arts called her in for an interview and she went in dutifully, but might as well have taken a number. The interview was perfunctory, and the young woman who spoke to her let Alex know that she was only one of legions who had come in to apply. She arrived back home feeling exhausted and discouraged. After hanging her coat up in the hall closet, she picked up the mail that had come through the mail slot and began to thumb through the flyers, catalogues and bills. Suddenly she stopped, her heart skipping a beat.

Her address on the envelope had been written in a neat, squarish hand that strangely resembled her mother's penmanship. For a moment, the sight of it made her feel weak. She looked at the return address. Framingham Prison for Women. Alex tore open the envelope and unfolded the single sheet of paper inside. The paper rattled as she gripped it.

Dear Alex,
I was surprised to get your letter. I don't really know what to say. Yes, I always knew I was adopted, but I didn't think too much about it. I figured if my birth mother didn't want me, why should I want to meet her? It never occurred to me that she might be hoping I would look for her.

You said you wanted to come and see me if I wanted to meet you. I didn't know you existed until I got your letter, but I guess if you want to come, why

*not? I am allowed to have visitors, so just come dur-
ing visiting hours. I am always here. Ha, ha.
Sincerely,
Dory Colson*

Alex sat down and reread the letter several times. She
felt as if she was standing at the edge of a cliff, looking
down. With each step she had taken so far, Alex had told
herself that she didn't need to go any further. There was
still time to drop the whole thing. It wasn't as if Dory could
come and visit her. The next step would be different though.
The next step would bring her face to face with this…sis-
ter. Maybe you should stop now, she thought. Maybe you
should forget about this and not pursue it.

But there was no stopping at this point. Tomorrow, she
thought, and wondered how long it would take to drive to
MCI Framingham.

ALEX PARKED IN the visitors' lot, got out of her car and
obeyed the order, printed on signs every few feet, to lock the
car. She straightened her jacket and the sweater underneath
it. She had carefully adhered to the visitors' dress code demanded on the MCI Framingham website. No denim, no
sweats, no camouflage or suggestive clothing. And she had
worn underwear, as the regulations required. She wondered
wryly if anyone would check, and then realized, with a
shudder, that it was quite possible that they would.

The prison sat at the edge of town but was clearly iso-
lated, a world unto itself. Approaching the red-brick building with its peaked dormers and a flag on a tall flagpole,
lifting and falling in the breeze, was almost like approaching a courthouse or a college classroom building. A closer
look revealed tall chain-link fences and loops of barbed
wire surrounding the open areas. Alex took a breath,

opened the front door and went inside. At that point, any façade of normalcy vanished. She followed the signs for the visitors' entrance and approached a small office walled off with Plexiglas. A uniformed guard sat inside, talking to another guard who was standing in an inner doorway.

'Excuse me,' said Alex. The man ignored her and continued to talk. A heavyset black woman sitting on an orange molded plastic chair in the hallway reading a paperback romance novel shifted in her seat.

'Excuse me,' Alex repeated as a few more moments went by and the guard did not acknowledge her presence. She lifted up a fist and went to tap on the Plexiglas.

The woman in the chair did not look up from her book, but murmured, 'Don't do that.'

Alex glanced over at her. The woman did not meet her glance but her mouth was set in a firm line. 'You best be patient,' she said.

Alex withdrew her fist and stood, uncertainly, looking at her. Finally the guard finished his conversation and turned his cold, silvery gaze on Alex. He did not ask what she wanted.

'Um, I'm here to see Dory Colson,' she said.

'Here's your number and a key,' he said, sliding a piece of paper out to her. 'Put all your things in one of those lockers.' He gestured toward the numbered cubicles against the front wall.

'Everything? I brought some photos. Can I bring them in…?' she asked. The guard had already turned away without replying.

Alex, frustrated by the guard's abruptness, put the key in the lock and jimmied it angrily, to no avail.

'Turn the key upside down,' said the other woman calmly, turning a page, her gaze still trained on her book.

Alex removed the key and tried again. The locker door opened. 'Thank you,' she said, jamming her purse inside.

'Can't bring nothing in. Put it all away,' said the older woman. 'Empty your pockets too. Just keep enough cash to buy a card for the vending machines,' she said, inclining her head toward a machine beside the lockers.

Alex looked at her, puzzled.

'They gonna want you to buy 'em something to eat. The machines got hot food. Hamburgers and the like. But you can't take cash inside.'

'Oh. OK,' said Alex. She walked over to the machine and read the instructions, depositing a ten-dollar bill. The machine clanked and spat out a card.

'You just hang onto that,' said the woman.

Alex did as she was told. She sat down across from her. The woman looked over her half-glasses at Alex.

'First time?' she said.

Alex nodded.

'You'll get used to it,' the woman said grimly.

'I guess you've done this before.'

'My daughter's here. Six years. Selling drugs.'

Alex grimaced. 'I'm sorry.'

'Who you here for?'

Alex somehow found the words possible to say. 'My sister.' Then she hesitated, trying to think how much to explain about the nature of Dory's crime.

'Number four hundred and twelve,' the guard barked.

The woman put her book down on her chair seat and got to her feet. 'That's me,' she said with a sigh.

'Thanks again,' said Alex.

The woman nodded and walked over to the door beside the guard's window. Alex watched her wait for a buzzer to sound and then the woman sighed, pushed the door open and went in. Alex shifted in her seat, sitting on top of her clammy hands, and waited for her number to be called.

The time dragged, and no one offered any explanations. Although she was not used to being treated rudely, Alex realized that she would accomplish nothing here by causing a fuss. Patience, she reminded herself. You don't want these people looking askance at you. Finally her number was called. She waited for the buzzer, opened the door and entered. The guard told her to stand in front of a scanner and empty her pockets. Luckily, she had been forewarned.

'I just have this card for the vending machines,' she said.

The guard nodded disinterestedly. He ordered her to pass through and, when she got to the other side, directed her to a room across the hall. 'In there,' he grunted. 'Sit down at a table. Doesn't matter which.'

'Thank you,' said Alex politely. She wanted to ask if Dory was already in there, but she didn't dare. She walked across the hall and entered the room, which was mainly empty. Her companion with the romance novel was seated at the far end across from a young woman with a rag tied over her hair and deep circles under her eyes. A tray of food rested, untouched, on the tabletop between them. Neither woman looked up at Alex.

Alex glanced around the room. She picked a table away from the others and sat down. It was Saturday and she had expected the place to be teeming with visitors but, in fact, it was almost eerily empty and silent, except for the constant barrage of announcements over the PA system.

She sat down, her heart pounding, and watched the door. She did not have long to wait. A guard came in with a prisoner in a dark blue jumpsuit. The minute Alex set eyes on her sister, she realized, with a start, that there was no doubt.

Dory Colson was tall and slim with frizzy, reddish-blonde hair in a ponytail and pale eyelashes. Her face was covered with a thin veil of freckles. She could have been a younger, slimmer and more beautiful version of Alex's mother, Catherine Woods.

Dory looked around the room and her vacant, gray-eyed gaze settled on Alex. She stared at her, unsmiling.

Alex stood halfway up in her seat and raised her hand. Dory spoke to the guard who had accompanied her and came gliding toward Alex. Alex stepped out from behind the table. She felt a sudden panic that she didn't know what to do. She felt as if she should embrace this person who was her sister, but she didn't want to. Then again, it seemed too weird to shake her hand. Dory settled the problem for her. She nodded abruptly and sat down in the chair across from Alex. Relieved, Alex resumed her seat.

'So,' said Dory in a low murmur, 'you found me.'

Alex was startled by those words and felt compelled to protest. 'Well, not me. Not really. My attorney has an investigator who…'

'I meant the prison,' said Dory.

'Oh,' said Alex, feeling flustered. 'Yes. It wasn't hard to find.'

She couldn't stop staring at Dory's face, at once so alien and so familiar. Unlike her mother, Dory's eyes were flat and lusterless. That wasn't the only difference. Where Catherine was warm, Dory was cool. There was a distant quality to her voice and her fleeting smile. But the ineffable resemblance in the arrangement of their features was uncanny. Alex felt almost angry at this prisoner for resembling her mother so closely. It seemed wrong, somehow. As if she had a claim to their mother that Alex never would.

Now that they were face-to-face, Alex suddenly struggled to think of what to say. Her brain felt utterly empty of any thoughts, except for an urgent desire to get out of this place which smelled of stale fried food and disinfectant.

Then she remembered the card which she was squeezing in her hand. The corners of it were cutting into her palm. 'I got this card,' she said. 'Would you like to get something… from one of the machines?'

Dory gazed at the array of vending machines with a flicker of interest that faded immediately. 'No. No, thanks,' she said. 'I'm watching my figure.'

'Really?' Alex asked, nonplussed.

Dory looked at Alex almost pityingly. 'No. I don't need anything.'

She may as well have added, 'from you.' The implication was there.

'I imagine the food's not too great here,' said Alex, feeling stupid that the only thing she could think of to say to this new-found sister was a comment about prison food.

'No. It's not good,' said Dory. 'Rice and potatoes. That's basically it.'

'You're sure you wouldn't like a hamburger or something?' Alex asked, gesturing vaguely toward the machines.

'I think they make those hamburgers out of potatoes,' said Dory.

It took Alex a moment to realize that Dory was joking, and then she laughed.

Dory smiled briefly. 'So. According to you, we are sisters.'

'Oh, we are sisters. Now that I've seen you, any doubts I might have had… If you knew how much you look like my mother…I brought along some pictures I wanted to show you. Of my mother and her family. I thought you'd be interested to see your relatives. But the guards made me leave them outside.'

Dory shrugged. 'There's a million rules around here.'

'You look just like her,' Alex said.

Dory frowned.

'Looking at you… It's like looking at a younger version of my mother. It's really…bizarre.'

A look of annoyance flitted across Dory's features. Alex abruptly stopped talking. She could see that Dory was irritated by this comparison.

'I mean, obviously, you look like yourself…' she stammered.

'What happened to her?' said Dory. 'You said she was dead.'

'My mother? She and my father were killed in a car accident in the spring. A drunken driver ran a red light.'

'Too bad,' Dory said evenly.

'Yes. Thanks.'

Alex knew it would be polite to ask about Dory's family. She was trying to mentally frame the question when Dory asked, 'Did your detective find out who my father was, too?'

Alex immediately thought of what she had heard about Neal Parafin, the troubled young man who shot himself as his car sat in the driveway of her mother's childhood home. 'No,' she said. 'Well, maybe…'

'What is it? Yes or no?'

'There's some possibility that it was this guy named Neal…'

'Doesn't matter,' Dory said, flicking her long, freckled fingers as if to dismiss the question.

There was something about Dory that made Alex feel anxious and hapless. 'I can do some more digging if you'd like,' she said. 'Try to find out for sure.'

'Don't bother. I don't really care. They didn't have any use for me.'

'It wasn't that my mother didn't want you,' Alex protested. 'She was just a young girl at the time. She couldn't take care of you. And Neal…Well, he wasn't even alive when you were born.'

Dory raised her eyebrows. 'Why not? What happened to him?'

'Like I said, I'm not certain that he was your father.'

Dory peered at her. 'What happened to him?'

Alex swallowed hard, wishing she had not even mentioned Neal. 'He… He committed suicide.'

Dory nodded and pursed her lips, staring at the tabletop.

'I'm sorry to tell you that,' said Alex. 'It must come as a bit of a shock.'

Dory shook her head. 'Not really,' she said, a studied indifference in her voice and gaze.

Silence descended. Alex felt almost panicky. Somehow she had thought that the biological bond between them would make it easy to talk, but the opposite was true. The fact that they had not even known about one another their whole lives made it seem almost futile to try and 'catch up'. Alex didn't want to bring up the crime which had precipitated Dory's long sentence in prison, and there didn't seem to be any way to ask about her older sister's past without mentioning it.

For her part, Dory seemed to have lost all interest in their conversation. She glanced up at the clock on the wall.

Alex felt a sudden flash of anger. She had come all this way, torturing herself with worry and doubt. And now, a woman in prison was too busy to spend any more time with her. 'Am I boring?' she asked coldly.

Dory seemed unfazed by her sister's chilly tone. 'I'm expecting a visitor.'

You *have* a visitor, Alex wanted to say, but she stopped herself. 'I thought there would be more visitors here,' she said instead, 'since it's the weekend.'

'Weekends are no better than the week,' said Dory.

'Except for Sunday.' Ever since Alex arrived Dory had seemed uninterested, but now, suddenly, her eyes lit up and her pallid skin gained a faint but discernible glow. 'On Sundays they bring in dogs from the animal shelter and they let you work with them out in the yard. I love animals, especially dogs. That's what I used to do. I used to be a pet sitter and a dog walker. That's how I made my living.'

'Really? I love animals too,' said Alex. 'I always had a dog and cats when I was a kid. I can't wait for my life to get a little more settled so I can get some pets.'

Dory's enthusiasm seemed to fade. 'I never had pets.'

'Not at all?' asked Alex, feeling privileged and guilty.

'My sister was a singer and she was allergic to pet dander. So we couldn't have animals around. Even after she left home and moved to Missouri, my mother said no. We couldn't risk it. Had to keep the place dander-free in case she came home unexpectedly.'

'Oh. That's too bad,' said Alex, startled by the offhand reference to the murdered Lauren.

A prison guard came up to the table where they were sitting, leaned over and spoke into Dory's ear.

Dory nodded and looked at Alex. 'My visitor is here. You'll have to go 'cause I can only have one visitor at a time.'

'Oh. OK,' said Alex.

Dory looked over Alex's shoulder anxiously. 'Marisol!' she called out. 'Over here.'

Alex, who was already standing, turned and saw a stout, brown-skinned woman in sensible shoes, a brightly-printed overblouse and a skirt, walking toward them. She wore glasses and carried a briefcase. Dory stood up, her frame graceful even in her prison jumpsuit, and briefly hugged her new visitor, who patted her on the back.

Dory then pointed to Alex, but spoke to Marisol. 'This is my sister. If you can believe it.'

'No kidding?' said Marisol. She turned her pleasant gaze on Alex. She was about Alex's age, with keen, dark eyes, straight white teeth and dimples. She extended her hand. 'Nice to meet you. I'm Marisol Torres.'

'Alex Woods.'

'Marisol is trying to get me out of this hellhole,' said Dory.

'Working on it,' said Marisol.

'Are you an attorney?' asked Alex.

'I'm in my last year of law school at New England University,' Marisol said. 'I volunteer for the Justice Initiative.'

'One visitor at a time,' bellowed the guard. 'You'll have to leave, miss.'

'OK,' said Alex, nodding. As had been the case when she arrived, she was uncertain how to take her leave. She wondered if she should embrace Dory, or at least take her hand. Once again, Dory eliminated the question.

'Sit, Marisol,' Dory insisted, taking her own seat. Then she looked up at Alex. 'Thanks for coming,' she said. 'It was…interesting to meet you.'

'For me too,' said Alex.

'Will you come back?' Dory asked.

'This is not a coffee klatch, ladies,' the guard barked. 'Let's go.'

Luckily for Alex, there was no time to answer.

SIX

ALEX BURST OUT of the front doors of the prison as if she had just finished serving a sentence herself. The January day had turned gray but the cold air was bracing. She felt as if she had been holding her breath the entire time that she was inside the facility. How could anyone survive in there? she thought. There was nothing about the place that would make you even want to live. Alex remembered that program with the dogs which Dory had mentioned. She lived from week to week, waiting to play with those dogs for a brief while. Obviously the most ordinary of pleasures was priceless behind those walls.

When Alex reached her car in the visitors' lot, she rolled down the windows despite the cold. She didn't want to be closed up, even inside her own car. She laid her head back against the seat and gulped in the air. You're free to go, she thought. And yet, she did not turn on the engine. Her visit with Dory had left her with more questions than answers, but the greatest question in her mind right now had to do with Marisol Torres. Why was she trying to get Dory out of jail? Dory had pleaded guilty. Wasn't that the end of it?

It's none of your business, Alex reminded herself. You came to introduce yourself and now you've done it. Nothing more could be expected of you. But still Alex sat in her car and did not move. Sooner or later, Marisol Torres was going to come out of that prison. Whatever reason she had for coming out here, Alex wanted to know about it. If there was a chance that her new-found sister didn't belong in prison,

Alex had to know. She had a right to know. Maybe, for no other reason than that, she cared enough to ask.

You should probably stay out of it, Alex told herself. But she didn't budge. She sat and waited. Half an hour passed, and several people came and went through the front door of the prison. As she looked at the dashboard clock for the fiftieth time, Alex was struck by an unpleasant thought. What if there was another entrance? Marisol was only a law student. Maybe she didn't have a car. Perhaps she came by bus, and entered the prison through another entrance. Alex was just about to convince herself that she must, indeed, have missed the law student's departure, when the prison door opened and Marisol Torres hurried out, pulling on her jacket. Alex hopped out of her car and met Marisol at the entrance to the visitors' lot.

'Excuse me,' she said. 'Ms Torres.'

Marisol, lost in thought, jumped at the sound of her name, and then smiled cautiously. 'Hi, Alex.'

'I wondered if I could talk to you for a minute.' Alex could see her own breath in the cold.

'About Dory?' Marisol said.

Alex nodded. 'I don't know if she told you anything about me…'

'She told me that you two had the same mother.'

'That's right. And, despite the fact that I never even met her before, I find myself feeling a little bit…concerned about her.'

'Well, that's good,' the law student said. 'She could use the support.'

'I wondered…What exactly is going on? I mean, about her case? What is there to look into? I understood that she pleaded guilty to her sister's murder.'

'She did,' Marisol said. 'But last year the public defender

who represented her came under investigation for breach of ethics. He has since been disbarred.'

'For what?'

'He made no effort to provide an effective defense for his clients. As you know, the Sixth Amendment guarantees that right.'

Alex didn't actually know which amendment was which, but she nodded.

'The cases of all his clients had to be reviewed. A huge job, as you can imagine. The Justice Initiative agreed to help. I was assigned to several cases. One of them was Dory's. I saw pretty quickly that she was badly served by this PD. I've been preparing a brief on her behalf for about six months now.'

'Wait a minute. Dory had a public defender? Isn't that what you get when you can't afford to hire an attorney?'

'That's right. They mostly serve the indigent.'

'Dory's family wasn't indigent, was it?'

'Dory was of legal age. Technically, no one else was responsible for paying for her defense,' Marisol said.

'I suppose not,' said Alex.

'Anyway, the primary job of a public defender is to arrange plea bargains, to clear the court's calendar. Which is fine, unless the attorney is deliberately misrepresenting the advantages and conditions of a plea to his client.'

'And you think that's what happened to Dory?'

Marisol grimaced apologetically. 'I can't really talk specifics about her case without Dory's permission. Attorney-client privilege.'

'Oh, I see,' said Alex.

'And I need to get going. My mother is taking care of my daughter and I want to have some time with her.'

'I understand,' said Alex. 'It's just that I feel like I need to know…'

Marisol pulled her car keys out of her briefcase. She walked over to a dented maroon Ford Taurus and unlocked the door. Alex followed her. Marisol set her briefcase down on the front seat. 'I'll be glad to talk to you,' she said, 'as long as Dory gives her permission. You'll have to ask her to contact me directly if it's OK.'

'I'm not sure how she would react to that,' Alex admitted. 'She seems a little bit suspicious as to why I wanted to meet her in the first place.'

Marisol chuckled. 'That sounds like Dory. Well, I speak to her almost every day. I'll ask her for you. Where can I reach you?'

'Would you? That would be great.' Alex fumbled in her purse for her business card and handed it to her, while Marisol fished in the pocket of her jacket and offered her own in return.

Marisol glanced at Alex's card. 'You live in Chichester? I grew up in Waltham. That's where I'm headed right now. My mom still lives there. Look, I'll speak to Dory and I'll be in touch.'

'Thanks,' said Alex. 'And thanks for helping her.'

'I do what I can.' Marisol waved as she slid into the front seat of her car and turned on the engine. She threw an arm over the seat and began to back out.

Alex watched her go and then, lost in thought, returned to her own car and headed for home.

IT WAS DARK when Alex got home, and she felt relieved that the day was over. Going to see Dory had been undeniably stressful. A childish, hopeful part of her, one that still secretly entertained the notion of guardian angels and love at first sight and other miracles, had wanted to believe that she and her sister would have an instant rapport. That had not happened. The reality was quite a bit more sobering.

Alex went into the kitchen and rummaged through her mother's cabinets. She found pasta in the cupboards and some vegetables that still looked edible in the fridge. She put everything on the counter and filled a pot with water for the pasta. Then she began to chop. Suddenly she heard a knocking on the front door. Her heart leapt. Seth Paige? she thought. She chided herself for her excitement, but then remembered that he had, indeed, agreed to come over and look at her father's books. Maybe he had chosen tonight to look through them. She noticed that the bottle of wine he brought her on Christmas Day was still on the counter. She knew where her mother kept the corkscrew. Maybe she would open it.

'All right,' she said. 'Just a minute, I'm coming.' She turned off the pot of boiling water and the burner under the sauté pan. Then she smoothed her hair as she went down the hallway. She pulled open the front door and looked out.

A black pick-up truck was parked directly in front of the house with the name 'Details' painted on the door. A man and a woman stood on the front steps. The woman was middle-aged with short, spiky gray-blonde hair, a fine-boned face and square jaw. Her well-shaped eyebrows arched over her light blue eyes. Her skin was lined, but she was obviously still attractive, wearing a bulky coat-styled sweater and little makeup. The man beside her was balding and his skin looked weatherbeaten. His eyelids were deeply creased, giving his gray eyes a sad expression. He was dressed in work boots and rugged, outdoors-man-style clothes.

Alex stared at them, disappointed. 'Can I help you?'

'Are you Alex Woods?' the man asked. He had a slight Western drawl.

'Yes,' said Alex cautiously.

'We heard you were looking for us.'
Alex frowned. 'I'm afraid there's some mistake.'
'I don't think so,' said the man. 'We're Dory's parents.'

SEVEN

For a moment Alex just stared. These were the people whom her sister had called 'mother and father'. The thought of it was jarring. 'I'm…this is unexpected,' she said.

'I'm Garth Colson,' said the man. 'This is my wife, Elaine. May we come in?'

Alex did not move. 'I'm sorry. I'm just a little…surprised to see you here.'

The couple exchanged a glance. 'According to our neighbor, you were looking for us,' said Garth.

Alex blushed, remembering the half-truths she told to Chris Ennis. 'I was. But how did you…. That is…how did you find me?'

'Dory called my phone and left me a message. She said you lived in Chichester and that you are her half-sister, and that you were coming to see her. After that, finding you was easy,' said Elaine Colson matter-of-factly.

'Oh, of course. I guess I probably should have…'

The woman shivered. 'It's chilly out here. May we come inside?'

Alex stepped away from the door. 'I'm sorry. Yes, sure,' she said.

'Thank you,' said Elaine. They walked in and stood uneasily, side by side, in the vestibule.

'Nice house,' Garth Colson said, inspecting the curved banister on the staircase. 'When was it built?'

'I'm not sure,' said Alex. 'The eighteen hundreds, I think.'

'Garth's an expert on old houses,' said Elaine.

'Please, come in,' said Alex, gesturing to the living room.

They followed Alex in. Garth stopped in front of the framed photos of her parents which Alex kept on the mantle. 'Look at this, honey,' he said.

Elaine walked up beside him and stared at one of the photos in silence. Finally she said, 'This must be your mother.'

'Yes, and my father,' said Alex.

'Dory looks just like her,' Garth said.

'That's what I thought,' said Alex. 'It was a little unnerving when I met her.'

Elaine turned her back on the photo. She picked a chair and sat down. Garth perched uneasily on the edge of an ottoman.

'Can I get you anything?' Alex asked.

Elaine shook her head.

Garth said, 'No, thanks.'

Alex sat down opposite them.

'I hope we're not interrupting,' Elaine said.

'No, I was just making a little dinner,' said Alex. 'All that anxiety. Makes you hungry.'

'What anxiety?' Elaine asked.

'Meeting Dory,' said Alex. 'It was very…emotional.'

'I imagine so,' said Elaine.

Garth nodded, avoiding her gaze.

'Look, I guess I owe you both an explanation,' said Alex. 'I did come by your house the other day. I talked to your upstairs neighbor.'

'Yes, we heard,' Elaine said in a chiding tone. 'You told Chris that you're my cousin. Why did you lie about that?'

'I don't know,' said Alex. 'I was trying to decide what to do. My attorney had located Dory for me, and I wasn't sure if I wanted to contact her. You see, my parents died recently and my mother left me a letter telling me that she'd given up a child for adoption, so I decided to look for her. I don't know if Dory told you when you spoke to her…'

'I didn't speak to her. I don't speak to her,' said Elaine.

Alex looked at her, confused. 'But you said that she told you…'

'I said that she left a message on my phone. I don't take her calls.'

'You don't?' said Alex. She looked at the composed, attractive middle-aged woman sitting opposite her. Then she looked at Garth Colson. He sighed and shook his head.

Alex looked back at Elaine. Her posture was perfect and her grooming was careful. Alex thought of her own mother with her messy strawberry-blonde hair and her softly rounded, middle-aged frame. Her sympathetic gray eyes. Alex could not imagine any circumstance where her mother would not speak to her. She just couldn't. 'Ever?'

'It's better this way,' said Garth.

Elaine's gaze was inscrutable. 'Dory left me a message as soon as she first got the letter from you, saying that you thought she was the child that your mother had given up.'

'I'm sure that came as a shock,' Alex said apologetically.

'I was surprised,' Elaine admitted.

'Well, I'm glad you aren't angry about it,' said Alex cautiously, although the woman she was looking at seemed far from content.

'As I said,' Elaine continued, 'I was surprised, but I tried to ignore it. Dory wanted me to supply some information. Obviously I wasn't going to do that. And then today, she called me as soon as you left. I listened to that message several times. Dory sounded quite pleased about it. Very pleased, in fact. As if this were some sort of validation. Her long-lost sister going out of her way to find her. To visit her.

She wanted to let me know about that right away.' This last was said in an accusing tone.

'Well, I hope she was glad that I came to see her,' said Alex carefully. 'It's not every day you meet a sister you never knew you had.'

Garth shifted his weight on the ottoman. 'We kind of thought that you might give up the idea of bonding with Dory when you found out she was in prison. When you found out why,' he said.

'I'll admit it—I almost did,' said Alex. 'That's why I came by your house. I guess I was hoping to talk to you about it. You know, to find out what you thought.'

'So why did you just run off?' Garth asked.

'I didn't run off,' Alex protested. 'It was just…incredibly awkward. I decided to go ahead and contact Dory. I realized that no one was going to talk me out of it. Despite what Dory had done, I was still curious to meet her.'

'You should have talked to us first,' said Elaine flatly.

Alex proceeded cautiously. 'You don't…approve?'

Elaine took a deep breath and steadied herself. 'Miss Woods.'

'You can call me Alex.'

'Alex, do you have any idea what Dory has put us through?' Elaine asked.

'Well, obviously, I know about what happened to…your other daughter.'

'Her name was Lauren. She was a beautiful girl. A treasure,' said Elaine, a slight tremor in her voice. 'She was on the road to stardom.'

'I'm sure she was,' said Alex. 'But it's Dory that I'm related to.'

Elaine sighed and shook her head. 'You look at Dory and you see this…sister that you didn't know you had. Locked up in prison like some princess in a fairy tale. I'm sure it must seem very romantic, finding your long-lost sister…'

'I wouldn't say romantic,' Alex protested.

'She didn't mean it like a boy-girl thing,' said Garth, trying to be helpful.

'She knows what I mean,' said Elaine. Then she looked up at Alex and held her gaze. 'I understand your curiosity. Believe me, I do understand that. But I feel that it is my duty to warn you that getting involved with her is a terrible mistake. Dory is dangerous…'

'Well, obviously, I know that she's in jail for murder.'

Elaine shook her head. 'When you say it like that, it sounds so…sanitary. Nothing could be further from the truth. Dory killed her sister. Her own sister. Brutally and viciously.'

'Not everyone is convinced of that,' Alex said stubbornly.

Elaine's eyes flashed and she let out a laugh that was almost a yelp of pain. 'So she told you about that business with the law student who has taken up her cause. We know about that, too.'

'The Justice Initiative has helped out a lot of innocent people,' said Alex.

'Innocent,' Elaine sputtered. 'Oh my God.'

'Alex,' said Garth, 'I beg your pardon, but you have no idea what you are talking about. This appeal is all about legal technicalities. The fact is that Dory pleaded guilty. Nothing will change that.'

'But her attorney has since been disbarred,' Alex insisted.

'It sounds as though he talked her into a guilty plea without even trying to help her.'

'Help her?' Garth yelped. 'Don't you think if she were innocent we would be doing our best to defend her? You don't know the whole story. She killed Lauren. No amount of legal maneuvering will change that.'

'It's too late, Garth,' Elaine interrupted him. 'She's already started believing her lies…I can see it in her eyes. She thinks we're terrible people, and that Dory is just a victim of injustice.'

Garth leaned forward and looked earnestly at Alex. 'We just want to set you straight before you go getting involved. This situation is complicated. Listen to what we're telling you. Walk away, young lady. While you still can.'

'Look,' Alex said, 'I can't put myself into your shoes. I mean, I don't know how you live with all this, losing your daughter like you did. But you're still Dory's parents. Doesn't that mean something?'

Elaine's expression was icy. 'She killed our daughter.'

'Your own, biological daughter, you mean,' said Alex.

'Now, just a minute,' said Garth. 'They were both our daughters.'

Elaine's tone was bitter. 'Do you have any children?'

Alex shook her head.

'I didn't think so. You couldn't possibly understand.'

Alex got up from her chair. 'What I don't really understand is what you intended to accomplish by coming here.'

Elaine stood up and Garth followed suit. He put a protective hand under his wife's elbow. Elaine looked again at the photo on the mantle. 'I came to pay a debt. I felt that I owed it to your mother.'

'My mother? Did you know my mother?'

'Not at all. We never met. But many years ago, your mother gave me a precious gift. I wanted a baby, more than anything in the world, and I wasn't able to conceive. When your mother gave up her baby, she made all my dreams come true.'

'Dory,' said Alex.

Elaine turned away from the photo, buttoned up her coat and knotted the belt. 'Be careful what you wish for,' she said.

EIGHT

THE NEXT MORNING Alex sat at her computer with a cup of coffee after a sleepless night, feeling as if her heart was made of lead. There was no denying the impression that the Colsons' visit had made on her. If they did not believe in Dory, why was she trying to see the good in her? The Colsons didn't seem like cruel or crazy people. Maybe they were right. After all, everyone in prison claimed to be innocent—even those who had committed the most heinous crimes.

She had bookmarked some of the most thorough articles about Dory's case. She read over them again, this time with a feeling of despair. The motive had been jealousy, ostensibly over this boyfriend, a doctor named Rick Howland, but Dory's parents seemed to feel that this was just an excuse. That Dory would have murdered Lauren sooner or later, no matter what. Alex Googled Rick Howland under physicians in Boston and found that there was a podiatrist of that name practicing on Huntington Avenue. She hesitated for a moment then dialed the number on her screen. She asked the receptionist for an appointment as soon as possible.

'Is it an emergency?' the receptionist asked.

Alex wondered what might constitute an emergency in podiatry. 'I'm in a lot of pain,' she said, realizing that this was, in fact, the truth.

The receptionist offered her an appointment at noon. Alex thanked her and hung up. Just then the doorbell rang and Alex picked up her coffee cup and went to answer it.

This time it actually was Seth Paige on the front step. Her heart barely registered the fact that he was there. In the light of day he looked different. Normal. She felt like an alien encountering a human. 'Hi,' she said dully.

'I came to look at your dad's books,' he said. 'Is this a good time?'

'Good as any,' Alex continued in a dull voice.

He followed her into the house.

'They're in here,' she said.

Seth walked into the office and gave a cursory glance at the shelves of books. 'Wow,' he said. 'What a great collection. I'd like to have all of them.'

'Take 'em,' said Alex.

Seth frowned and turned to look at her. 'What's the matter with you?' he asked.

Alex shook her head. 'Long story.'

Seth sat down on the edge of her father's desk. 'Go ahead. I'm in no hurry. I've played about all the games of cribbage with my dad that I can stand for one lifetime. I wanted to see the books but, honestly, coming over here was my excuse for getting out of the house.'

Alex smiled wanly. 'I can't talk about it,' she said. 'It's too much.'

'Well, let me see if I can help boil it down. I know about the sister in prison. I know you went to see her.'

'How did you know that?' Alex asked, taken aback.

Seth shook his head. 'How long have you lived in this neighborhood? Your Uncle Brian told Laney Thompson. He's been keeping tabs on you through the Thompsons.'

'I don't believe this,' Alex protested.

'Be glad they care,' said Seth. 'So, what happened?'

Alex sighed. 'Well, I went to see her.'

'How was that?' he asked.

Alex hesitated. 'Difficult. Upsetting.'

'No shit.'

'Then her parents came by here last night. They basically said that Dory was bad to the bone, and that I should stay as far away from her as possible.'

'But you don't feel that way?' he asked.

Alex shook her head. 'I don't know what I feel. They know her better than I do. I spent half an hour with her. Maybe they're right,' she cried. Then she exhaled. 'I just don't know.'

'Then look farther,' he said.

Alex looked at him in surprise. 'You're not going to tell me to stay away from her?'

'Why would I do that?' he said. 'You're an intelligent woman. Make up your own mind.' He looked over his shoulder. 'Have you got a plan for those cartons over there?' he asked, pointing to a pile of boxes from the liquor store.

She shook her head.

'Look, Alex, I'm not trying to be flippant,' he said. 'I just think you have to trust yourself. Do you know what you're going to do?'

Alex shrugged. 'I located her old boyfriend. I thought I might go and talk to him. Maybe he can shed some light on what happened.'

'You may as well,' he said. 'I would if I were you.' He walked over to the bookshelf and reverently pulled down a volume.

'You would?' she said.

He turned a few pages in the book, and then looked up at her. 'If I wanted to know more, yes, I would. Obviously you are not satisfied with what you know now.'

'No, I'm not.'

'So go,' he said.

Alex hesitated. 'You're right. I'm gonna do it. But you can stay and look at the books.'

'I'll come back another time,' Seth said, setting down the volume on the desk and following her out of the office. Alex opened the front door for him.

'Anytime,' she said, and then blushed at the eagerness in her voice.

Seth did not seem to notice. 'There's no hurry,' he said.

TOO IMPATIENT TO wait for the train, Alex drove into town and parked in a lot near Copley Square. She walked to the podiatrist's office, located in a relatively new high-rise block along the wide boulevard that was Huntington Avenue.

She gave her name to the receptionist.

'Can you fill out these forms for me?' asked the receptionist, handing over a clipboard. 'Do you have insurance?'

Alex handed over her card.

'Your co-pay is thirty dollars,' said the receptionist.

Cheap enough for a chance to talk with the man for whom Dory had murdered her own sister. Alex gave the receptionist cash and sat down to fill out the forms. The man in the seat nearest to her was wearing one normal shoe, and one with the sides cut out so that his socks were exposed. Alex tried not to look too closely. She handed the clipboard back and thumbed through a magazine until a patient limped out of the doctor's office and began to discuss her bill with the receptionist.

'Ms Woods,' the woman said, pointing to the office door.

Alex went inside and sat down in a metal chair in the examining room. The walls were decorated with charts showing the musculature of the foot, interspersed with photos of a tall, shaggy-looking dog with what appeared to be eyebrows over soulful brown eyes and a handlebar mustache. In a few minutes, the white-coated doctor entered, a chart held protectively across his chest. He was on the short side, with thinning dark brown hair and a pleasant, unremarkable face.

'Thanks for seeing me, Dr Howland,' she said.

'Miss Woods. What seems to be the problem?' he asked. 'You left it blank on your chart.'

'The problem is…' Alex thought about how to say it. 'I have recently learned that I am Dory Colson's half-sister.'

The doctor recoiled and stared at her.

'I only met Dory the other day for the first time. You can imagine that this is all very disturbing—to find out that the sister you never knew you had is in prison for murder.'

'So you're not here as a patient,' he said.

'No,' she admitted. 'I just wanted a chance to talk to you. I was afraid you might avoid me if I called looking for information.'

'You know you could have handled this better. You didn't need to take up valuable time in my practice.'

'I gave your receptionist my co-pay,' Alex said with a slight smile.

He did not seem to be amused. 'What do you want from me?' he asked coldly.

'I guess I want you to…fill in some blanks for me. If you would.'

He did not agree, but he did not tell her to get out. Alex pressed on. 'You and Dory were dating at the time of Lauren's murder?'

He leaned back against the examining table. 'Yes. That's right,' he said.

'How did you meet?'

'I was one of her clients. She took care of Iago for me during the day.' He looked at the photos on the wall and his eyes softened. 'My dog is very highly strung. He needs to get out during the day. I answered Dory's ad in the free paper. She had great references. It turned out that she was…

excellent with dogs. And she was a great-looking woman. I got to know her over time. One thing led to another.'

'So you and Dory were involved?' Alex asked.

'Well, why not?' he asked defensively. 'We were both single people. We both liked animals.'

'I'm not criticizing,' said Alex wearily. 'I'm just trying to understand. Her parents don't seem to have a shadow of a doubt that she is guilty. They are completely convinced that she killed her sister. And that you were the cause.'

'That is just not true,' he scoffed. 'I spoke to her sister a few times, just because she was there when I came by to pick up Dory. And she had had surgery on her foot at Boston General. I knew her surgeon. He's a colleague of mine. Anyway, she asked me a few questions. I answered her. It was nothing at all. It was common courtesy. It wasn't even a flirtation.'

'But Dory believed that it was,' said Alex.

The doctor shook his head. 'Nothing I could say would convince her otherwise. She and her sister—it was a bad relationship. In fact, once the sister came home for her surgery, my relationship with Dory started to go downhill.'

'Why?' asked Alex.

Rick Howland shrugged. 'That was all she could talk about. Lauren this and Lauren that. She was obsessed with that sister. I told the cops this. She could hardly think about anything else. We went from being two people having a pretty good time together to an endless monologue from Dory about all the ways that she detested and distrusted Lauren. It was terrible.'

Alex frowned at him. 'And you're sure you didn't contribute to this?'

He leaned forward and looked Alex in the eye. 'There was nothing going on between me and Dory's sister, Lauren. It was all in Dory's mind.'

Alex hesitated. 'Do you ever see Dory anymore?'

'No,' he said firmly. 'Never. She's crazy. I don't want to see her.'

'So you think she did it. You think she killed Lauren.'

Rick Howland shrugged. 'She said she did.'

'Were you surprised by that?'

Rick considered the question. 'Yes,' he said at last. 'Actually, I was. She wasn't really warm and fuzzy, but she loved those animals so much. I couldn't imagine her ever hurting an animal. I guess I assumed that she would never hurt another person. But when it came to her sister all bets were off.'

'So you didn't want to see her anymore?'

'In prison?' he asked. 'I'm not a masochist.'

'But if you cared for her…'

'Not that much. There are other fish in the sea,' he said brusquely.

'The Justice Initiative is trying to get her a new trial,' said Alex.

'Good luck,' said the doctor.

'So even if she were exonerated, you still wouldn't want anything to do with her?'

The doctor looked at her, his eyes wide. 'No,' he said. 'In fact, I'm seeing someone else now. I don't want anything to do with Dory Colson. If you're smart, you might want to avoid her as well. Now, if you'll excuse me, I have actual patients waiting.'

Alex thanked him and left the office. Out on the sidewalk she felt like a balloon whose air had all leaked out. She was not sure what she had hoped to hear from Rick Howland, but she knew that she felt worse for having talked to him. While he wasn't exactly against Dory, he certainly wasn't in her corner. Alex felt her phone vibrating in her pocket. She pulled it out and glanced down at the screen.

There was a text message from Marisol Torres. *Dory says I can talk to you. Let me know when you want to meet.*

Alex hesitated, then texted her back. *I'm in town. Meet at your office?*

THE JUSTICE INITIATIVE was located in a brownstone building which formed part of the New England University Law School. Alex spoke to the receptionist on the first floor. She was directed up three flights of steps to Marisol Torres's small, narrow office. On each floor the building seemed to buzz with activity.

The door was open, but Alex tapped on the door frame. Marisol looked up and greeted her with a smile. She moved some boxes and folders so Alex could sit down. 'Sorry about this mess,' she said. 'I think this room was somebody's storage closet when the building was a private home. No windows and you can barely fit a desk in here.'

'It's cosy,' said Alex, sitting down on a swivel chair on casters, which was wedged firmly in place by cardboard boxes filled with papers. On Marisol's desk was a photo of a bright-eyed little girl in a striped T-shirt with ribbons in her hair.

'Is that your daughter?' Alex asked.

Marisol sighed and looked fondly at the picture. 'That's my Iris. Everything I do, I do for her.'

'She's adorable,' said Alex.

'Thanks,' said Marisol, settling into her own chair. 'So, I spoke to Dory, and told her you were curious about her case, and she said that I could tell you anything you wanted to know about it.'

'I have a lot of questions,' said Alex.

'I'll try to help.'

'I guess my first question is a legal one,' said Alex. 'How

can you win an appeal for someone who's already pleaded guilty to the crime?'

'Basically we will be pleading that Dory was denied her right to counsel because she was advised by her attorney to plead guilty. He said that she could never win at trial.'

'And she could have?'

'No one can answer that. But Dory told the police that the day Lauren died, she and her sister argued—the prosecution had a witness to corroborate that—a dry cleaner who came to the family's apartment in the South End to make a delivery. Then Dory claims that she went out for a walk. When she returned, she found her sister's body.'

'What actually…happened? I mean, the crime,' Alex asked, grimacing.

'Well, Lauren's body was found in the kitchen at the back of the house at the garden level. The door to the garden was unlocked when the police got there. Lauren was found on the floor, stabbed several times. The murder weapon was a knife from the block on the kitchen counter. Dory was covered with blood when the police arrived. But that was easily explained. She said she was trying to revive Lauren.'

'I read in the newspaper accounts that Dory and Lauren argued about this guy, Rick Howland,' said Alex. She did not mention that she had just come from Dr Howland's office.

Marisol nodded. 'Oh, yes. The foot doctor with the Spinone.'

'Spinone?' Alex asked.

'That's his dog. He and Dory had only recently started seeing one another. Socially, so to speak. Dory seemed to see Rick as quite a prize catch, and she was sure Lauren was trying to steal him away from her. In fact, she was always very jealous of Lauren. There's no disputing that. But there's no evidence of any entanglement between Doctor

Howland and Lauren. No emails. No calls. Nothing. Lauren lived in Branson, Missouri, and rarely visited Boston.'

'So, it's possible that Dory was being…'

'Paranoid. Yes. I'm afraid so.'

Alex frowned. 'Everybody agrees that she had a motive. And an opportunity, obviously. What makes you think she could have won at a trial?'

'Ah,' said Marisol, raising her index finger. 'This is where the attorney's negligence comes in. Dory said she took a walk after their argument to clear her head. In his effort to convince Dory to take a plea, her attorney, the public defender in question, told her that there was not a single witness to back up her story. He claimed to have canvassed the neighborhood and that nobody remembered seeing her. He said there was no one to support her alibi.'

'How is that helpful?' Alex asked.

'It turns out,' said Marisol, pausing for effect, 'the neighbors were never asked. That much they do remember. No one ever came around from the public defender's office to even ask if they remembered seeing her. Dory claimed that she walked up to Copley Square and that she bought a bottle of water in the Back Bay station. No one ever questioned the clerk who was on duty that day, or showed the clerk her picture. The attorney just didn't bother to try to corroborate her story.'

'Were there cameras in the store? Security cameras?'

'Yes—not that the attorney checked on that.'

'Did they show Dory?'

'Well, I've looked at the footage,' Marisol said. 'It was a cheap camera, so the film is grainy. And sadly, the owner was using it to spy on his clerks. So the only visible face was the clerk's. Everybody else was shot from behind. And it was a cold day so they were all wearing scarves and hats and collars up.'

'What about a receipt?' Alex asked.

'Dory threw it away,' said Marisol. 'The attorney told her that without alibi witnesses there was no hope for an acquittal, and she needed to take a plea or go down for life.'

'And she took it,' said Alex.

'Yes. And she never should have. This was a murder case,' Marisol said. 'The brief will show that her defense lawyer made no effort to confirm her alibi. That alone should demonstrate that she was not defended adequately, and the judge should grant her a new trial, especially with what they already know about this public defender.'

Alex tried to sound positive. 'You seem pretty hopeful about this.'

'I am,' said Marisol. 'The brief is being reviewed right now by one of the attorneys who help us. Harold Gathman. He's already applied for a court date for the judicial review.'

'Good,' said Alex. 'But if she does get a new trial, there's still no way to prove her alibi. Especially after all this time.'

'We'll cross that bridge when we come to it,' Marisol said.

Alex nodded.

Marisol sat back in her seat. 'So, we can count on your support.'

'Yes,' said Alex doubtfully.

Marisol frowned at her. 'Dory said she thought you might be willing to help with some funds.'

'Funds?' said Alex, knowing she had never made any such offer.

'The law school could really use any financial contribution you might want to make. Everything costs money,' Marisol said.

Alex stood up. She was a little bit put off by the fact that Dory had offered her financial assistance without even asking. She couldn't help remembering her attorney, Mr

Killebrew's warning. Prisoners were known to take advantage of people from the outside. People who cared about them. But there was no doubt that this was a good cause, she reminded herself. The Justice Initiative. It was worth supporting. 'Of course, I will. This is important work that you're doing.'

'I like to think so,' Marisol said.

NINE

ALEX DROVE HOME, parked the car in the garage, lowered the door, and was about to go into the house when she remembered that she had nothing in the house to eat for dinner. She thought about getting back in the car and heading for the grocery store, but the thought of major shopping was unappealing. She decided to walk the three blocks to the nearest convenience store to get herself a hero sandwich or something equally decadent. She needed to stretch her legs, breathe some fresh air and think about what she had learned from Rick Howland and from Marisol. Overall, it wasn't encouraging. The podiatrist had suggested that Dory was obsessed with her jealousy of Lauren. Obsession implied a kind of madness.

Alex's conversation with Marisol Torres had left her frustrated. She had to admit to herself that she had hoped to learn that there was some irrefutable proof of Dory's innocence which was motivating the Judicial Initiative to represent her. In fact, it turned out to be, as the Colsons had said, all about legal maneuvering. Marisol was focused on the misdeeds of the public defender, and she might very well win the appeal. But in a new trial, how would anything be different? While she knew that everything Marisol had told her was legitimate, it seemed to beg the question: had Dory killed her sister? No one is going to answer that for you, she thought. Either you believe her or you don't.

The afternoon was growing dark and Alex shivered in her coat. She thought about that day, when Dory said she had gone out for a walk in the South End of Boston. If it had happened in the summer, people would have seen her on the street. But on a cold day like this people were in their homes, not sitting out on the front steps watching passers-by. If I had to prove that I was out walking today, she thought, how could I do it? There was no one looking out at her and, even if they were, she was covered in a coat, hat and scarf. It would be hard to tell at a passing glance if she were a man or a woman. A few cars went by but it was nearly dark, and who would remember seeing someone hurrying along, bundled up against the weather?

Alex trudged along in the cold, and was glad to arrive at the brightly lit convenience store. She picked up a basket at the door and began to put a few things in it. Not too much, she thought. She needed everything, but this was only a stopgap measure. She still had to carry it home.

She brought her items up to the counter and set them down.

'Pretty chilly out there, isn't it?' said the clerk.

Alex shivered reflexively. 'It really is. I wouldn't be surprised if it snowed.'

The clerk nodded as he rang up her order. 'They've been saying on the TV that it's going to. Twelve dollars and ninety-nine cents,' he said.

Alex handed him the money.

'You want your receipt in the bag?' he asked.

'No, I'll take it,' she said, stuffing the slip of paper in her coat pocket.

'Stay warm,' he said as Alex moved out of the way of the person who was now behind her.

Alex gathered up her bags and headed for the door, opening it with her shoulder. She dreaded going back out into the cold. She put her head down against the wind and began the short, unpleasant walk home.

She went into the house, turning on all the lights, and carried her bags to the kitchen. She flung her coat on a chair and began to put the things she had brought back with her into the cupboards and refrigerator. Feeling guilty, she had decided to skip the sandwich and had bought, instead, some eggs and a ready-made salad. She could make an omelet with the cheese she already had in the refrigerator... She emptied both bags and realized that she didn't have the salad.

Damn, she thought. I paid for it. I know I did. She didn't want to go all the way back to the store and start complaining, but it was a four-dollar salad. She looked in the bag for the receipt and then in her wallet, to no avail. Then, going over the transaction in her mind, she remembered that she had stuffed her receipt into her coat pocket. She picked up her coat off the chair and fished into the pocket, past the gloves and a wad of tissues, and pulled it out. She looked it over. No salad was listed. I'm losing it, she thought. I could have sworn... All that was listed was juice, bread, milk and a package of Oreos. Oreos? She hadn't bought Oreos. And then she looked again at the receipt. This was not her receipt from today. It was a receipt from...Alex stared at the little slip of paper. At the bottom the date and the time of the transaction at the convenience store was printed. It was from two weeks ago.

Alex was distracted from her missing salad by another thought. On the day that Lauren was killed, Dory had bought a bottle of water at Back Bay station. That receipt could prove that she was where she said she was. Dory said that she'd thrown it away. She probably didn't even remember what she did with it. What if there hadn't been a trash can handy? Dory might well have jammed it into her coat pocket, just as Alex had done at the convenience store. Alex frowned, picturing it. It was possible. It could have happened that way.

Alex gazed at her own jacket as if she were seeing it for the first time in a new way. Had that receipt for a bottle of water been jammed in there, covered by lint and tissues, in Dory's coat pocket? And if it was, whatever became of that coat?

She picked up her phone and searched for the number at the prison, punched it into her phone and prepared herself to sound desperate while she listened to it ring. A family emergency, she thought. I'll say it's a family emergency. She expected resistance from the person who answered, but a woman with a harsh voice said, 'Just a minute,' when Alex asked to speak to Dory. Alex marveled at the lack of restriction on a phone call. No one seemed to be concerned.

By the time Dory picked up the phone, Alex was drumming her fingers impatiently on the dining room table. She jumped when Dory said hello.

'Dory,' she said. 'It's me. It's Alex.'

'What do you want?' Dory asked suspiciously.

Obviously there weren't going to be any pleasantries. Fair enough, Alex thought. 'Something occurred to me. I have a question.'

'About what?' Dory asked.

'Dory, what happened to the clothes you wore that day? The day Lauren was killed?'

'The clothes I wore?' Dory sounded skeptical.

'Yes. Your clothes. What happened to them?'

'The police took them,' said Dory. 'They had blood all over them.'

Alex was silent for a moment, her thoughts filled with this grisly image.

'Well, when I found her, I lifted her up. I tried to help her,' Dory said defensively. 'That's why they had blood on them. I got it on my clothes when I tried to help her. I had to give them all to the cops. I don't know if they keep shit like that...'

'Everything?' said Alex, deflated.

'Shoes, socks, the works,' said Dory.

'Your coat too?' Alex asked.

'Probably,' said Dory. And then she was silent for a moment. 'No. Not my coat. I wasn't wearing my coat when I found her. I must have hung it up when I came home.'

'Are you sure about that?'

Dory hesitated again. Then she said, 'Yeah. When we went to the police station, my dad gave me one of his old work jackets to put on over the bloody clothes. He said I should wear the parka so we could throw it in the wash when I got home. He didn't know I wasn't coming back home.'

Alex felt her hope rising. 'So what happened to your coat? The one you wore out on the walk?'

'I don't know,' said Dory irritably. 'Why?'

'It might be nothing,' said Alex. 'What did the coat look like? Describe it.'

'Why?'

'Humor me,' she said.

Dory sighed. 'It was a black pea coat from Gap. Size eight. The belt was attached to it. Sewn onto it. I always liked that coat.'

'And that's the last time you remember wearing it?' Alex asked. 'When you went out for that walk?'

'I guess so. Why are you asking me all this?'

'Look, it's probably nothing. I don't want to get your hopes up.'

'No danger of that,' Dory said.

Alex heard some noise on the other end of the line.

'I gotta go,' said Dory. She hung up without another word.

Alex thought about what she needed to do. First, she had to go to the Back Bay station and see if there was a trash can in that little shop. Of course it was several years ago but if there was none now…

All right, she thought. Steady. If there was no trash can, the next thing to do was to go to the Colsons' South End apartment to try to locate that coat.

She shook her head and consciously derailed her train of thought. She realized that she should clear this idea with Marisol. She might have already thought of it, already tried it. Alex could call and ask her. But even as she thought it, she realized that she didn't want to. She felt sure that Marisol would try to talk her out of it. It was a complication she didn't need to make her case. But Alex wanted to try, to see if there was a way to help. If it didn't work out there wouldn't be any harm done, she thought. But if she asked, and Marisol told her not to do it…

Alex knew better than to ask permission when she wasn't willing to take no for an answer. She'd explain afterwards if nothing came of it. She glanced at the clock. It was rush hour. There would be lots of trains. If she drove to the Chichester station, she could be in the Back Bay in half an hour. She put her groceries in the refrigerator and threw her coat back on.

TEN

ALEX BOUGHT A bag of peanuts and wolfed them down while she looked around in the dim, fluorescent light of the shop. No trash can. She looked outside the door. None there either. 'Excuse me,' she said.

The clerk, a young woman with heavy eye make-up, stared at her.

Alex held up the empty peanut bag. 'Do you have a trash can here?'

'No,' she said. 'Take it out on the street. There are trash cans out there.'

'Not even behind the counter?' said Alex.

The clerk looked at her as if she had grown a horn in the middle of her forehead. 'Take your trash outside.'

'What do you do when you have something to throw away?'

The clerk shook her head. 'My boss says let the city pay to haul the garbage. He says I can take it outside or bring it home with me.'

'That's terrible,' said Alex, but she felt her heart lift hopefully as she walked out of the Back Bay station and surveyed the block. There were no trash cans on this side of the street. She saw one on the other side. Would someone cross the street to use it? Maybe not, Alex thought.

The streets were teeming with cars and pedestrians hurrying home in the darkness. Alex thought about her next stop. Elaine and Garth Colson lived about ten blocks from here. They would probably be home, having dinner. She wasn't quite sure what she was going to say to them. She only knew that she needed to get into that apartment. She merged into the river of people on the sidewalk, and headed in the direction of Dory's former home.

THE SMELL OF Italian food cooking emanated from the apartment along with the plaintive, vibrant voice of a woman singing about lost love to the sound of an electric fiddle. Alex pressed the buzzer in the vestibule and waited, still not sure of what she was going to say. The door opened and Garth Colson stood there, frowning at the sight of her. Then his brow cleared. 'Oh, hello, Alex,' he said. 'I thought you were our dinner guests.'

'I'm sorry. I didn't mean to interrupt,' said Alex.

'Oh, it's nothing special. It's just our neighbors.'

'I was wondering if I could talk to you.'

'Come in. Come in,' he said. 'I'm cooking my famous spaghetti and meatballs and I have to get back to it. Elaine's not home yet. Come on in. Hang up your coat.'

Alex stepped into the apartment where Dory had grown up and looked around curiously. Inside, the house seemed elegant but comfortable. The wallpaper was a dark rose color and the hardwood floors were scuffed. There was a big mirror to the right of the door and, beneath it, a table with a Chinese bowl flanked by brass candlesticks.

On the other side of the front door was a chipped, ceramic umbrella stand stuffed with umbrellas and a long line of hooks surmounted by a shelf which was fastened to the wall. On the shelf were a riotous pile of hats, most of them knitted and of bright colors. From the hooks hung an assortment of garments, some several layers deep. Beneath them were several pairs of boots, neatly lined up.

Alex walked over to where the coats were hanging. Was it possible, she wondered, that Dory had come home that long ago day, thrown her coat on a hook and forgotten it? Maybe the Colsons left it there, as if in hope that one day their daughter would return. Or, more likely, distracted by the horrible events of the day, they might not have noticed it and never gotten around to removing it. Alex knew better than most, after clearing out her parents' house, how clothing could pile up and stay in place, unused, sometimes for years.

Garth, who had disappeared into the kitchen, came back out into the hallway, wielding a wooden spoon. 'Can I get you a beer or a glass of wine?'

'Oh, no,' said Alex. 'Thank you, anyway.'

Once Garth had returned to his cooking tasks, Alex shrugged off her own coat and quickly ran her hands over the collection on the hooks. She had to pull the coats back without pulling them off, and sort through them. She was looking for a pea coat, not a long coat, so that eliminated some of the candidates. She rummaged through looking for jacket-length coats, and her heart leapt when she saw a dark jacket with a bathrobe-style belt sewn into it. In the dimness of the vestibule, which was lit by a chandelier, Alex couldn't tell if the jacket was black or navy. But it was definitely the right style. She wrestled it out from among the others and quickly examined the inside of the neck. Gap. Size… She could not make out the number of the size because it was nearly worn away. But the coat was made for a slim person. It could have been Dory's size.

Shifting her own coat to her other arm, Alex reached into the pockets of the pea coat. Her heart sank when she realized that each pocket was filled with wads of Kleenex, change, dog treats and scrunchies. And multiple small pieces of paper. One of them might be exactly the receipt she was thinking of.

Suddenly she heard the key in the lock, and she withdrew her hand from the pea coat pocket and folded the flap down over it, smoothing it as she did so. She stepped away from the hooks as the door opened. Elaine came in, wearing a plaid coat and carrying a book bag. She stopped short when she saw Alex and shook her head.

'What are you doing?' Elaine asked bluntly. 'How did you get in here?'

Alex hesitated. 'Just hanging up my coat. Your husband let me in.'

'Come with me. Bring your coat. Garth,' Elaine called out as she set off through the apartment.

Alex pulled her coat back on and followed Elaine down the hallway. They descended a short staircase to a great room with a fireplace, with a cozy brick kitchen at the other end of the ground level. Elaine set her book bag down beside a chair and laid her own coat over the back of it. Then she walked up to her husband who was standing by the stove. 'Where are Joy and Therese?' she said, putting a finger into the sauce on the stove and tasting it.

'Not here yet,' said Garth.

'Why did you invite her?' Elaine asked.

'Alex? She just arrived. I didn't know she was coming,' said Garth. 'But she's welcome to stay. I made plenty.'

'Never mind that, Garth,' said Elaine. She turned to Alex. 'What are you doing here?'

'I'm here on kind of a mission,' Alex admitted. 'I'm trying to help Dory.'

'Ah, yes. I've heard,' said Elaine. 'She's left me several voicemails.' She shook her head. 'You didn't listen to a word we said.'

Alex blushed but refused to apologize. She imagined the lonely voicemail from Dory, speaking to a mother who never picked up the phone. 'Elaine, I know that you warned me, but I find I can't turn my back on her.'

Elaine looked exasperated. 'What exactly are you hoping to accomplish?'

'I'm hoping to help her prove her alibi.'

'Her alibi.' Elaine snorted and opened the refrigerator door. She pulled out a bottle of water. 'Garth, do you need anything in here?' she asked.

'Get me that jar of garlic,' he replied.

While Elaine searched in the refrigerator, Alex looked at the assortment of photos affixed to the open refrigerator door with magnets. The largest photo was of a beautiful young woman onstage, her arms extended out in a plea, her gaze troubled, her mouth open and lips forming an oval. Her shining blonde hair cascaded over her shoulders and she was wearing jeans, boots and a gauzy top over a camisole. When she looked more closely, Alex realized that all the photos were of the same person. In one photo, she was a young teenager accepting a bouquet, her golden hair in a long braid down her back. Another was a headshot. Her sweet eyes snapped with life. Lauren, Alex thought.

There were no photos of Dory.

'Is that Lauren?' Alex asked.

Elaine closed the door and handed Garth the jar he was seeking. Then she tilted her head and listened, her eyes misting. 'Yes. That's our Lauren. She had such a beautiful voice.'

Alex was suddenly aware of the CD that had been playing since she arrived. 'Oh, is that Lauren singing?' she asked.

Elaine frowned at her. 'Isn't that what you asked me?'

'I meant the pictures,' said Alex. 'I'm sorry—I don't really know country music. But you're right. She does have a beautiful voice. It's so clear.'

'There's a lot you don't know,' said Elaine.

Alex, who had not been asked to sit, shifted from one foot to the other. 'Like what? What is it that I don't know?'

'Elaine,' Garth said in a warning tone.

Elaine scowled and Alex could see that she was debating with herself whether or not to heed his warning. Finally she made up her mind. 'This was not the first time,' she said.

Alex frowned. 'What do you mean?'

'There's no need to bring this up,' said Garth.

Elaine ignored her husband's warning. 'Do you know what it means to have your record expunged?' she asked.

'Well, I imagine…' Alex's voice trailed away. 'No, not really.'

Garth muttered something unintelligible. He set the spoon down and turned on his wife. 'Elaine, stop. I understand how you feel, but stop. This is a stranger you're telling all this to. And she doesn't need to know this stuff.'

'She wants to know about Dory. I think she has a right to know, before she gets herself in any deeper. If you don't want to hear it, why don't you go upstairs and see what's keeping Joy and Therese.'

Garth shook his head and sighed as he walked out of the room. Alex heard the door to the apartment slam.

'What were you saying? About a juvenile record?' she prompted.

'Expunged. It's something they do for minors,' said Elaine crisply. 'It's a way of clearing the criminal record of a minor, so that it doesn't affect their whole lives.'

'Now that you mention it, I think I have heard of that,' said Alex.

'When she was fifteen years old, Dory took a razor to school and sliced the face of one of her classmates,' Elaine said calmly.

Alex stared at her.

'We knew she was troubled by the time that happened,

but we tried to support Dory. We made excuses for her. That the other girl was picking on her. It cost a fortune for the lawyer to arrange it, but her record was expunged. We never dreamed…' Elaine heaved a sigh and looked at the spot in front of the double French doors which led into the garden, as if she could still see her daughter's body lying there on the floor.

'This incident at school. Maybe she was provoked,' Alex said.

Elaine looked back at Alex in disbelief. 'You're determined to take her side.'

'I'm not,' Alex protested. 'I'm just trying to understand.' But there was no question that she was shaken by this revelation about Dory's violent past. What kind of person attacked another student with a razor?

The sound of voices filled the hallway and Garth came back into the kitchen, trailed by Therese and a tired-looking woman with dark curly hair shot through with gray. She was wearing an ill-fitting polyester suit and flowered blouse.

'They were on their way downstairs,' said Garth. 'Alex, these are our neighbors. Joy and Therese Ennis.'

'Oh, this album is my favorite,' exclaimed Therese, closing her eyes to be transported by the music. She twirled around, her delicate frame graceful as she moved to the music. 'Nobody could sing like Lauren.'

Elaine smiled indulgently at the teenager. 'She thought the world of you,' she said. Then she turned to Joy. 'Where's Chris tonight?' she asked.

'He started teaching a calligraphy class at the Y,' said Joy.

Looking at Joy, Alex could faintly discern the lovely, even dreamy young girl that she had once been in that photo upstairs from her student days. She still had the fetching mole by her lips and wide, beautiful eyes, but they were encircled by shadows.

'At least they're paying him for it,' she said in a resigned tone.

The song ended and Therese opened her eyes. Her gaze fell on Alex and she frowned. 'Hey, you were here before,' she said accusingly.

'That's right,' said Elaine. 'She was pretending to be a relative.'

'Joy, do you want a beer?' Garth asked.

Joy Ennis nodded. 'I could use one,' she said. 'I had a crappy day at work. Nice to meet you,' she said to Alex, offering a handshake.

'I'm Alex Woods.' She thought about mentioning her relationship to Dory, but it seemed like a guaranteed conversation-stopper. 'What do you do?' she asked instead.

'I'm an insurance adjuster. I work downtown in the Hancock Building.'

'That must be interesting,' said Alex politely.

'Not really. But it pays the bills. Somebody has to. My husband's a flower child. He works part-time at a food co-op and still takes classes.'

Garth, who seemed determined to lighten the atmosphere, smiled at Alex. 'What about you, Alex?'

'No, thanks. I'd better get going.' She gestured vaguely toward the front of the house and began to back out of the room. She had the sudden thought that, as she left the apartment, she might be able to pick up Dory's coat from the hook in the hallway and carry it off. Everyone was down here in the kitchen. There would be no one to see her take it and, clearly, no one would ever miss it.

'You can go out this way,' said Elaine, in a tone that brooked no disagreement. As if to emphasize the point she walked over to the garden door and pulled it open. Then she flipped a switch beside the door, illuminating the walkway surrounded by bushes and plants. 'It's dark,' she said, as if to explain her gesture.

'That's all right. I'll just…' Alex stopped mid-sentence as Elaine came over to her, subtly steering her to the French doors.

'Do you understand now?' she said quietly. 'I told you that you didn't know everything.' In a louder voice she said, 'Follow the path out. It leads up to the street.'

Alex hesitated, realizing that Elaine was not going to give her the choice of how to leave the apartment. And Alex didn't want to make a scene. She walked out the double doors to the garden. When she reached the foot of the steps leading up to the street, the lights beside the door were abruptly shut off, leaving her in total darkness.

ELEVEN

FROM UNDER A street light on the corner, Alex called the Justice Initiative and asked to speak to Marisol. A light snow had begun to fall, and she could see the sparkling showers of flakes descending in the glow of the street light.

'She's not here,' said the person who answered the phone. 'Do you have her number?'

'Yes,' said Alex. In a way, she was almost relieved. She didn't really want to have to tell Marisol about her visit to the Colsons' apartment. Elaine's account of Dory's youthful arrest was undeniably upsetting. But there was still the matter of the coat. Alex had, at least, found it. She decided to send Marisol a text, saying that she thought she knew where Dory's missing receipt might be. She composed the text, sent it, and then walked back to the station and boarded the next train back to Chichester.

There was a car parked in front of her house when she arrived home. She looked closer at it and saw that it was a dented Ford Taurus. Marisol got out of the Taurus and walked around to the backseat passenger-side door. She lifted a little girl from her car seat and set her down on the front walk. Together they walked up toward the house as Alex pulled in the driveway.

'What are you doing here?' Alex said.

'I got your text,' Marisol said. 'What is this all about?'

'You drove out from the city?'

'No, I was picking up Iris at my mother's. In Waltham.'

She leaned down to the child whose hand she was holding. 'Iris, this is Miss Woods. Say hello.'

The bright-eyed child became immediately bashful. 'Hello,' she whispered behind her fingers, which she had placed in her mouth.

'Nice to meet you, Iris,' said Alex.

'So, what gives?' Marisol asked.

Alex shook out her key chain and sighed. 'Come on in. I'll tell you about it.'

Alex opened the door and picked up the mail. She gestured for Marisol and Iris to follow her inside.

'Can I get you something, Iris?' Alex asked. Although she didn't know what she might have that a child would like. 'Some orange juice?' she suggested.

Iris shook her head.

'I may have some toys she could play with but they're up in the attic,' said Alex.

'You've got a TV, haven't you?' Marisol asked bluntly.

Alex nodded and went into the living room, turning on the TV and the lights.

Marisol settled her daughter on the sofa under a wool throw. 'OK,' she said. 'You watch for a while. Mommy won't be long.'

Iris nodded obediently and Marisol followed Alex. 'Any mother who says she doesn't use the TV for a babysitter is a liar.'

'I'm sure that's true,' said Alex. As she kicked off her shoes and padded back to the refrigerator in her bare feet, she explained to Marisol her thoughts about the receipt.

'I figured that if the receipt was still in Dory's coat pocket, the time and date on it might be just what we need to corroborate her story.'

'What did you do?' Marisol asked, frowning.

Alex told her about her trip to the store at Back Bay

station, and then to the house where Dory grew up. She offered Marisol a bottle of beer from the refrigerator but Marisol declined it.

'I'm driving,' she said. 'Precious cargo.'

Alex poured herself a glass of wine and indicated that they could sit down at the kitchen table.

'Well,' she said, 'I went to the Colsons' apartment and, believe it or not, I found the coat, still hanging in the foyer.'

Marisol groaned and clapped a hand over her eyes. 'Tell me you didn't take the receipt.'

Alex took a sip of wine and sat back, affronted. 'What's the matter with you? That's what I went there for.'

Marisol shook her head. 'Oh, no.'

'Well, given your reaction, I guess you'll be glad to know that I never got the chance. I don't even know if it was in the coat,' Alex admitted. 'Her mother came home and basically kicked me out of the house.'

'You told her mother what you were looking for?' she asked anxiously.

'I considered it,' said Alex. 'But I decided against it.'

Marisol exhaled noisily. 'Whew. Good,' she said. 'You should have asked me before you did something like that.'

'I didn't think I needed your permission.'

Marisol waved her hands as if to dismiss the subject. 'Anyway, it's all right. Everything is all right.'

Alex felt irritated by this response. 'Now it's all right?' she demanded. 'I don't understand. I didn't get the receipt. I doubt that Elaine Colson will let me back in that house again. I thought it was a good idea so I did it. Now I'm not so sure.'

'It was a good idea. It was a great idea,' said Marisol. 'It's just that we can't be the ones who come up with this receipt. The police have to do that. Otherwise, it's considered contaminated. They won't let us use it as evidence for the appeal.'

'Oh,' said Alex, thinking how close she had come to stuffing the contents of Dory's coat pockets into her handbag. 'Of course. I didn't realize.'

'No harm done,' said Marisol. 'We know the coat is there. That's the important thing. We'll see about getting a search warrant for it.'

'The police would do that?' Alex asked. 'Search Elaine's house?'

'No. But I can probably obtain a warrant for that particular item.'

'If that receipt is in there, will it prove that Dory didn't kill her sister?'

'Not exactly,' said Marisol. 'She could have gone out for a walk, come home and killed her sister then. After all, it was Dory who found the body. Dory who called nine-one-one.'

Alex frowned at the law student. 'I'm confused. Do you believe her or don't you?'

Marisol held up her palms. 'I'm just saying what a judge might say.'

'Then why are we bothering? If the receipt doesn't confirm her story, it doesn't even matter.'

'Oh, it matters,' said Marisol. 'It could be a game changer. With the receipt, we can gauge how long it would have taken Dory to walk home. And we know what time she called nine-one-one. That receipt may prove convincing evidence that she did not have sufficient time to commit this crime.'

'Really?' asked Alex, suddenly hopeful again.

'If, as you suspect, it's still in her coat pocket. Well, I shouldn't get ahead of myself. We don't actually have it yet.'

'No, right,' said Alex, sipping her wine. For a moment,

they were both silent, lost in thought. 'There was something else,' said Alex.

Marisol waited, her eyebrows raised.

'It turns out that Dory spent some time in a juvenile facility. Apparently, she…injured a girl with a razor blade at school. Her record was expunged.'

Marisol paled slightly. 'You're sure about this?'

'You didn't know, did you?' Alex said. 'That's what Elaine thought.'

'There's no way I could know, if it was expunged.'

'Does it make you wonder,' said Alex, 'if maybe…'

Marisol shook her head as if to shut off the flow of Alex's words. 'Hey, this appeal is on solid ground. One thing has nothing to do with the other.'

'Not legally, maybe…' said Alex.

'Legally is all I'm concerned with. Look,' said Marisol, getting up from her chair. 'I better get going. It's bath time and story hour for us. Luckily my mother already fed her. Thank heavens for my mother.' She walked out into the hall and called out to Iris. 'Come on, Iris, we're going.' She crouched down and began putting Iris's little jacket back on her.

Alex chewed her lip. 'Does this…change anything for you?'

'What do you mean?' the law student asked.

'Well, I mean, about Dory. What you think about her case?'

Marisol shrugged. 'This case is about a defendant being entitled to a vigorous defense. And now, thanks to you, we may have actual, physical proof that she was poorly defended. If we find that receipt, that new trial is a given. I feel very confident about that.' Then Marisol peered at her. 'Why? Does it change things for you?'

'I guess I find it a little…worrisome.'

Marisol patted her forearm. 'If we find that receipt, that's all we need. It's not DNA, but it's enough. Just focus on that.' Marisol bent down and scooped her child up in her arms. 'It is going to be a long day tomorrow. I have to get that warrant, and find out how all this is going to affect the appeal I've already written. That was good work, Alex. Really.'

Alex smiled weakly. 'Goodbye, Iris.'

'Say 'bye,' Marisol instructed the toddler.

''Bye,' Iris whispered sweetly.

'I'll be in touch,' said Marisol, heading out the door.

Alex felt a little surge of anxiety. For Marisol, this was a legal exercise. After all, Dory wasn't her sister. 'Drive carefully,' she said. 'That snow is slippery.'

Marisol smiled, flashing her beautiful teeth and cradling her daughter. 'I am always careful,' she said.

TWELVE

THE NEXT DAY, Alex tried to resume the cleaning out of the house, but she could not concentrate on the task since all her thoughts seemed to revolve around Dory, the coat and the awaited call from Marisol. Finally she pulled on a jacket and some boots, stuffed her phone in her pocket, and headed out of the house. She had a destination in mind. In downtown Chichester there was a store which took up half a block and sold used books and CDs. She thought she would ask the proprietor if he would accept the books that Seth didn't want. Or, if Seth didn't come back to look through them, accept them all. It was mostly an excuse to get out of the house.

The walk downtown was chilly but bracing. By the time she got to the store, Alex was feeling slightly more human. She opened the door and the smell of mold and dry paper greeted her. She tried not to inhale. The portly, bespectacled man behind the counter was busy going through some bags of books which had just been brought in by another customer. Alex had to wait her turn.

While she waited, she began to look through the CDs. There was a vast collection of rhythm and blues, opera and even folk music, but very little in the way of country western. She searched through the meager collection in vain.

'Are you following me?' asked a voice behind her.

Alex turned around and blushed at the sight of Seth Paige, who was holding half-a-dozen CDs in his hand. She did feel a little bit as if she had conjured him with her thoughts. 'Oh, hi,' she said. 'Actually, I think you're following me.'

'That could be. I love this place, don't you?' he asked.

Alex nodded. 'I wanted to ask the owner if he would take any of the books you don't want.'

'I am going to get those out of your way. I came back yesterday to have a look, but you weren't there,' he said.

'No,' said Alex. 'I've been pretty busy.'

He seemed to be waiting for her to elaborate, but she hesitated, not knowing where to begin. Seth frowned and glanced down at the rows of CDs divided by music style and artists. 'So, you're a country music fan?' he asked.

'No. Not really. I was just looking for a CD of Lauren Colson. Dory's sister. She made a couple of albums...'

'A country and western singer from Boston? That's a little odd, isn't it?'

'Well, her father was from out west. I guess she grew up listening to country music with him. Once her career got going, she moved to Missouri.'

'Branson?' he asked.

'Yes. How did you know?'

'That's a big country music town. It's like Nashville West.'

'Are you a country fan?'

'No. Just some fact that stuck in my flypaper mind. Actually, I don't know one country song from another,' he said, smiling. 'They're all about Jesus, angry redneck women and pick-up trucks, aren't they?'

'I don't know. I don't listen to country either,' Alex admitted. 'But I can't help being curious. She doesn't have her own section though.'

Seth began to thumb through a section called Miscellaneous C&W women. 'Maybe she's in here.'

'Maybe,' said Alex, watching as he flipped through the

plastic boxes. Just then, her phone buzzed in her pocket. She pulled it out and looked at the caller's name. 'Oh, I have to get this,' she said. 'Marisol?'

'Can you get over here?' Marisol asked. 'It's important.'

'On my way,' said Alex.

HALF AN HOUR LATER, Alex arrived, breathless, at the Justice Initiative, and clattered up the stairs to Marisol's office. The door was open and Marisol was jamming papers into an already stuffed file cabinet. Alex planted herself in the doorway. Marisol straightened up when she saw her, smiling.

'You got the coat,' Alex said.

Marisol grinned broadly. 'It was just where you said it would be. The police searched through it in my presence. The receipt was there, in her pocket. Date and time,' she said.

Alex let out a cry of surprise.

'And, in the nick of time too. The hearing date has been set for Friday.'

'Friday? Oh my God,' said Alex. 'Did you tell Dory?'

Marisol sat down at the desk and indicated the nearby chair. 'Not yet. I thought I'd wait till you got here to call her. We'll put her on speaker.'

'OK,' said Alex, sitting down.

Dory sounded depressed when she came to the phone.

'Dory, hi. It's me. It's Marisol. Alex is here with me. We both wanted to tell you this news,' said Marisol.

'What news?'

'You tell her, Alex. You found the missing piece on this one.'

Alex blushed with pleasure and began to explain about the receipt. 'Marisol got a warrant for the police to confiscate that one item of clothing, and there it was. In the pocket of your pea coat. Right where you left it three years ago.'

'Wow,' said Dory. 'Really? What are the chances it would still be there?'

'It was still there,' Alex affirmed.

'This is good, right?'

'Yes,' said Alex.

'It's excellent,' said Marisol. 'It couldn't have come at a better time. We found out today that your hearing is set for Friday. With this new evidence which supports your alibi, I feel very confident that we will win the appeal for a new trial.'

Dory was silent for a moment.

'We thought you'd want to know right away,' said Alex.

'I do. I don't know how to thank you.'

'I'm just glad we found that receipt,' said Alex.

'Wow. Me too. What did my mother say?' Dory asked.

'Your mother?'

'Yes. Was she upset about the police coming into the house?'

'I…don't know,' said Alex. 'I wasn't there.' She frowned at Marisol.

'I hope she wasn't too upset,' Dory fretted.

'She'll get over it,' said Alex impatiently.

'Listen, Dory, you and I have a bunch of things to go over before Friday. Tomorrow I'll come up to the prison with Mr Gathman, who is going to actually be pleading your case in court.'

Alex looked at the law student quizzically, pointing at herself and then at the door.

Marisol shook her head and frowned. 'I'll see you tomorrow, Dory.'

'OK. Whatever you think,' said Dory. 'Listen, Alex. And Marisol. I'm really grateful to you both. I can't believe you're doing all this for me.'

'I'm glad to do it, Dory,' said Alex, feeling a surge of affection for her.

'You're lucky your sister came along when she did,' said Marisol.

'I know,' said Dory sincerely.

Tears rushed to Alex's eyes. She took a deep breath.

'I'll speak to you tomorrow,' said Marisol. 'Try not to worry. Everything is going to be all right.'

'Promise?' Dory asked, in the voice of a small child.

'You get some rest,' said Marisol.

When they'd hung up Alex leaned back in her chair and found that, despite her lingering misgivings, she was genuinely happy and excited. When she set out to find her sister, she had never dreamed that she would be involved in an effort to save her from a life in prison. But it was getting closer. She could feel it. Then she looked at Marisol and saw that she seemed preoccupied.

'What's the matter?' she said. 'Aren't you excited?'

'I am,' Marisol said, nodding.

'But…'

'There's something else you and I need to discuss,' she said.

Alex frowned. 'What's that?'

'Well, if the judge does grant her a new trial, her attorney will be asking for bail.'

'Bail? How could she get bail?' Alex asked.

'The judge has the right to grant her bail, with very limiting conditions, until the new trial takes place. Or until the DA decides not to refile the charges. This is kind of a long shot. But, there are precedents. We need to consider the possibility.'

'OK,' said Alex slowly.

'Dory would need to have someone to pay the bond. It's ten per cent on the amount of the set bail, which is returned at the time of trial. I don't know how much money that would be but, if the judge agrees to it, I don't think he'll set an exorbitant amount. He wouldn't agree to it unless he was pretty well convinced that she was wrongfully imprisoned.'

Alex felt the question in Marisol's statement. 'My parents had insurance and some savings. I guess my mother would want me to do that. Yes, I'm sure she would,' she said.

'Good,' said Marisol. 'That's one thing settled. Also, in this unlikely event, the judge is going to ask who is willing to accept responsibility and take her in.'

Alex grimaced. 'Her mother definitely won't do that.'

'What about her father?' said Marisol. 'Does he feel the same way?'

'I'm not sure. I mean, I would think if the judge grants a new trial, they might be willing to look at Dory in a different light. Certainly if they drop the charges. That would be a reason for them to consider that she might, indeed, be innocent.'

'It's possible,' said Marisol.

'Well, we won't know until it happens,' said Alex.

'But our attorney needs to know before he makes the request for bail,' Marisol said. 'The judge will want specifics.'

'I really hope they would agree to take her in,' said Alex. 'She is their daughter, after all.'

'Or there's you,' said Marisol.

'Me?'

'She's your sister,' said Marisol. 'You've got that big old house to yourself. It's not as if you don't have room for her.'

Alex looked at her anxiously. It was one thing to try to be supportive of Dory's cause, to pay a bond. It was another thing to imagine living with her in the house. 'You probably think I'm terrible,' she said. 'Frankly, I feel guilty for hesitating. But I barely know Dory.'

'I don't think you're terrible. Let's be honest. The woman has been in prison for murder. And now we've learned that she had a violent incident in her past. Anybody would be concerned. That's why I thought I should warn you.'

'Do I need to answer you right away?'

'No. But soon.'

'I want to get to know my sister. I do. But…I think I will try to talk to her father. I'm sure, if she had a choice, Dory would rather be with her family. In the home she knows.'

'Wasn't there some poem about home being the place where, when you have to go there, they have to take you in?' Marisol said.

'Robert Frost.'

'I always liked that phrase. Anyway, I wouldn't worry. The chances are slim to none that, even if they agree to a new trial, any judge would grant her bail.'

'But he might,' Alex said.

'Is that what you want?' Marisol asked.

Alex hesitated. 'I want her to be able to go home.'

'Wherever that might be,' Marisol said.

THIRTEEN

AFTER SHE LEFT Marisol's office, Alex drove directly to Jamaica Plain in search of Garth Colson. She knew that Details, the architectural salvage firm which Garth owned, was situated in a large warehouse in that traditionally blue-collar neighborhood bordering the Jamaica Pond. Details served everyone from high-end designers to construction workers and weekend do-it-yourselfers. Alex parked her car down the block and entered the warehouse, picking her way through the historic remnants to reach the spot where Garth was working.

She found him sorting through a collection of brass and crystal doorknobs. He stood at a counter surrounded by piles of wooden window frames, Mexican tiles and an assortment of cement garden statues. Ornate mantelpieces, floating free from any fireplace, leaned against walls. Grecian columns stood alone on the cement floor.

Garth looked up when she called his name, and his expression darkened.

'Mr Colson, can I talk to you?'

'I suppose so.' He pointed to a free-standing oak church pew. 'Have a seat,' he said.

Alex nodded her thanks and sat down on the curved wooden bench. It was chilly in the high-ceilinged warehouse, and Garth was dressed for it. He wore a dusty parka, jeans and boots. His half-glasses hung on a chain around his neck.

Alex made no attempt to disguise the reason for her

visit. 'Dory is having her hearing on Friday. To decide if she gets a new trial,' she said.

'I didn't know it was going to happen so soon,' he replied without enthusiasm. 'Of course, we're not really in touch.'

'That's why I came here to see you. The fact is, if the appeal is successful, and Dory is granted a new trial, the attorney is going to ask for bail.'

'Bail? She's not going to get bail,' Garth scoffed.

'It's unlikely, but not out of the question.'

'Hmmph,' Garth murmured. He frowned and resumed his search through the doorknobs without comment.

Alex hesitated in the face of his silence. 'If that happens,' she said, 'the judge will need to know that Dory has somewhere to go and someone who can take responsibility for her. I was hoping that you and Elaine might be willing to do that.'

Garth shook his head. 'That's not going to happen. My wife doesn't even speak to Dory if she calls. She's not going to let her back in the house.'

'You could ask her,' Alex pleaded.

'I don't need to ask her. This is not something she's about to forgive and forget. Look, you have no idea what you're asking.'

'But if the court decides that Dory didn't have justice, and that she deserves a new trial, I would expect that her family would at least support her.'

Garth shook his head, and seemed to be weighing a crystal doorknob in his hand. 'Doesn't matter what the court says. Some things can't be denied.'

'Like what,' said Alex angrily.

Garth sighed. 'It's not just what happened to Lauren. Obviously none of us will ever get over that. Or even that incident in school. There's a whole history there. You know, Elaine and I tried for years to have a baby with no luck.

Then the adoption was another long procedure. We were just waiting to take Dory home with us when Elaine realized that she was pregnant.'

'So you were doubly blessed,' said Alex.

Garth frowned. 'People always say things like that. But it's not that simple. As they grew up, the two of them never got along. Dory was always the aggressor. She would pull Lauren's hair, or knock her over. It was like she wanted to… eliminate Lauren from day one. Of course, Lauren wasn't much more than preschool age when we realized that she had this beautiful voice and this…knack for performing. Elaine has a beautiful voice too, you know. But no one had ever really encouraged her as a child. So Elaine devoted herself to being sure that Lauren had every chance for success. She had to home school Lauren so that she could take her to all her lessons and auditions. It was the only practical thing to do, but Dory always took it personally.'

'But she must have felt like Lauren was your favorite child. Could you blame her for being jealous?' Alex asked.

'I didn't blame her. I just didn't realize how vicious it had become. Since she moved to Branson for her career, Lauren was hardly ever home. On those brief visits all we wanted was for those two to get along. But that never happened. You know, when Dory started dating that doctor…'

'Rick Howland,' said Alex.

'That's right,' said Garth. 'Rick. She finally seemed happy. Everything was Rick. We were kind of hopeful about it. We thought she might be calming down. Might even get married and move out of the house. But no. In the end, it became about Lauren.' Garth shook his head. 'That was our mistake. Thinking her jealousy was under control. If it hadn't been the dog-loving podiatrist, it would have been something else.'

Alex began to shiver. 'Maybe this guy, Rick Howland,

and Lauren were involved. Some men are born cheaters. It's his word against Dory's? Why do you choose to believe him?'

Garth's gaze was implacable. 'Why? Because I knew my daughter.'

Even though she was still wearing her coat, Alex was trying to keep her teeth from chattering. 'Lauren, you mean?' she said acidly. 'Lauren, who could do no wrong?'

'No,' said Garth sadly. 'Lauren, who was gay.'

Alex stared at him.

Garth smiled at her with bitter satisfaction. 'That's right. There was no way that Lauren was trying to steal Dory's boyfriend. She only liked girls.'

'I don't understand. Didn't Dory know that?' Alex asked, incredulous.

'No one knew. Especially not Dory. We had to keep it from her. She would have used that information against her sister. Lauren was making a mark in country music. Believe me, I grew up out west. I know. There is no room for gay people in the country and western world. None whatsoever. Do you remember what happened to that pretty thing, a country singer, when she came out a few years back? Her career was over. Dried up overnight. I think it's wrong, but it's a reality. Lauren had worked too hard to have her dream.'

Garth's phone buzzed and he pulled it out and looked at it. He frowned. 'I better take this. It's Elaine.'

He got up, walked away from the desk and spoke into the phone. Alex could hear the murmur of his voice and see anguish on his face. Finally Garth folded up the phone and stuffed it into a pocket inside his parka. He looked at Alex, unsmiling.

'She was calling me from work,' he said. 'She's fit to be

tied. She just got back to the school. She had to go home because the police came to take some old coat of Dory's.'

'I know about that,' said Alex.

'I thought you might. You better just go, Miss Woods. And keep on going if you know what's good for you.'

'Come to the hearing, Mr Colson,' she pleaded. 'You might find out that you have not been entirely fair to Dory.'

'Oh, I'll be there,' he said wearily. 'You can be sure of that.'

Alex hesitated, then got up from the church pew. She realized that she was not going to get anything more from the Colsons. She also realized, as she picked her way back through the salvaged embellishments, that Dory's only hope for getting out on bail now rested entirely with her.

FOURTEEN

'ALL RISE,' SAID the bailiff. Everyone stood up and watched as the judge left the courtroom by the door behind the bench. He was returning to his chambers to deliberate, his black robe billowing out behind him.

An excited murmur went up in the courtroom. Alex leaned over the railing and tapped Marisol on the shoulder. 'What do you think?' she asked.

Marisol smiled and gave her a thumbs up. 'I think it went well.'

'I thought so, too,' said Alex. In a two-hour hearing, Harold Gathman, the attorney from the Justice Initiative, had presented the brief convincingly, and the new-found receipt provided a dramatic moment. Gathman's explanation of the new timeline, which seemed to put Dory outside of the house when the crime occurred, had drawn a gasp from the assembled spectators.

The prosecutor from the district attorney's office, which had been inundated with such cases as a result of this public defender's ineptness, argued, somewhat dispiritedly, that Dory had entered the guilty plea voluntarily and should continue to be held accountable for the crime.

Alex glanced over at Dory, who was seated on the other side of Gathman. She had a distracted look in her eyes. Manacled and dressed in a dark-blue prison jumpsuit, she was staring ahead, seemingly lost in her own thoughts, and oblivious to all that was going on around her. Alex slid down the row of seats until she was behind Dory. She tapped her sister gently on the upper arm.

Dory started and looked around.

'Marisol thinks it went pretty well,' Alex said.

Dory gazed at her. 'Does she?'

'Yes, definitely. I think he's going to rule in your favor. You're going to get that new trial.'

Dory nodded. 'Did you notice? My parents are here. Do you think I will get a chance to talk to them?'

Alex had seen Dory's parents though she preferred not to look at them again. For one thing, they were seated across the center aisle, behind the district attorney's table. Elaine was wearing a large, laminated, circular button on her blouse which bore a photo of Lauren Colson.

'Yes, I noticed they were here,' she said.

'My mother looks good,' Dory said.

'I guess so,' said Alex carefully.

'Chris and Joy are here too,' said Dory, nodding toward the family sitting behind her parents. 'And Therese. They live upstairs from us. Suddenly all these people are rooting for me.' She smiled. 'A couple of my pet-sitting customers came. One of my high school teachers is here.'

Alex looked back at the courtroom full of strangers. Chris Ennis sat, arms folded over his chest and long legs extended beneath the seat in front of him. Therese, looking fragile, sat between her father and her mother, her posture upright, her eyes wary, as if she were a little bit intimidated by the courtroom. Joy had her arm draped protectively over the back of Therese's chair. Alex had seen them come in quietly during Gathman's presentation of the brief. 'Amazing,' she agreed. She doubted they were here in support of Dory, but Dory seemed so genuinely surprised. Alex didn't want to spoil the moment for her.

'Alex!' Marisol hissed.

'What?' Alex asked, moving back to her seat.

'Did you see the button Dory's mother is wearing?' Marisol asked indignantly. 'What's wrong with that woman? It's lucky there's no jury here to see that. It's as if she is trying to sabotage us.'

'I know. I saw it,' said Alex. 'And she's sitting behind the prosecution table. But Dory is convinced that she came here to support her today.'

Marisol shook her head. 'Talk about a blind spot.'

'A lot of people showed up. That's for sure,' said Alex. She swept the courtroom with her gaze, and then her heart jumped as she recognized the familiar features of a dark-haired man at the back. He nodded at her.

'Who's that?' Marisol asked, following her gaze. 'He's a hunk.'

'Seth Paige. He's a neighbor. Frankly, I'm surprised to see him here. I guess he's curious about this dysfunctional family.' But secretly, she was flattered that Seth had taken the time to come. 'How long do you think we will have to wait?' she whispered over the rail to Marisol.

'Well, I can't say for sure, but if he thought it was going to take all afternoon, he probably would have dismissed us. As it is, I think he's going to rule pretty quickly. Let's hope so.'

'Right,' said Alex. Dory glanced down in her direction, and Alex gave her a thumbs up. Dory nodded gravely.

'Here he comes,' Marisol whispered. 'That was quick.'

Sure enough, the door beside the bank of flags opened and the judge strode in, glancing at no one and resuming his seat on the bench. A hush fell over the courtroom. Judge Nardone cleared his throat and looked out over the assembled spectators through his black-rimmed glasses. 'I'm ready to rule on this case,' he began. 'There are times when it is in the best interests of a defendant to enter a guilty plea and avoid the risk of a jury trial. When a defendant pleads guilty, it is presumed that such plea agreement has been entered into with the sober advice of counsel, and it represents an informed decision on the part of the defendant reflecting their best interests. In this case the defendant was urged to accept a plea agreement, even though her attorney, who is now disbarred, made no attempt to represent her interests, conducted no investigation, and then assured her that he had. Defendants have a right to expect that their attorney will provide counsel. That is their right under the constitution. In this case, the defendant was deprived of that right.

'The defendant is also entitled to a trial by a jury of her peers. If the defendant's attorney had indeed been advocating on her behalf, he might have located this receipt, which was presented as evidence by Mr Gathman today, and used it in a jury trial to provide an alibi for his client. We will never know what the result might have been in such a trial, but it is fair to assume that, with this receipt entered into evidence, the defendant could reasonably have been found not guilty.

'Thus, it is the decision of this court,' he said, 'that the defendant received ineffective assistance of counsel which influenced her decision to plead guilty. Her conviction and sentence are hereby set aside and this case is remanded to the fifth circuit court where it originated. The district attorney in that jurisdiction will have two weeks to decide whether or not to refile charges.'

Whoops and cries erupted in the courtroom, and the judge banged his gavel on the bench. Alex, who had been holding her breath, felt as if she had been struck by an electric shock. Marisol turned in her chair and they grasped hands for a moment. Then Alex looked at Dory. Her eyes were wide. She was staring at the judge as if she wasn't sure she had heard correctly.

'Order,' the judge said sternly, banging the gavel again. 'We're not finished here. A motion for bail has been filed pending the outcome of the appeal. Mr Gathman?'

Gathman rose to his feet. 'Thank you, Your Honor. In light of this new evidence, and the fact that it might well have led to an acquittal had there been a trial, it is our contention that the defendant should be freed on bond while she awaits the district attorney's decision and, if necessary, her new trial.'

The judge's face betrayed no emotion. 'This court is inclined to agree with you. If bail is granted, where would the defendant reside?'

Dory turned and looked at her parents. She had already been informed that she was going to live with Alex if bail was granted, but her gaze was a bald plea, a last-minute appeal. If she was thinking that their position might have softened as a result of this decision in her favor, she was doomed to disappointment. Garth Colson glanced at her and looked away. Elaine stared straight ahead and did not meet her gaze.

'Your Honor, the defendant's sister, Alex Woods, has offered the defendant residence in her home and Ms Colson will reside there permanently—that is to say, between now and the trial, if indeed another action is brought. I have submitted to you all necessary financial and residential information.'

The judge frowned at the papers on his desk. 'Permission for the defendant to reside with her sister at her home in Chichester is granted with the following conditions…'

The judge began to enumerate the conditions for Dory's bail. She had to report to a probation officer and was not allowed to leave the jurisdiction. As he was speaking Alex looked at Dory, who tore her gaze reluctantly from her unresponsive parents. Her expression was indignant, her eyes glazed with angry tears. Alex felt a stab of pity for her.

'Therefore,' the judge continued, 'within these limits outlined by the court, the defendant will be free to go on bail. Bailiff, release the prisoner.'

The khaki-uniformed bailiff came up to Dory and indicated to her that she should hold out her hands. Then he began to unlock and remove her handcuffs. He carried them back to his position by the bench as Dory rubbed her wrists gingerly.

'I will speak to both attorneys in my chambers please,' said the judge. 'Good luck to you, Ms Colson. This hearing is adjourned.'

He banged the gavel, got up and, as the bailiff cried out, 'All rise,' left the courtroom. Dory buried her face in her hands. Harold Gathman put a consoling arm around her shoulders. 'I'm very pleased for you,' he said, beaming and patting her back. Marisol appeared beside them and Dory hugged her.

'Thank you,' she whispered. Then Dory turned to Alex. 'Thank you,' she said. 'Thank you so much.'

Alex smiled at her gently. 'You're welcome.'

Dory turned away from Alex as Garth and Elaine approached. She pulled her shoulders back and stared at her parents, her chin trembling.

'I'm happy for you, Dory,' said Garth. He put his arms awkwardly around his daughter. Dory was rigid in his embrace. She disentangled herself and looked directly at her mother.

'Are you happy for me?' she asked.

Elaine's expression was impassive. 'Yes, of course,' she said.

'So why can't I come home?' Dory asked in a raw voice.

'Why would you say you killed your sister if you didn't?' Elaine demanded. 'Explain that to me.'

'Let me come home,' Dory insisted.

'Honey, don't,' said Garth. 'This is not the time or place. We'll talk about this another time. Come on,' he said to Elaine. He put a hand under her elbow and began to steer her from the courtroom.

'She'll come around,' said Marisol reassuringly. Dory covered her eyes with one hand.

Harold Gathman leaned over to Alex. 'Make sure she is at court for every proceeding related to the new trial and you'll get the bond back,' he advised her.

'I will,' said Alex. 'What happens now?' she asked.

'Well, I'll go talk to the judge and we'll dot all the i's and cross all the t's. Once we're done with the judge you'll be free to take your sister home. Then, either the charges will be dropped, or we will prepare a proper defense for a new trial. I don't think we'll have too much trouble with that. I'll throw it back to Marisol. This is her case, after all.'

'She knows a lot about it, that's for sure,' said Alex.

The attorney nodded and packed up his briefcase. 'Dory,' he said.

Dory turned and looked at him.

'There are going to be a lot of reporters wanting to talk to you. Do not speak to them. Just say that you're happy. That's it. Nothing else. Don't say a word about a possible new trial or anything like that. Do you understand?'

'How come?' Dory asked.

'This granting of bail for you could be controversial. Don't say a word or you could find yourself back in Framingham. Understood?'

Dory nodded somberly.

'I've planned a little celebration for Dory at my house,' said Alex. 'I hope you'll stop by.'

'Certainly,' said Gathman.

Alex turned around to see if Seth was still in the court-room. She wanted him to come to the celebration too. But he had disappeared.

Chris Ennis, Joy and Therese stood off to one side. Joy was looking at the screen of her iPhone. Therese appeared to be weeping, wiping tears away from her red face.

Alex walked over to speak to them.

'I don't really understand this whole thing,' said Chris. 'Did she do it or didn't she?'

That's the million-dollar question, Alex thought. 'It was nice of you to come today,' she said.

'We wanted to be here for Garth and Elaine,' said Joy. 'And for Dory. We're not taking sides.'

'My dad made me come,' said Therese, her confusion obvious in her eyes.

'We're going to have a little celebration at my house. You're welcome to join us if you'd like to,' said Alex.

'I've got to get back to work,' said Joy. 'And Therese needs to get to school.'

'I'll take you both,' said Chris. 'But thanks for invit-ing us.'

'Why are they celebrating?' Therese cried. 'What is there to be happy about?'

Dory, hearing Therese's voice, turned and looked at her neighbors. 'I thought you said you were here for me,' she said.

'Why would we come here for you?' Therese said bit-terly. Joy tried to restrain her, but Therese would not be quiet. 'Lauren is dead. Doesn't anybody care about that anymore?'

'Therese, stop,' Joy insisted. She reached out a hand to

Dory, who spurned it. 'She's just upset. Don't mind her. We're happy for you, Dory.'

Dory stared mutely as Chris and Joy each took an arm and shepherded their weeping daughter from the courtroom.

FIFTEEN

'THIS WILL BE your room,' said Alex, stepping aside so that Dory could enter the guest bedroom which she had made up for her.

Dory walked in and looked around. 'It's nice,' she said carefully. 'Not as nice as my room at home. But it's OK...'

Your room at home? Alex thought. The home where you are not welcome? She forced herself not to say what she was thinking. Instead she walked over to the closet and opened the door. 'I put a few of my things in here for you. I think we're the same size.'

'How did you know my size?' Dory asked.

'The pea coat?'

'Oh, right,' said Dory, coming over and running the fabric of a shirt through her fingers. 'These are nice.'

Alex could hear the murmur of people talking downstairs. Marisol had entered the house and the spirit of the occasion, helping Alex to uncover a tray of sandwiches she had bought and set out glasses for champagne. 'We better get back to your guests,' she said.

'I think I'll change into this,' said Dory, choosing an olive-colored knit dress from the closet.

'OK, well, come down when you're ready,' said Alex. She pulled the door shut and went down the stairs. Harold Gathman was at the foot of the steps, talking to a woman who was wearing a hacking jacket and Ugg boots.

'Mr Gathman, I'm glad you could come.' Alex extended

her hand to the woman he was talking to. 'We haven't met,' she said.

'I'm a friend of Dory's,' the woman said before Alex could even introduce herself. 'Regina Magill. I was one of Dory's best customers. I'm kind of a dog broker. I put people together with the dogs they want. I always recommend Dory to the new owners to take care of the dogs. You never met a better girl. So good with animals. Animals can tell, you know. You can't fool them. They know people.'

Alex smiled and nodded politely, thanking her for coming. Then she went through the house to the kitchen. Marisol was pouring champagne into plastic cups and handed one to Laney Thompson, who had come from across the street for the occasion. 'Is Seth coming?' Alex asked Laney. 'He was at the courthouse.'

'I'm sure he'll be here,' said her neighbor.

'We're going through this at a clip,' said Marisol. 'Have you got any more?'

'Out on the back porch. I'll go get one,' said Alex. She slipped out the back door, where she had stashed a few bottles of champagne in a cooler filled with ice. She lifted the lid and wrestled one out. Out of the corner of her eye she saw a movement in the trees which flanked the porch. She looked up, peering out into the gloomy yard, and saw a man with a camera trying to conceal himself behind a tree.

Alex set down the champagne bottle and went to the porch door, opening it. 'What are you doing?' she demanded.

The man came out from behind the tree. 'Just wanted to get a few pictures,' he said apologetically.

'This is private property. You can't just come into my yard and start taking pictures.'

'Hey, this is news,' he said. 'You're living here with a confessed killer.'

'Who do you work for? Get off my property or I'll call the police.'

The photographer lifted his camera and took her picture.

'All right. That's it,' Alex cried, pulling out her phone as she descended the steps and strode in his direction. The man backed away from her and then began to lope out the yard.

'Bastard!' she yelled after him.

The back door opened and Seth came out onto the porch.

'Hey. What's happening out here?' he asked. 'I heard yelling.'

'You're here,' Alex said. She was still shaking from her encounter with the cameraman.

'I wouldn't miss it,' he said. 'This is the most interesting thing that's happened in this neighborhood in years. So what was going on out here?'

Alex walked back to the house and up the porch steps. 'Some idiot with a camera wanting a picture of Dory. He had to settle for one of me before I ran him off.' She sighed. 'I hope that's not what we have to look forward to.'

'I wouldn't be surprised,' he said. 'This is going to be big news for a while.'

'I suppose so.' Alex sighed again. Then she looked at him shyly. 'I saw you in court.'

'Well, I have to admit I was curious. I'm no attorney but it sounded to me as if she may not have to stand trial on these charges. That Justice Initiative lawyer presented a pretty strong case.'

'I hope you're right. It would be good to have this over with.'

'Not looking forward to this house guest?' he asked.

'It's not that,' said Alex. 'It will actually give me a chance to get to know her.'

'But…'

Alex hesitated. 'No. No buts…She is my sister. You know, I'm still not used to saying those words.'

'You sound convincing,' he said. 'Oh, by the way…' He reached into the inside pocket of his jacket and pulled out a square plastic case. He handed it to Alex. 'I found this after you left.'

Alex put the champagne bottle under her arm and looked at the CD that Seth had just given her. The cover photo of Lauren Colson was soft and sexy, and the title of the album was *Love You Only*. Alex looked at it and then up at Seth.

'Thanks,' she said. 'That was so nice of you.' She studied his face. She had often been attracted to men who were difficult and forbidding. Men who didn't seem to listen to what she said unless she got angry with them. Seth's face was very masculine, but it had an open quality. An attentiveness. He was interested in her life, and he made no secret of it. Although maybe that was all it was on his part. Simple curiosity.

'It took me a while to go through that crazy collection of his,' Seth said. 'It's open 'cause it's used.'

'Did you listen to it?'

'I did,' he said. 'As I told you, I'm not a country fan, but she did have a beautiful voice. Very soulful.'

'I don't think I'll play it while Dory's here.'

'What are you not doing while I'm here?' Dory asked. She had stepped out onto the back porch. She was wearing the olive-colored knit dress, which fit her slim frame and smoky eyes perfectly. Her reddish hair looked like it was flecked with gold.

Alex slipped the CD inside her sweater and then turned back to Dory. 'Oh, I was telling Seth that I want to spend a lot of time with you—while you're here. You look nice,' she exclaimed.

Dory was unsmiling. 'What's going on out here?'

'Your sister chased off a photographer who was lurking around, trying to get a picture of you,' said Seth.

'Of me?' said Dory.

Alex lifted the bottle of champagne. 'Yes. I came out here to get this and I saw this guy trying to hide behind a tree in the yard. I told him to get lost and leave us alone.'

'I'm not supposed to talk to those people. I had enough of them when…you know…before.' Dory turned to Seth. 'Who are you?'

'Dory, this is Seth Paige. He's a…neighbor.'

'I thought he was your boyfriend,' said Dory.

'No,' said Alex, feeling herself blush. 'I don't…have a boyfriend.'

'Whew, it's freezing out here,' Dory said. She shivered and grasped her own upper arms. 'I'm going back inside.'

'Good idea,' said Seth, opening the back door. He turned to Alex. 'Are you coming?'

'In a minute,' said Alex. 'You go ahead.' She clutched the bottle to her chest and looked out at the now empty yard, wondering if it was going to become commonplace to have journalists and curiosity seekers lurking there. She wasn't used to being suspicious of people. She was raised in a home where the door was always open.

She glanced back into the house. She could see people drinking, eating and celebrating, as they often had in the days when her parents were alive. Doug and Cathy Woods were never reluctant to have a party. Their hospitality was casual and inclusive. Alex thought that they would probably be proud of her for what she was doing today. Making a celebration of Dory's release. Giving her a place to stay, in spite of her misgivings. It had been a difficult decision but, in a way, she felt cornered. If the court was willing to free Dory, how could Alex refuse her sanctuary? She told herself that she had nothing to fear from Dory. They were virtual strangers, and this house was little more than a temporary haven, a place to land when Dory had nowhere else to go.

Suddenly Alex felt a wave of sorrow and anxiety break over her, so strong she felt as if it could knock her down. She missed the life she used to have in this house with people who loved her. She held onto the door frame for a moment, shivering, and gazed in at the cozy scene. She could see that Dory was talking to Seth, her gaze focused on his handsome, bespectacled face. Every so often she would reach up and absently touch his forearm with her hand, as if to reassure herself that she was free. As if to prove that she could touch anyone she wished, and no one could stop her.

ALEX FINISHED PUTTING out the trash and came inside to put the last of the dirty dishes in the dishwasher. Dory, still wearing the olive dress, came into the kitchen and watched her load up the glasses.

'That was nice of you. Thanks,' said Dory.

'Did you enjoy it?'

Dory shrugged. 'Sure.'

'Well, it's not every day a person gets sprung from prison,' Alex said.

'No, that's true,' said Dory. She sat down on one of the kitchen chairs and tapped on the surface of the table.

'So, you were talking to Seth.'

Dory looked up at her suspiciously. 'And?'

'Nothing,' said Alex. 'I just noticed you two talking.'

'He's very nice. And smart,' said Dory.

'He is. He's an instructor at the University of Chicago. That's a really good school.'

'I didn't go to college,' said Dory ruefully. 'I'm probably

not smart enough for a guy like him. Although I did used to go out with a doctor.'

'Hmmm…' murmured Alex, thinking about Rick Howland.

'Well, Seth will probably be going back out to Chicago any day now. He only came home to help his father out when he had surgery.'

'Doesn't mean I can't get to know him,' said Dory.

There was something in her tone which made Alex feel vaguely uneasy. 'I didn't mean that,' she said. 'Dory, would you mind helping me clean up?'

'I thought I'd get one day off,' Dory said.

'Everybody has to help around here,' Alex said lightly.

'Everybody?' Dory asked. 'Who else is there?'

'I meant both of us,' said Alex.

'Then say that,' said Dory. She picked up a broom and began sweeping the kitchen. 'I've been thinking about something,' she said.

'What's that?' Alex asked.

Dory carefully made a pile of crumbs with the broom. 'I was thinking it might be a good idea if we got a dog. You said you always had pets,' Dory reminded her.

Alex took a deep breath. 'It's true. I did. And I like animals. But I don't know if this is the right time for a dog.'

'Why not?' Dory asked.

'Well, there's a lot to do in the house. And I'm not sure where I'll…where we'll be living. You know, in the future…'

'You wouldn't have to take care of the dog. I know everything about taking care of dogs.'

Alex wiped off the counter and frowned. 'I suppose you do.'

'That photographer that was here. That's not going to be the last time that happens,' Dory observed.

Alex nodded. 'You're probably right.'

'A dog would keep them away.'

'Well, maybe. Let's think about it,' said Alex.

Dory shoved the broom back into the pantry. 'Oh, I get it. You make all the decisions. I don't get a vote.'

'I just want to think about it,' Alex protested.

'It's just like being back in prison,' said Dory.

Alex struggled to hold her temper. 'Isn't that a little bit of an exaggeration?'

'What do you know about it?' Dory asked.

Alex counted to ten, trying not to get into an argument on this first night together. 'I don't want you to feel that way,' she said. 'This is your home now. I want to feel like you belong here.'

'This is not my home,' said Dory. 'I don't belong anywhere.' She left the room. Alex could hear her trudging through the house and mounting the stairs toward her room. The room that now confined her.

SIXTEEN

THE DOOR TO Dory's room was open. Alex looked in. Dory, dressed in a pair of Alex's old jeans and a roomy sweater, was studying her reflection in a full-length mirror attached to the closet door. Determined to make a fresh start, Alex decided to ignore that nasty exchange from the night before. After all, it had been an emotionally draining day. She rapped on the frame of the door. 'Morning,' she said.

'Morning,' Dory replied, her voice a little bit froggy.

'Did you sleep all right?' Alex asked with a forced cheerfulness.

Dory nodded. 'Pretty well, actually.'

'Good,' said Alex.

'These clothes are not going to work,' said Dory.

'Really?' said Alex. 'They look like they fit you.' She came over and stood beside Dory. Seeing their reflections, side by side in the full-length mirror gave Alex a start. Despite the difference in their coloring, there was definitely a resemblance between them. They actually looked like sisters.

'They're too short,' said Dory, lifting up one leg and displaying the hem of the jeans. 'They don't look right.'

Alex did not see the problem. She and Dory were about the same height. Dory was nitpicking. Maybe, Alex thought, she didn't want to wear someone else's clothes. That was understandable after nearly two years in a prison jumpsuit.

'Well, why don't we go shopping?' she suggested. 'We could get you some new things.'

'I'd rather have my old things,' said Dory. Alex frowned. 'What do you mean?'

'I want to go to my house and get my own clothes.'

Alex grimaced. 'Oh. I don't know if that's a good idea, Dory.'

'Why not?' she demanded. 'It's my stuff. It belongs to me.'

Alex did not want to argue about it. 'I guess that's true,' she said. 'Maybe I could go by your parents' apartment and pick up a few of your things.'

'I'll go too,' she said.

Your mother does not want you there, Alex thought. But she couldn't bring herself to say it out loud.

'Besides, you don't know what I want. Or where anything is. I can find what I need in no time. I'll just go in my room and grab a bunch of stuff. And then I'll leave,' Dory said, sounding like the soul of reasonableness.

Alex did not relish the thought of showing up at the Colsons' apartment with Dory, but her sister's request did not seem extreme when she thought about it. Why shouldn't Dory have her own clothes if she wanted them? 'All right,' she said. 'We can stop over there.'

'Now?' Dory asked.

'I have a few things I have to do this morning.'

'I almost forgot,' said Dory sourly. 'You make the decisions.'

Alex's temper flared. 'Look, if you want to walk down to the station and go by yourself, be my guest. But it would be a little difficult to carry all that stuff back here on the train.'

Dory did not answer or look at her.

'If you want to go in the car, you'll have to wait till I'm done.'

'I'll wait. I need my stuff,' said Dory.

Alex started down the stairs. Dory followed behind her.

'How come there are so many boxes everywhere?' she asked.

'I'm trying to clean this house out. It has to be cleaned out if I want to sell it.'

'Why would you want to sell it?' asked Dory. 'It's a beautiful house.'

Alex felt surprised, and almost foolishly pleased by the remark. 'I'm glad you like it.'

'Of course I like it,' said Dory. 'I wish I had a house like this.'

'Well, you do, in a sense. You live here now,' said Alex.

'That's not the same thing,' Dory said as she walked into the kitchen and began opening the cupboards. 'I'm just a guest.'

Alex wanted to say that's not true. You're my sister. But she knew that she would sound hollow and insincere. She decided to change the subject. 'What do you want for breakfast?' she asked brightly.

Dory stared into one of the cabinets. 'What choice do I have?' she asked.

By LUNCHTIME ALEX could stall it no longer. Dory was sitting patiently by the door with her shoulder bag in her lap, like a pup holding a leash. Alex sighed and picked up the car keys.

'Do you have something to put the clothes into?' she asked.

'I have suitcases in my room at home,' said Dory.

'OK,' said Alex. 'Maybe we should call first.'

'No,' said Dory. 'Let's go. If we call first they'll say we shouldn't come.'

She's not oblivious. She does know, Alex thought. 'All right.' Just then her cell phone rang and she looked at the

name. The Orenstein Gallery. 'I have to take this,' she said
to Dory and turned her back on her.

'Hello,' she said.

'Ms Woods? This is Margo, calling from the Orenstein
Gallery. If you are still interested in the position, Louis
Orenstein would like you to come in for a second interview.'

'Absolutely,' Alex cried. 'I absolutely am. When should
I come in?'

'Monday afternoon at two?' said Margo.

'I'll be there,' said Alex. 'And thank you.'

She ended the call and turned happily to Dory. 'Sorry
to keep you waiting. It's a second interview for a job I really want.'

'What kind of job?' Dory asked.

Alex explained the parameters of the job as they walked
out to the car, got in, and pulled out of the driveway. Dory
listened intently.

'This is a really prestigious gallery. Louis Orenstein
has discovered the work of some of the best artists around
today. I would really like to work there,' said Alex.

'Would you be gone all day, if you got the job?' Dory
asked.

'Well, yeah,' said Alex. 'I mean, it's a full-time position.'

Dory nodded and looked out the car window as the
streets of Chichester flashed by. The day was gloomy, and
snow was predicted for the night. Everything seemed to
wear a blanket of gray. 'It's so quiet around here,' she said.
'I'm not used to that.'

'I'm sure the prison was a noisy place to live,' said Alex,
sensing the complaint in her words.

'It was noisy,' said Dory. 'I wouldn't want to go back
there for anything. But this place is like living in a cem-
etery.'

Alex knew she shouldn't take Dory's remark personally,

but she found it impossible not to be offended. Thanks a lot, she thought. She no longer felt like talking to her.

They rode the rest of the way into Boston in silence. Alex thought about parking in a lot, near the Colsons' apartment, but decided to give the on-street parking a try. It would be easier to move Dory's belongings that way. Luckily there was a spot open halfway down the block. Alex eased into it and parked the car.

Dory hopped out before Alex turned off the engine, and rushed up to the building where she had always lived. Alex hurried to catch up with her. Dory pulled a ring of keys from her purse as they climbed the steps.

'Oh, no. Wait a minute,' said Alex. 'You can't just let yourself in. We have to knock.'

'I've lived here all my life,' Dory exclaimed, affronted.

Alex shook her head. 'Absolutely not. Either you put those keys away or we're leaving right now.'

Dory glowered at her, but stuck the keys back into her purse. They went into the vestibule and pushed the buzzer for the Colsons' apartment.

There was a rather long wait, and then the door opened. Elaine stood staring at them.

'Hi, Mom,' said Dory.

'Hello, Dory,' said Elaine.

'We came to get my clothes,' said Dory in an apologetic tone.

'I cleared out a lot of your clothes,' said Elaine.

Alex thought about the coat, still hanging on the hallway peg. She doubted that Elaine had done any such thing. 'She doesn't need that much,' she said.

'Did you throw my stuff away?' Dory asked plaintively.

'Some of it,' said Elaine.

Alex suddenly felt angry at this woman. 'Why don't you just let Dory collect her things and we'll be on our way.'

Elaine turned her chilly gaze on Alex. 'Why don't you stay out of this?'

'Well, I can't really do that, can I?' snapped Alex. 'We live together now.'

Elaine hesitated for a moment and then stepped away from the door. 'All right, but don't hang around in your old room.'

'I won't, Mom,' said Dory, and her voice sounded timid and thick with tears.

Shoulders slumped, she entered the apartment, followed by Alex and her mother. She began to look around her, her eyes shining. 'It smells so good in here. Were you baking?' Dory turned to Alex. 'My mother is the best baker.'

'Just go get your stuff,' said Elaine, pointing down the hall. 'We'll wait in the kitchen.'

Alex kind of wanted to go with Dory, fearful that she would collect so much stuff that they would be hours getting it out of the apartment. But she didn't want to antagonize Elaine any further. She followed the older woman down the steps to the kitchen.

There were two places set at the table for lunch, and Therese Ennis sat in one of the seats. There was something medieval-looking about Therese. With her long, wavy hair and her frail form clad in a gauzy dress, she had the appearance of a maiden, languishing. The teenager frowned when she saw Alex. 'How come you're here?' she said accusingly.

'Dory wanted to get some of her things,' said Alex.

'Oh,' said Therese. She took her fork and began to poke at the food on her plate.

'You said you were hungry. Now don't play with it, Therese. Eat it,' said Elaine. She turned to Alex. 'So, I guess you're pretty pleased with how this all turned out.'

'It's not over yet,' said Alex. 'I'm hoping that the district attorney will decide not to refile the charges against Dory.'

'So that my daughter's killer can get away scot-free?' asked Elaine.

Alex shook her head and did not reply. 'Dory, hurry up,' she called out. Dory's answer from the depths of her room upstairs was unintelligible. Alex sank down into a chair to wait.

Therese picked at her lunch and kept glancing surreptitiously at Alex.

Alex frowned at her. 'What are you looking at?'

Therese shook her head. Then she said, 'I'm just wondering…'

'Wondering what?' Alex asked.

'Aren't you afraid of her? After…what she did?'

Alex gave an exasperated sigh, trying to cover the fact that the teenager had struck a nerve. 'I'm trying to help her get on with her life. She's my sister.'

'All the more reason,' Therese observed.

'Look, this really isn't any of your business,' said Alex.

'Don't be rude to Therese,' said Elaine. 'She is welcome here. Therese was invited.'

Just then Alex heard the sound of suitcase wheels rolling across the wood floors upstairs and thudding on the steps. She looked up as Dory began to descend the stairs to the kitchen. Alex stood up.

'Have you got what you need?' she asked.

Dory had stopped dead in her tracks and was staring at Therese. 'What is she doing sitting there?' she demanded. 'That's my place.'

Elaine sighed. 'Therese is having lunch with me. She often does on Saturday. Why?'

Tears welled up in Dory's eyes. 'That's not fair. That's my place.'

'You don't have a place here. You lost your place here when you stabbed Lauren,' said Elaine bitterly.

But Dory was not listening. In a flash she was around the table and grabbed Therese by the hair, twisting a large clump of it between her fingers. 'You get out of my seat,' she growled.

Therese's head jerked back and she let out a fearful cry.

'Dory, for God's sake,' said Alex. 'Let go of her. Right now.'

'No, I won't,' Dory insisted, tightening her fingers in the girl's thick curls. 'Get out of my chair, Therese, or I swear I'll…'

'Stop it!' Therese cried.

Elaine rushed to put a protective arm around Therese and glared at Dory. 'Get your hands off her or I swear I will have you back in jail so fast you won't be able to see straight,' she said in a quiet, menacing tone.

Dory blushed and released the clump of Therese's hair.

'Here, take your stupid chair,' Therese cried, jumping up and cowering behind Elaine. 'Just leave me alone.'

'Never mind, it's not her chair,' said Elaine. She turned to Dory. 'Get out of my house before I call the police.'

Dory stared at her mother. 'You would call the cops on me?'

'I'm going to,' said Elaine. 'I'm going to tell them I have a dangerous lunatic in my house.'

Dory closed her eyes and began to shake her head as tears seeped out from under her eyelids and ran down her cheeks. 'Why…' she moaned.

Alex took charge. She pulled Dory along by the arm without another word to Elaine or Therese. Dory stumbled along and mounted the stairs with Alex leading the way. Alex grabbed the polka-dotted suitcase at the top of the steps and rolled it, leading Dory and her belongings out of the apartment and the building and into the street below.

ONCE THEY WERE in the car and en route back to Chichester, Alex glanced over at Dory. 'What the hell were you doing back there?' she chided her. 'You could have had your bail revoked for assaulting Therese.'

Dory sat hunched in the passenger seat, her arms crossed over her chest. She raised her chin defiantly and did not reply.

'Look,' said Alex. 'I'm sure it's difficult to see someone sitting in your place. But between Lauren's…death and you going to jail, your mother has lost an awful lot. Maybe Therese is some comfort to her.'

'She could have me back now if she wanted,' said Dory. 'But who is she making lunch for? Therese. My mother always treated Therese like her own little china doll. Always fussing over her.'

'Why would she do that?' Alex asked.

'Oh, she felt sorry for her. Chris and Joy are always fighting,' said Dory disgustedly.

'That's tough on a kid,' Alex said.

Dory looked over at her. 'Did your parents fight?' she asked.

Alex shook her head. 'No. Not really. They got along really well.'

'Mine didn't either,' said Dory. 'My father just does everything she says. It's easier that way.'

'I'm sure that's true,' said Alex.

'I don't know why Chris and Joy don't get divorced. People get divorced all the time,' said Dory.

'Maybe they want to stay together for Therese's sake,' said Alex.

Dory shook her head. 'I don't think so. She walked out on both of them.'

'Who?' Alex asked, confused.

'Joy. She left Chris. And Therese. That's why my mother

feels sorry for the kid. Joy was gone for a while. But then she came back.'

'How long was she gone?' Alex asked.

'I don't remember. Six months maybe…'

'Wow. That must have been hard on Therese.'

'Oh, don't you start,' said Dory irritably.

Alex sighed. Change the subject, she thought. 'So, are you glad to have your things back now?' she asked.

'Yes,' said Dory. 'I can't wait to change into my own clothes.'

As if, Alex thought, there was something disgusting about my clothes. She stifled the urge to make a cutting remark. Leave it alone, she thought. Keep the peace. But at what price? she thought. And for how long?

SEVENTEEN

IT BEGAN TO snow around midnight and continued on till morning. When Alex woke up and looked out her window the streets were silent, the tree branches laden, the driveways and curbs adrift in snow. She lay under the covers, still half asleep, thinking how lovely it looked outside her window.

Suddenly Dory appeared in the doorway to her room. She was wearing a down parka over her nightgown and shivering. 'The power's out,' she said.

Alex looked at the clock radio beside her bed. It read four o'clock. She tried to switch on the bedside lamp to no avail. 'Damn.'

'No heat, either,' said Dory.

'Oh. I guess not,' said Alex. 'Not if the power's out. Sorry.'

Dory shrugged. 'Not your fault,' she said. 'You didn't make it snow. I'm going downstairs.'

Before Alex could reply, Dory vanished from the doorway. Alex slid down under the covers and relished the warmth. Once she got out from under these covers it would be a struggle to stay warm. There was no telling when the power would be back on. She wasn't really looking forward to a day in the cold and the dark with Dory.

She closed her eyes and felt the beginning of a headache. She needed to be able to wash her hair before her interview tomorrow. She couldn't meet Louis Orenstein looking like this. Oh, well, she thought. Stop feeling sorry for yourself. Maybe the power is out in Boston as well.

She thought she would try to go back to sleep, and she had nearly succeeded when she smelled something cooking. Bacon. Alex sat up in bed, frowning. Suddenly she heard a voice calling her name. 'Alex. Breakfast.'

Alex forced herself to get out of bed. She hurried to the closet, threw on several layers of her warmest clothes and headed for the stairs. When she got down to the kitchen, she saw Dory standing at the stove wearing a parka, boots and gloves, and wielding a spatula. Coffee was steeping in the glass push pot, and there was a pile of bacon and pancakes on a plate next to the oven. Dory was busy flipping eggs.

'Wow,' said Alex admiringly.

'Snow day,' said Dory amiably. 'We need a good breakfast.'

'So the range top works,' said Alex.

Dory pointed the spatula at the piles of food. 'As you can see.'

'That's great. I am hungry.' She went over to the china closet and took out some plates. She set them down on the kitchen table.

'I thought we'd eat in the living room by the fireplace,' said Dory.

'Oh,' said Alex, in the mood to be agreeable. 'OK. That's a good idea. I'll go get a fire started.'

'Already did it,' said Dory.

Alex's eyes widened. 'Really? Wow.'

'What?' Dory asked suspiciously.

'Nothing, I'm just…lucky you're here.'

Dory smiled and flipped an egg.

In truth, it was beyond the scope of the fireplace to heat up the room. If you stood five feet away from it, it was as cold as being outside. But Alex and Dory pulled their chairs near to the hearth and sat huddled with their plates on their laps, eating their breakfast. Alex ate twice what she normally had for breakfast.

'I guess you liked it,' said Dory.

'It's really good. Were you a girl scout or something?'

Dory shrugged. 'My dad's from Colorado—in the mountains. We'd drive out there sometimes to see his family, and one year we camped along the way. My mother and Lauren hated it. Lauren was always worried about her hair and manicure. But I liked it. My dad taught me how to build a fire and all that.' Alex watched as Dory calmly related a family anecdote and asked herself the question she had asked herself a million times these last few weeks.

Did you kill her?

It seemed unimaginable that this slender, fragile woman who had just cooked her breakfast could have stabbed her own sister to death. She didn't dare ask the question.

Dory frowned at her. 'What?'

'Oh. Just thinking that your camping experience came in handy today,' said Alex.

Dory nodded and finished her breakfast. Alex took their plates into the kitchen and stopped to pull some extra blankets from the downstairs linen closet on her way back. She handed one to Dory, who was shivering by the fire. Dory put it over herself gratefully. Alex resumed her seat and did the same.

'Did you ever go camping?' Dory asked at last.

Alex shook her head. 'My parents weren't really…outdoorsy. They liked going to museums, restaurants. City stuff.'

Dory nodded and looked thoughtfully at the photo on the mantelpiece. 'What was my mother like?' she asked offhandedly.

Alex took a deep breath and thought about her mother.

'She was…a wonderful person. She was very smart. She worked part time as an accountant. But I think what she liked most was just being home with us. She liked being a wife. And a mother. She had an easy laugh. You could tell her anything. She always made me feel…appreciated. Loved.'

Dory nodded. 'She sounds nice.'

'I wish you'd have known her,' said Alex, meaning it.

Dory shrugged. 'Just wasn't meant to be.'

They were silent for a minute.

'Do you think you'll have kids someday?' Dory asked.

'I hope so,' said Alex. 'I mean, I'd like to get my career going first. And ideally, find the right guy to have kids with. But, yeah. Eventually. What about you?'

'I don't really think so,' Dory said, staring into the fire.

'You don't like kids?' Alex asked.

'I just don't think so,' Dory said in a tone of finality, as if she wanted to close the door on the subject.

Alex nodded and then she shuddered. 'Man, I hope the power comes back on. I don't know how we're going to keep warm all day.'

Dory straightened up and spoke in a no-nonsense tone. 'We'll go out and shovel. That will warm us up.'

Alex winced and looked at the icy windowpanes. 'You want to go outside?'

'Don't be a wuss,' said Dory, standing up. 'It'll be good for us.'

THEY STUMBLED THROUGH the snow to the backyard shed where Alex was able to find two shovels. Then they went out into the driveway and began to dig out.

Sure enough, it wasn't long before they were warmed up, and even though she got a blister on her palm and her back began to ache, Alex kept on shoveling. It was preferable to going back into the freezing house, and there was something undeniably congenial about doing this task with Dory. It almost felt as if they really were sisters.

Alex straightened up and leaned on her shovel. 'This is kind of fun,' she said to Dory.

Dory looked up at her. 'No slacking off,' she said.

'Aye, aye, captain,' said Alex, smiling to herself and resuming her task. They were almost done with the front walk when Alex saw a large figure, bundled up and heading in their direction. Between the man's knit watch cap and the scarf wound around his neck, Alex saw a pair of black glasses frames. She lifted her hand in greeting. Seth waved back.

When he got closer Alex said, 'We're not doing your driveway. Don't even ask us.'

'Damn,' said Seth. 'How'd you know what I wanted?'

Dory straightened up and smiled shyly at him. 'Hi, Seth.'

'Hi, Dory,' he said. 'You two did quite a job here.'

'I had to force her,' said Dory.

'It's true,' said Alex. 'It's just that it was so cold in the house, it seemed like it might be warmer if we got moving. Do you guys have power?'

'Just came back on ten minutes ago,' he said.

'Oh, great,' said Alex, although she felt vaguely disappointed. It seemed as if the snowy morning without electricity had brought her and Dory closer together. She almost hated to see it end.

'You better watch it!' Dory cried. Both of them turned to look at her, and just then a snowball exploded on the shoulder of Seth's parka.

He gave Dory an exaggerated menacing glare. 'Oh, you're in trouble now, little lady,' he said. Reaching quickly down, he packed a snowball and hurled it at her, grazing her jacket.

Dory let out a whoop and lobbed another at Seth. They exchanged fire for a few moments, and then Seth turned and pelted Alex's sleeve with a snowball. Alex bent down and quickly packed a snowball to lob back at him.

'Hey, no fair,' he cried as the snow turned to powder against his forearm. 'Two against one.'

'She's not on my team,' said Dory. She aimed at Alex, and the icy orb hit Alex right in the face.

Alex turned on her. 'Oh, is that the way you're going to be?' She threw one at Dory that fell short.

'That's right,' said Dory, an edge in her voice. She hit Alex in the face with another snowball.

'OK, cut that out,' said Alex, wiping her face. 'That hurt.'

'Stay out of it, then,' said Dory.

Suddenly there was an uneasy feeling in the air, as if the passing storm had doubled back on the house.

Seth clapped his hands together, knocking off the snow. 'That's probably enough for me, anyway,' he said.

Alex brushed off her coat. 'Do you want to come in for a warm drink or something?' she asked.

'The game's not over!' Dory cried. This time the icy snowball hit Alex near her temple.

'OK, stop, Dory!' Alex shouted.

'No!' Dory cried, pelting her again.

Seth held up his hands. 'Halt. We surrender.'

'Alex, you suck at this game,' Dory said.

'Girls, girls. I'm on my way down to the store,' said Seth. 'I told my dad I'd get him some soup. I'll get enough for all of us. You two are welcome to come down for lunch.'

Alex hesitated and looked in Dory's direction. But Dory had jammed her shovel into a snow bank and was wading through the drifts back toward the house.

'Maybe another time,' said Alex.

Seth frowned at Dory's retreating figure. 'You don't think she took that seriously, do you?'

Alex shook her head. 'I don't know. Honestly.'

Seth hesitated, as if choosing his words carefully. 'Look, Alex, are you sure this is a good idea, having her living here with you? I know you want to think the best of her and give her the benefit of the doubt, but you don't know what she's really like,' he said.

'It might not be for much longer, if the DA decides not to refile the charges.'

'And if he does? You could be looking at a year or more.'

'If she doesn't stay here, she goes back to prison,' said Alex. 'I'm not going to do that to her. Not over some stupid snowball fight.'

'Just because something's stupid doesn't mean it can't be dangerous,' he said grimly.

Alex looked back at the house, which looked beautiful and inviting, banked with snow. Dory had disappeared inside. 'I'm trying to be patient,' she said. 'We just need to get…used to one another.'

Seth kicked into a mound of snow with the toe of his boot. 'Who are you trying to convince?' he asked. 'Me or yourself?'

EIGHTEEN

THE NEXT MORNING Alex hopped onto the train just as the whistle that signaled 'departure' began to blow. She pressed the rectangular plate in the door between the cars and the door slid open to admit her. Alex began to lurch down the aisle between the seats and then stopped short.

'All right,' she said, trying to suppress a smile. 'Now I'm sure of it. You're following me.'

Seth looked up and smiled, seeming genuinely pleased to see her. 'What are you doing on this train?'

Alex took the seat beside him. Her arm brushed his, and she felt a current pass between them. 'I might ask you the same question,' she teased him.

'I'm going to meet my old advisor from grad school,' he said. 'He invited me weeks ago, but I couldn't get away because of my dad. But he's doing better. And now that Janet is back...'

'Your sister came home?' Alex said.

'Yeah. The kids have to start back at school. So she's right around the corner if he needs her in an emergency. And it gives me a chance to finish up a few things I meant to do. Tonight we're going to have a family dinner and I'll give the monsters their Christmas presents and all. I finally got them wrapped. Better late than never.'

Alex understood the implication of what he was saying. 'You're going back soon?' she said. She tried to sound offhanded, but she could hear the disappointed note in her own voice.

'End of the week,' he said.

'Really?'

Seth nodded. 'I've got a lot to do out there. I can't put it off.'

Alex nodded, avoiding his gaze. 'Well, I'm sure your dad will really miss you,' she said. She pulled her iPhone out of her purse and began to study the screen, languidly flipping it with her index finger.

'What about you?'

'I really don't have time to miss anybody,' she said. 'I've got my hands full.'

'No, I meant, why are you going into the city today?'

Alex smiled brightly, pretending not to be embarrassed at having misunderstood him. More than anything, she wanted to get up and move to another seat so that, if her face betrayed her dismay, he wouldn't be able to see it. 'Actually, I have a second interview at the Orenstein Gallery today. It's an outstanding gallery. I'm really hoping to get this job.'

'I hope you do,' he said, 'if that's what you want.'

'It is,' she said, studying the screen as if she were longing to give it all her attention. 'It's exactly what I want.'

They rode the rest of the way in silence. Alex rose abruptly from her seat as the conductor called out 'Back Bay' and gave her seat mate a friendly smile. 'Well, if I don't see you, have a good trip back.'

'Take care,' he replied. He looked up and Alex thought that his eyes seemed a little bit sad. But then she told herself that she was imagining things. It wasn't as if anything had actually happened between them, although she had certainly wished, more than once, that it might, and she had the completely unfair sense that he was abandoning her in a difficult situation.

'You too,' she said, giving him a brief wave as she made

her way to the exit. He doesn't owe you a thing, she reminded herself as she waited in the space between the cars for the train to stop. He was just being nice.

IT WAS CLEAR to Alex, after about five minutes, that the second interview at Orenstein's Gallery was a formality. Louis Orenstein outlined what her duties would be and suggested that the more extra work she took on the more likely she was to advance in the art world. Then he stood up and embraced Alex, kissing her, European style, on both cheeks. 'Welcome to the gallery,' he said.

Alex thanked her new employer profusely and, after filling out more paperwork and agreeing to start the next day, she virtually floated out of the building and onto Newbury Street. I have the job, she thought. Her first thought was to call her mother and tell her. And then she realized, for the thousandth time since the fatal accident, that it wouldn't be possible, and her heart grew heavy. She could still remember the happiness, the excitement in her mother's voice, in her eyes, when Alex would arrive home with good news. I'll have to settle for remembering it, she thought.

Her very next thought surprised her. She wanted to tell Seth. Immediately she knew that she would not be doing that either. How stupid would that seem? A neighbor from down the street, calling him to crow about her new job when all he was thinking about was getting on a plane to go back to his real life. No. She would not be calling Seth.

And Dory? she thought. She tried to imagine Dory being happy and excited for her. Wasn't that what sisters were supposed to do? she wondered. But she could not picture it. She felt as if she had no one to share her news with, and it made her feel a little bit resentful. She had tried to do all she could for Dory. And yet, when she had exciting news, she suspected that Dory was not going to want to hear it.

Walking back toward the Back Bay station, Alex crossed Boylston Street where the Justice Initiative had its offices. Hesitating, she decided to stop in and see if Marisol was there. Alex walked into the offices and was directed immediately to the law student's tiny office.

'How's it going?' Marisol asked warily.

Alex nodded. 'Fine. It's going fine.'

'You two getting along OK?'

'As well as need be,' said Alex.

'Oh, I see,' said Marisol. 'So what brings you to town?'

'Actually, I just a got a job at the Orenstein Gallery as Louis Orenstein's assistant. I'll be helping to choose the artists he's going to feature. I start tomorrow.'

'Oh, congratulations,' said Marisol sincerely. 'I know that gallery. It's great. Way out of my league price-wise, but beautiful stuff. You should be very proud to be working there.'

'Thanks,' said Alex, smiling. 'I am.'

'It was nice of you to share this news,' said Marisol.

Alex understood. Marisol was busy and wanted her to get to the point. 'I was just wondering,' she said, 'if you knew how long it would be before the DA makes his decision. You know, whether to refile the charges or not.'

Marisol shook her head. 'I don't know. But it should be soon. They usually don't dawdle with these decisions.'

'And what happens if they decide not to refile?'

'Then Dory is free to live her life without restrictions, and you get your bond money back.'

Alex nodded. 'You'll let us know.'

'Right away,' Marisol promised.

Alex left, walked back to the station and rode the train to Chichester. It was already growing dark as she got into her car and drove the short distance to her house. As she got out, she looked down the street to the house where Seth's father lived. She thought she saw several cars parked in front, and the house was cheerfully alight. But there was no coach light on outside her own house. It was as if nobody was expected. And the interior seemed to be lit dimly, if at all. Home sweet home, she thought.

She sighed and walked up to the door. As she pulled open the storm door, wild, angry eyes leapt at her from the shadows of the hallway. Shattering, ear-piercing barks assailed her.

Alex jumped back and cried out as the dog, his canine teeth dripping with saliva, his muscles straining, pressed forward, forcing her to stumble back toward the door.

'Remus, stop,' Dory said, materializing in the gloom of the hallway and trying ineffectually to grab the dog's collar. 'Stop it. She lives here.'

'Dory, what the hell…' Alex cried out.

At this, the dog redoubled his efforts, his nails scratching the floor as Dory finally got a grip on him and held him back. His barking spiraled up the stairwell and reverberated through the house.

'Remus, that's enough,' Dory insisted. 'You be a good boy.'

'Get that dog out of my face,' said Alex.

'OK, OK. Don't get all bent out of shape.' Dory pulled some kind of treat from her pocket and waved it in front of the dog.

'You're rewarding him?' Alex cried. 'For attacking me?'

Dory's eyes flashed. 'I know how to handle dogs,' she said. 'Just back off, Alex.'

'You want me to back off?'

'Yes, just shut up for a minute. I've got this.'

The dog, seeming to sense their dissension, began to growl.

Dory bent over and looked the dog in the eye, waving the treat. 'Here you go. Take it easy,' she said.

The dog became interested in the treat and simmered down, only letting out the occasional bark. Dory gave him the treat, brushed her hands together and straightened up. 'See,' she said. 'Problem solved.'

'Whose dog is that? Where did it come from?'

'He's our dog,' said Dory brightly, running a hand over the dog's shiny coat. 'Isn't he pretty? My old customer, Regina, brought him over while you were out.'

'How could you just get a dog without consulting me? I said I wanted to think about it.'

'What is there to think about?' Dory asked. 'You said you liked dogs.'

'What breed is this dog?'

'Some kind of Lab mix,' said Dory vaguely.

'That dog is no more a Lab than I am,' Alex protested. 'That's a Pit Bull.'

'The correct name is American Staffordshire Terrier,' said Dory. 'And so what if he is part Pit Bull? They can be wonderful dogs. It's all in how they're handled.'

'Everybody knows they're dangerous,' said Alex.

'That'll work for us. People are afraid of these dogs. If those journalists come nosing around again, you need a dog that can guard his territory. Remus will protect us.'

'And who will protect me from Remus?' Alex demanded.

'You'll get used to him,' said Dory unsympathetically.

'No,' said Alex. 'I don't want to get used to him. He's going back. We're taking him back right now.'

Dory looked at her coldly. 'Excuse me?'

'You heard me,' said Alex. 'Have you got a crate for him? We'll put him in the car and take him back to Regina.'

'We can't,' said Dory.

'Why not?'

'She…had to go away. She won't be back for several days.'

'How convenient,' said Alex.

'You think I'm lying?' Dory challenged her.

She and Alex stared at one another. Remus began to growl low in his throat.

'You better shut that dog up,' said Alex, brushing past Dory and starting for the stairs. 'He's going back the minute Regina gets home. End of discussion.'

Alex thought she heard 'bitch' breathed into the air, but she didn't stop on her way up the stairs.

LYING ON HER BED, staring at the ceiling, Alex couldn't help feeling sorry for herself. This was a big day. She'd got the job she wanted and she should be celebrating. Instead she was alone in her room and downstairs her sister, an accused murderer, patrolled the house with a Pit Bull. She knew the Pit Bull's bad reputation wasn't the dogs' fault. Any dog lover knew that. It was the people who owned and abused them. That didn't mean the dog wasn't dangerous. What did they know about this particular dog anyway? And how could Dory simply take it upon herself to get this dog, without any thought to what Alex might want?

Alex sighed. Face it, she thought. The fact was that she felt imposed on, and cornered by Dory and her mercurial moods. You haven't really given her much of a chance, she argued with herself. Stop being so negative. Dory had been through so much. She'd been longing to have a dog all her life, and now she had the opportunity. Was it too much to ask? You'd been thinking of getting a dog anyway, she reminded herself.

Alex turned over on her stomach. She undoubtedly was

in a bad mood because Seth was leaving. She probably wouldn't see him again—maybe not till next Christmas. For all intents and purposes, it was a relationship that was never going to happen. Perhaps she wouldn't have reacted so badly to the dog if she hadn't had that news about Seth today. Maybe in the morning, she thought, yawning, Dory and I can talk it over. Arrive at some kind of compromise. Maybe you're just a spoiled only child who is too used to having her own way to tolerate anybody else's choices.

As she chided herself and tried to count her blessings, she drifted off and fell into a deep sleep. She began to dream, at some point, that she was walking down a dark street and suddenly someone came up behind her. In her dream, she was trying to pretend that she didn't know they were there. But the sound of their breathing was getting louder and closer. Suddenly she felt something cold touch her face. Alex was instantly awake.

Inches from her face, Remus hovered beside her, panting. In the darkness of her room, his eyes were like ebony marbles. His teeth gleamed in the moonlight. Standing above him, holding his leash, stood Dory. She was dressed in dark clothes, her hair sticking out wildly from her head. She was staring down at Alex, studying her, her gray eyes blank and cold.

Alex's heart hammered and she let out a whimper of terror. 'Jesus Christ!'

Remus started to growl.

Dory jerked his leash. 'Heel,' she said.

'What are you doing in here?' Alex whispered.

'We heard something,' said Dory. 'A sound coming from your room. We came to check on you.'

In the darkness, Dory's eyes seemed to glitter. Alex could not help it. She wondered if those eyes were the last ones that Lauren ever saw. She began to shake.

'What's your problem?' said Dory.

'Nothing,' said Alex.

'You look scared.'

'Please get that dog out of here,' Alex whispered.

Dory studied her, and for a moment Alex had the distinct feeling that she was about to refuse. Then what will you do? Alex asked herself.

'Remus, come,' said Dory. She turned, tugging on his leash.

'I'm sorry,' Alex said. 'Thanks for…being concerned about me.'

But Dory and the dog were gone.

NINETEEN

THE NEXT MORNING, as she was heading out of the door, Alex called up the stairs to Dory, who had not yet come down to breakfast, and said that she was leaving for her new job. There was no response.

'Dory,' Alex yelled up the stairs. 'Can you answer me?'

Dory did not come to the top of the stairs. 'I heard you!' she shouted.

Alex was almost relieved not to have to see her. She left the house and decided to walk down to the station since she was getting an early start on the day. She hadn't been able to get back to sleep once Dory and Remus had appeared by her bedside. She finally decided to just get up and iron her clothes. For her first day of work Alex had picked a stylish black suit with a short, closely-fitted jacket and a box-pleated short skirt. She ironed the suit carefully, polished her boots and made herself a good breakfast. At least she would look ready for her first day on the job. It was no substitute for a night's sleep, but it was better than tossing and turning, sleepless, in the bed. She walked in the morning cold to the train station, wrapping her wool coat tightly around her and avoiding the piles of snow with her high-heeled boots. She did not have long to wait for the next commuter train to Boston. She hopped on and found a seat, where she stared out the window at the winter landscape, all the while trying to get herself mentally ready to sound intelligent and knowledgeable about art.

The day in the gallery flew by as Louis included her on speakerphone in conversations with two sculptors and a painter, and heaped her with museum and gallery references to track down and assess for him on the Web. Every time Alex looked up from her work and saw herself surrounded by exquisite paintings and sculptures bathed in the spotlights of the spacious gallery, she felt happy and lucky to have found work here. Judging by her first day, she was in exactly the right place. It was almost six o'clock and she was finishing up a printout on the sale prices of a certain painter's work when the door to the gallery opened and a stout woman dressed in cheap polyester and wearing a limp ponytail walked in.

Alex looked up and then beamed. 'Marisol!' She got up to greet the law student.

'Hey,' said Marisol in a hushed voice.

'I'm so glad you came over. You don't have to whisper, you know.'

Marisol made an engagingly self-conscious grimace. 'I feel like I'm in the temple of art here.'

Alex shook her head. 'Just the marketplace,' she said, pretending a nonchalance she did not yet feel about the paintings and objects on display. 'So, what brings you over here?'

Marisol frowned slightly. 'I wanted to hear what you thought about the news,' she said.

'News?' Alex asked.

'Well, I spoke to Dory earlier. I thought she would have called you.'

'What happened?'

'We heard from the DA's office. They have decided not to refile the charges.'

'Really. For real?' Alex cried.

Marisol smiled and nodded. 'It's over.'

'Wow,' said Alex, sagging against the wall. 'What a relief.'

'She sounded pretty happy,' Marisol admitted. 'I thought she would have given you a call.'

It doesn't matter, Alex thought. This means I don't have to have her under my roof any longer. But she didn't say it. 'I'll call her,' she said instead. 'Oh, thank you, Marisol. You are going to be an amazing attorney. If I ever get in trouble, I'll know who to turn to.'

'Try to stay out of trouble until I pass the Bar then,' said Marisol.

'How can I ever thank you?'

Marisol smiled bashfully. 'I'm just glad it all worked out.'

Alex reached in her pocket for her phone.

'I'll be going,' said Marisol. 'Good luck.'

Alex gave her a hug as she headed for the door. Then she punched in Dory's number.

The phone rang a few times before Alex heard Dory's voice. 'Hello.'

Actually, Alex only heard Dory's voice dimly, given the noise in the background. 'Dory, it's Alex. Marisol was just here at the gallery.'

'Oh,' Dory shouted. 'Did she tell you?'

'Yes,' said Alex. 'The charges aren't going to be refiled. You're free.'

'Yes, I am,' said Dory.

'Are you excited?'

Dory said something unintelligible.

'What's all that noise?' Alex asked. 'I can barely hear you.'

'We're celebrating. I'm at my mother's.'

'Your mother is hosting a celebration?' Alex asked, incredulous.

'When I called them with the news, my dad insisted,' Dory admitted.

'Well, that's very nice,' said Alex. She wondered if Elaine had been consulted about this spontaneous celebration. Alex couldn't imagine it. But she hoped, for Dory's sake, that Elaine's position might have softened as a result of this news. Alex knew how badly Dory wanted to have her mother's approval or forgiveness or whatever it was that was missing between them.

'What?' Dory asked someone in the background who was speaking to her. 'Oh, yeah,' she said into the phone. 'You can come over if you want, Alex.'

Not much of an invitation, Alex thought. But she thought she would go anyway. It was certainly an important event. For one thing, it marked the end of her official responsibility for her half-sister. She thought of last night, of waking up to find Dory and that dog beside her bed. She shuddered involuntarily. Not a minute too soon, she thought.

'I'd be happy to,' she said.

ALEX WALKED OVER to the Colsons' apartment in the South End, feeling grateful for how quickly the snow had melted and been packed down by the city traffic. The sidewalks were clear, and her high-heeled boots were not the same handicap they had proved to be this morning when she walked to the station.

She mounted the stairs to the vestibule and pressed the buzzer. There was a short wait and then the door opened. Garth Colson was standing there, holding a bottle of champagne and looking distinctly unburdened and about ten years younger than he had the last time Alex had seen him.

'Alex, come in,' he said. 'We're just having an impromptu celebration. I guess you heard. Dory will not have to stand trial after all. The charges have been dropped.'

'I did hear,' said Alex. 'It's great news.'

'Come in. Hang up your coat,' said Garth, pointing to the hooks beside the door. Then he smiled bemusedly. 'You know where the coats go.'

'I do, indeed,' said Alex. She put her coat on a hook, adjusted the fitted jacket and skirt on her black suit, and followed him down the hall and then down the steps into the family room.

The scene which greeted her made her stop short. Dory was sitting beside Elaine on the sofa. Elaine sat up straight, her back rigid. Her eyes looked bruised and wary. On the opposite side of Dory, Alex was startled to see Seth, looking somewhat uncomfortable. He caught Alex's eye. She glanced at him and looked away. Chris, Therese and Joy were also in attendance. The Ennis family had apparently been recruited to join in the celebration and were doing their best to appear enthusiastic.

Dory looked up at Alex as she came in. 'Hi, Alex,' she said.

Alex summoned all the friendliness she could muster. She walked over to Dory, bent down and gave her a hug. 'Congratulations,' she said. 'I'm so happy for you.' She deliberately did not speak to Seth, who was so close she could inhale his familiar, disturbing scent.

Dory grabbed her hand as she was straightening up. 'Thanks, Alex,' she said. 'I mean it. I owe you.'

'Not at all,' said Alex. 'I'm just glad it worked out.'

'I'm glad I have a sister,' said Dory with uncharacteristic warmth.

Alex saw a grimace of distaste twist Elaine's face. She hunched her shoulders, as if to escape from Dory's arm that pressed against her.

'Me too,' said Alex. 'I'm glad too.'

Garth approached with a glass of champagne and handed it to Alex. She took it and began to sip.

'So, Dory,' said Joy, who was still dressed in her rumpled work clothes, but was wearing bedroom slippers. 'What do you do now?'

Dory shrugged. 'Get back to my life, I guess. Try to connect with my old customers. Maybe meet some new people.' She looked pointedly at Seth, who smiled briefly and looked away.

'You going to continue living with Alex?' Chris Ennis asked.

'I don't know,' Dory said evasively. 'If I want to get my old customers back, I probably need to live here. Besides, Alex has probably had enough of me.'

Alex felt cornered as all eyes turned to her. I have had enough, she thought. But she would never say it in front of these people. In fact, looking at the way in which Elaine seemed to recoil from her daughter's touch, Alex felt the old sympathy for Dory rising again. 'We didn't do that bad,' she said.

Just then the doorbell buzzer sounded again.

Garth looked around the room. 'Who's that? Who else did you invite?' he said pleasantly to Dory.

Dory shook her head.

Garth dutifully began to mount the stairs again.

Therese, who was sitting on a wooden chair beside her mother, spoke quietly into Joy's ear. Joy nodded and patted her daughter on her bony knee. 'We will,' she said, a half-smile lifting the dimple and beauty mark on one side of her face. 'We'll leave in a few minutes.'

Seth, excusing himself to Dory, pushed himself up out of the corner of the sofa and came over to where Alex was standing. Alex looked at him coldly and refused to ask the obvious question.

Seth did not wait to be asked. 'I saw your car in the driveway so I stopped by your house this afternoon. I wanted to find out how your interview went at the gallery,' he explained in a low voice. 'Dory told me you got the job and you started today. How come you didn't call me?'

Alex remembered thinking that she had wanted to call him, but had convinced herself that she would sound needy and foolish if she did. 'It didn't occur to me,' she lied.

'How did the first day go?' he asked.

'Fine,' said Alex. 'I think I'm going to like it there. So, you were hanging out with Dory this afternoon?'

'We weren't "hanging out,"' he protested. 'We were talking a little bit, and I was still at your house when the call came. Dory was all excited, naturally enough, and wanted to tell her parents herself. So she asked me to drive her here.'

'You don't have to explain,' Alex said, feigning indifference.

'Yes, I do,' he said. 'I saw your expression when you saw me here.'

'I was just surprised,' Alex protested.

'Anyway, that dog she bought nearly bit my head off,' Seth said.

Alex nodded grimly. 'Remus. He's a handful.'

'I was trying to imagine your delight yesterday when you came home and were greeted by that barking maniac.'

Alex smiled. 'You're right. It was bad.' Then she could not resist adding: 'I wasn't pleased about the dog either.'

Seth burst out laughing.

Dory turned to look at him. 'What's so funny?' she asked suspiciously.

'Nothing,' said Alex.

Seth composed himself and waved off Dory's concern. When she looked away again, he spoke in a low voice to Alex. 'So, are you relieved?' he asked. 'She's free to go now.'

Alex nodded slightly. 'To be honest, yes,' she said.

Not looking at her, Seth put his arm around her waist and gently tugged her toward him. Alex allowed him to hold her like that for a second and then pulled away. Dory turned and gazed at them with an alert, flinty expression in her eyes.

Just then Garth reappeared at the top of the short staircase, flanked by two men, one white and one black, in overcoats and suits. The three of them descended the steps, their faces grave, as silence fell on the festivities.

'Um, folks, we have an official visit here. This is Detective Spagnola and Detective Langford,' said Garth.

'More cops? This is overkill,' Chris Ennis exclaimed.

Therese looked warily at the two detectives and burrowed against her mother.

Alex had to stifle a gasp herself. What now? she thought.

Dory looked at the policemen in alarm. 'What's going on?' she demanded. 'Why are you here?'

'I called them,' said Elaine. 'I asked them to come.'

TWENTY

DORY JUMPED UP from the sofa and stared at her mother, who was looking quite satisfied with herself. 'You called them?' she cried. 'Why? This thing is finally over.'

Elaine's gaze seemed to crackle. 'Over? It's not over for me. In case you've forgotten, your sister, Lauren, was murdered. Just because the charges against you were dropped does not mean that this case can be put to rest. What happened to my baby? I still want answers. If it wasn't you who killed Lauren, who was it? They're the police. They need to start all over again.'

Garth frowned at his wife. 'Couldn't you have let Dory have this one day?'

Elaine sniffed. 'I thought you, of all people, would understand.'

'You were right to call us,' said Detective Spagnola. 'We are officially reopening this case. We've been over the file, and we need to question again all the people we talked to three years ago.'

Chris Ennis stood up abruptly. 'Well, I guess the party's over.' He turned to Joy and Therese. 'We may as well head back upstairs.' Following his lead, Joy and Therese stood up to go.

Detective Langford frowned at him. 'You live in this building?'

Chris nodded. 'My wife and my daughter and I.'

'And your name is…'

'Christopher Ennis. And this is my wife, Joy. And my daughter, Therese.'

Detective Langford consulted a list he had on a clipboard. 'Mr Ennis. You were living here when Lauren Colson was murdered.'

'Yes, we were,' said Chris. 'But we answered all these questions when it happened. We really have nothing new to offer. None of us were home at the time it happened.'

'Why don't you just sit back down for a minute,' said Detective Langford.

'Why do we have to stay?' Therese asked her mother.

'Look,' said the detective. 'Obviously somebody messed up when they were questioning witnesses and suspects, and now we need to re-question friends, family, anybody who was in the building or had access to the building. What about you, ma'am?' he asked, turning to Alex.

'What about me?'

'Name?'

'Alex Woods.'

'You a friend of the victim's? Or the family?'

Alex knew better than to give him the long version. 'I never met the Colsons until a few weeks ago. I never knew Lauren Colson at all.'

'Me neither,' said Seth. 'Seth Paige. I just gave Dory a ride here today.'

Dory glared at him. 'Thanks a lot, Seth. We're not even friends?'

'I didn't mean it like that, Dory,' he said. 'I only meant for their purposes.'

The detective consulted his list. 'You two can leave,' he said.

'Thanks,' said Seth. He turned to Alex, as if to ask her if she was coming. Alex was looking at Dory.

'I'm sorry this had to happen right now,' she said.

Dory shook her head. 'Lauren. It's like she's still here.'

'Are you staying with your parents or coming back to my house tonight?' Alex asked.

'I don't know,' said Dory irritably.

'Well, if you want me to I can bring your stuff to town tomorrow. But you still need to pick up the dog.'

Dory looked at Alex and shook her head. 'You said you liked animals. What a joke. You're too selfish. I can't imagine you ever having a dog of your own.'

'Dory,' Garth warned her. 'Where did you get the dog?'

'My old customer. Regina Magill. She brought him out there.'

'We'll get Regina to take the dog off your hands,' said Garth. 'Don't worry.'

'I'll decide what happens to my dog,' Dory said.

'Fine,' said Alex grimly. 'I'll wait to hear from you.'

OUT ON THE street Seth said, 'Can I give you a lift? I'm parked right at the end of the block.'

Alex hesitated. Then she said, 'OK.'

She followed him to his car and clambered into the front seat, grateful when the heat began to rise. She couldn't stop shivering. As Seth maneuvered the car out of the space, Alex closed her eyes and tipped her head back, exhausted after the sleepless night before and the upheavals of the day. Before she knew it, she was asleep. She opened her eyes again when the car jerked to a halt in her driveway.

'Sorry,' she said. 'I wasn't much company.'

'Doesn't matter. You were tired,' he said.

'I was,' she replied. 'Well, thank you.' She opened the car door.

'I think I better go in with you,' he said.

'Why? Don't be silly.'

'Remus might be in an ornery mood.'

As if Remus had heard what Seth said, he began to bark frantically from inside the house.

'What can you do?' Alex asked doubtfully.

'I'm a dog whisperer,' he said.

'Right.'

'Just wait,' he said, getting out of the driver's side.

Alex didn't want to admit it, but she was glad he was coming in with her. She followed him up the shoveled walk to the front door, opened it and let him precede her into the house. Remus barked like he was possessed by the devil, the shrill noise echoing up the stairwell.

Seth began murmuring and, in a short time, Remus was quiet. Seth straightened up and turned to Alex.

'Ahem,' he said. 'What did I tell you?'

'You're right,' she said. 'I've got to hand it to you.'

Seth hesitated in the doorway.

'Can you stay for something to drink?' she asked.

'I can't stay long,' he said. 'I have to pack.' Alex shrugged. 'Beer?'

Seth nodded and followed her into the kitchen. Remus, his nails clacking on the floor, brought up the rear.

Alex got them each a drink and they sat down at the kitchen table.

'Nice party at the Colsons, eh?' he asked.

She laughed in spite of herself. 'That was horrible. Poor Dory.'

'She brings it on herself,' he said.

'Maybe,' Alex admitted. 'But her mother just won't cut her any slack.'

'There's worse things than losing your mother, I guess,' he said.

Alex raised her glass and clinked it with his beer bottle.

'True,' she said.

They sat in silence for a moment, each contemplating their own losses. Then Alex said, 'So, is it Friday you're leaving?'

'Actually, I'm leaving tonight,' he said.

'Tonight?'

'Yeah, I'm not flying. I'm going to drive out. Obviously it's going to take a lot longer to get out there, so I'll just do five or six hours tonight and then I'll stop somewhere and pick it up tomorrow.'

'Guess you're in a hurry to get going,' she said.

'The sooner I go, the sooner I get back.'

Alex looked up at him and frowned. 'Get back?'

'I'm going back to resign from my position. I'm driving the SUV so that I can clear out my place and bring back my stuff.'

Alex felt her heart leap in her chest. 'What are you talking about? You're coming back here?'

Seth nodded. 'This thing with my dad was kind of a wake-up call. You know, I'm pretty fond of that old guy, and I can see that his health isn't all that it might be. And he's the only parent I've got left. I guess talking to you made me hyperaware of that this vacation. And there's Janet and the kids. They're my family. It's important to be around them. I'm tired of living so far away.'

'So you're just quitting your job and moving home?'

'You make me sound like a slacker,' he teased her.

Alex blushed.

'No. Remember the other day on the train when I told you I was having lunch with my old advisor? He's been trying to get me to come back and teach in his department at the university for several years now. This time I told him I was ready to do it. It's semester break so I figured I better make the leap before the new semester started.'

Alex stared at him. 'You're really moving back here?'

'Yep,' he said. He was quiet for a moment. 'What do you think?'

Alex could not meet his gaze. 'I'm…really glad,' she said.

'Good.' Seth smiled, then extended his hand across the table. 'Because my family isn't the only reason I want to come back here,' he said.

Alex could feel the warmth of his gaze on her. She hesitated before reaching out and putting her hand in his. She felt as if her hand was going to burst into flame. 'It isn't?'

Seth shook his head. 'Nope.'

They sat like that for a moment, both tongue-tied. Then Seth let go of her hand and stood up. 'So as much as I'd like to stay here and discuss this with you, I've got to get a move on. It's a long drive.'

Alex stood up, smiling, and walked with him to the front door. 'I'm so happy you're coming back,' she said.

Seth leaned towards her, as he had on Christmas Day, but this time he kissed her on the lips. Alex almost gasped from the surprise. She answered the question in his kiss with her own, and they were soon entwined in each other's arms.

Alex could have stood that way all night, reveling in the reality of what she had only imagined—holding him, and being held, but suddenly Remus began to bark and the front door opened. Alex and Seth reluctantly surfaced from their kisses and turned, feeling intoxicated, still clinging to one another, and looked in the doorway.

Dory stood there, staring at them. 'Well,' she said. 'What a surprise.'

Alex pulled away from Seth and tugged down on her suit jacket. 'Dory. Hi.'

'What do you know?' she said, pushing past them in the vestibule. 'Don't let me interrupt. I just came to get my things like you asked me.' She started up the stairs, every step heavy.

'I think I better go,' Seth whispered.

Alex nodded and they kissed again, quickly. 'Have a safe trip,' she said. 'Drive carefully. Hurry back.' She followed him to the doorway.

''Bye, Dory,' he called out from the foot of the stairs. There was no reply.

Out in front of the house, Garth Colson's black truck sat idling. Alex could see someone at the wheel though she couldn't swear that it was Garth. Seth stole one more kiss from her before he jogged out to the car in the driveway.

She waved as he pulled out and drove down the street. Then she went back inside. Dory was coming down the staircase, awkwardly hefting the polka dot suitcase and a couple of tote bags.

'I can't take the dog,' she said abruptly. 'My mother still won't have a dog in the house. You'll have to keep him here until Regina gets back.'

'Dory, you don't have to leave,' said Alex. 'You can stay here.' She hadn't expected those words to pop out of her own mouth, but suddenly her heart was so light that she couldn't begrudge Dory anything. In fact, she felt positively inclined to be generous to this difficult sister.

'Oh, don't worry about me. I want to leave,' said Dory. 'I didn't realize what you were up to.'

'What do you mean?' Alex asked uneasily.

'You said you didn't have a boyfriend. But obviously, you do.'

'Really, no, I didn't,' said Alex. 'We just…started…'

'Maybe it was because you could see that I was just getting to know him. You didn't want that, did you? Him liking me, and not you. I guess I really didn't have much of a chance, did I?'

Alex sighed. 'Dory, that is not what happened at all.'

Dory gazed at her. 'Don't tell me that's not what happened. Don't lie to my face. I have eyes.' She hauled her things to the door and started out.

'Do you need a hand?' Alex asked.

'From you?' Dory asked. 'No. I don't need anything from you.'

'Dory, don't,' said Alex. But she might as well have been talking to the wind. Dory had stepped off the front porch step into the darkness and was gone.

TWENTY-ONE

ALEX ATE A grilled cheese sandwich, ran a bubble bath and submerged herself. And the whole time, her heart felt like it was going to burst with happiness. Seth, she thought. She had felt the attraction to him from that first night at Laney Thompson's party, but it hadn't seemed possible. He lived in Chicago and, for all she knew, was involved with someone else. He was six years older, and she told herself that he probably still saw her as one of the little kids from the neighborhood. And yet she had felt breathless each and every time she saw him. And now, to know that he felt the same way…That it was real! That he was coming back here to live. That they were going to start a relationship. It wasn't a feeling you had that often in life. That glorious tipping sensation when you were first falling in love. Yes, she thought. Falling in love.

She dried off from her bath, put on her oversized T-shirt and bathrobe, and whirled in her bedroom, hugging herself. For maybe the first time since she had set foot in this house after the accident, she felt happy. Hopeful. Alive. And they knew it. She felt sure that they knew it. She could feel her parents' love for her like a glow around her, and she almost felt, impossible though it was, that they had had a hand in it. 'Thank you,' she whispered to the silence in the house which now seemed not depressing, but benign. And even though she knew rationally that this could not have been the case, she still said, 'Thank you for Seth.'

She went downstairs and tried to read, to calm herself

down, but it was no use. For a little while she thought about Dory. She couldn't help feeling vaguely guilty about Dory's disappointment over Seth. She felt that Alex had deceived her. It would be difficult to convince Dory that there was nothing between her and Seth until this very night. But it wasn't up to Alex to persuade Dory of that, she reminded herself. It wasn't as if Seth had led Dory on. Alex knew better. He'd just been nice. Alex wasn't sure that Dory knew the difference.

Alex thought about Elaine calling the police to come and interrupt the celebration of Dory being officially cleared in the case of her sister's murder. It was almost as if she could not bear the idea that Dory wasn't guilty. Why? Alex wondered. How could a mother feel that way? She should have been delighted that Dory was no longer a suspect. Instead it seemed as if her only aim was to remind Dory that she did not believe her, did not trust her. And all that Dory wanted, it seemed, was to be welcomed back into her mother's affections.

Maybe, Alex thought, she wasn't being fair to Elaine. After all, someone murdered her daughter, right there in her own home, and Dory had pleaded guilty. Could she really be blamed for believing in her guilt? And now there was no one to blame, but Lauren was still dead. That pain would never go away and Elaine would probably never be at peace until she knew who had killed her. So, who was Lauren's killer? Alex wondered. Maybe the police were not looking far enough for the murderer. They seemed to be focusing on the people in Boston but Lauren had lived far away, in Branson, Missouri. Could it have been someone from her life in Branson who wanted her dead?

Or maybe a crazy fan. Everybody had read about them. Maybe someone followed her to Boston from her other life. Thinking about Lauren's murder reminded her of that

CD that Seth had bought for her at the second-hand bookstore. To be sure that Dory didn't see her with it, Alex had slipped it into a drawer in the dining room that same day and not looked at it since. She went into the dining room, opened the drawer and pulled it out. Back in the living room she popped the CD into the sound system and sat down to listen. The first track was some coy number about a biker at a bar. Alex listened to a few bars and skipped over it. The second track was the title song, 'Love You Only' set to the wailing accompaniment of an electric fiddle. The plaintiveness in Lauren's voice was unmistakable. Alex unfolded the liner notes and read along with the lyrics.

No one knows or understands me
No one thinks I've done enough
No one's close, or ever can be.
No one wants to know it's rough.
Mama tells me to do more
Or my moment will be lost
Says I'm gonna end up poor.
I say what's it gonna cost?
Lost my passion and my youth,
All I'm left is tired and lonely,
And I've finally faced the truth.
I'm condemned to love you only.

As a rule, Alex hated country music. It always sounded whiny and sentimental to her ears. But once in a while a country song could capture her with its sincerity, and she found herself replaying 'Love You Only' several times.

Maybe it was because she knew something about this singer. She knew the mama in Lauren's life, and wondered if the song was autobiographical, or if she had written the lyrics in the persona of a fictional character. It was tempting to read it as autobiographical, and she certainly felt a jolt of recognition when Lauren described her mother as demanding and difficult to satisfy.

Alex had assumed, from the start, that Lauren had been lavished with love and attention while Dory was neglected. But, when she thought about it, Elaine was the same person, even if she treated her daughters differently. Perhaps she had overlooked Dory, but maybe her great love for Lauren had taken the form of pushing her unmercifully, and never being satisfied with the results. No wonder Lauren was lonely.

Clearly she had suffered from a love affair gone bad. Was it someone from Branson? Alex wondered if the police had looked into Lauren's personal life there at all. Probably not, since Dory presented them with the ideal suspect. Maybe I'll mention that to Dory, Alex thought. Or to Elaine. The sooner someone else was arrested for Lauren's murder, the sooner Dory might be truly forgiven by her mother.

For a moment Alex felt her sister's sadness and lamented it. She looked over at Remus, who was resting quietly on the bed which Dory had bought for him. 'We can't abandon her, Remus,' she said. 'We have to try to help her.' Surprisingly she realized that she actually meant it. She and Dory were not done with one another. They were still sisters and Alex was not going to give up on her, even if she had installed the worst dog ever in Alex's home. 'I mean you,' Alex said to the dog who was curled up on the bed, snoring.

In the midst of a dream, Remus snorted and covered his eyes with one of his sinewy forelegs.

Alex smiled. Everything seemed endearing to her right now. Even the Pit Bull. She flicked on the television, watched it without really seeing it and finally turned it off. She wondered how far Seth had gotten. She didn't even know the route he was taking. He was probably on the Mass Pike, heading west. She thought of calling him, and then decided against it. He didn't need to be distracted while he was driving. They had all the time in the world to talk when he returned.

Alex looked at the time on the cable box. She still had work tomorrow, even though today seemed to have changed her life forever. She had woken up this morning feeling lonely and disgruntled and now everything had changed. She didn't even feel like the same person. But, she reminded herself, she had the same new job. And she needed to at least try to get some sleep. Finally she got up, turned out the lights and climbed the stairs to her bedroom. She set the alarm, tossed her bathrobe over the foot of the bedstead and crawled under the covers. She thought she would lie awake, stimulated by all the unexpected events of the day, but in no time she was fast asleep.

THE BARKING WOKE HER.

Alex struggled up on one elbow and looked at the illuminated numbers on her clock. It was after three. What is he barking about? she thought.

She didn't hear any noise in the house, but something was making Remus go crazy. Well, she thought, it wasn't as if it took a great deal to make this dog start barking. He was so damn skittish. Maybe a car backfired on the street, or the wind snapped a tree branch against the window. Whatever it was, he sounded like he was in it for the long haul. Alex hated getting out of the warmth of her bed. She wished she could just yell down the stairs at him and make him stop, but there was no way that would work.

She took a deep breath. It's nothing, she told herself. It's probably nothing. But she knew she wasn't going to get back to sleep if he kept that up. She got out of bed, put on her bathrobe and slippers and went out to the stairs. The house was as dark as she had left it when she went to bed. She turned on the stairwell light, yelling, 'Remus. Remus!'

The dog continued to bark. It was a high, strangled bark that grated on her nerves. Dammit, she thought. What was his problem? She went down into the living room and turned on a lamp by the door. His bed was empty. He was somewhere else on the first floor. Probably by the back door, she thought. There might be a raccoon traversing the backyard, and Remus heard it with those super-sensitive ears that dogs had.

'Remus, what is it?' she demanded.

She shuffled through the house, glancing into her father's office and the dining room, turning on a lamp on each one. He wasn't in either room. She went to the end of the hall toward the kitchen. Even in the dark, she could see him. His shiny, muscular black frame was straining forward and the barking was incessant. She called his name and he turned to look at her.

'What is it?' she asked. 'What are you barking about?'

She walked into the kitchen and flipped the switch beside the door which illuminated the track lights over the counters. Remus looked at her and then continued to bark, all his attention riveted to the closed door of the pantry.

Did I close that? she wondered. She couldn't remember. She often left it open, but this time she may have shut it. Perhaps there was a mouse in there, Alex thought. It wouldn't be the first time. There hadn't been a cat living in this house since her parents died. Laney Thompson across the street had adopted Castro after the accident. So now that the coast was clear, the mice could definitely have returned. That was probably it, Alex told herself. Mice. Nonetheless, she felt her heart beating hard in her chest at the sight of the dog, snarling and barking implacably at the door.

Murmuring soothing words to him, she reached out to

the pantry doorknob, getting ready to open it, when suddenly her eye fell on something on the floor beyond the pantry door. Her heart thudded with anxiety. It was too big to be a mouse. A rat? she thought. In the half-light of the track lighting, she could not make out what it was. She held her breath, waiting for it to skitter off in some direction. But the object lay still, and did not move.

'What is that thing?' she demanded aloud, although there was no one to answer her question. She went over and crouched down, reluctantly reaching for the small, dark form, her heart pounding. She touched it and immediately cried out as a shudder ran up her spine. The thing on the ground was cold and slimy. 'What the hell?' Alex cried. Grimacing and wanting to flee from it, she forced herself to hold her ground instead. She reached out with two fingers and gingerly picked it up.

Even in the dim light she could see that it was the size of a small envelope and purplish in color. Repulsed, Alex wanted to drop it, but she kept a hold on it, and dangled the object in front of her eyes to examine it. It was some kind of organ meat. A piece of liver.

What the fuck? she thought, struggling to get to her feet without throwing the hunk of liver away from her. The dog began to bark like a lunatic. Over the barking Alex heard a door squeak, tried to turn and saw a shadow on the wall. Before she could register what was happening or cry out, she felt a thudding against her back, and then a searing pain which took her breath away. She crumpled to the floor, landing on top of the piece of liver which she had dropped, as her knees and all the strength in her arms gave way and let her fall.

TWENTY-TWO

SHE HEARD A murmur of voices, and thought that they were talking about her. But she didn't recognize them, and couldn't make out what they were saying. She wanted to see who it was. She wanted to ask them something. But what was it she wanted to ask?

Alex forced herself to open her eyes. The very act of raising her eyelids was painful. She blinked and looked around the room where she lay. It was completely unfamiliar, but she knew that it had to be a hospital. There were machines attached to her by lines, blinking neon numbers and whooshing sounds. She had absolutely no memory of arriving here.

She tried to move and gasped with the pain of it. She realized that she was encircled with gauze and tape, and she felt as if someone had sawn her in half, like one of those magician's assistants.

She let out a whimpering cry. Anything more would have hurt too much. A blonde, heavyset nurse in scrubs appeared in the door to her room and hurried over to Alex's bedside. She peered at Alex, and smiled when she saw that her eyes were open.

'Hey, there,' said the nurse. 'You decided to come back to us.'

Alex tried to speak but her lips were dry. The nurse picked up a glass with a straw and gave her a sip. Alex wanted to suck down every drop of water in it but the nurse wrestled it away from her.

'Don't overdo it. Just take it easy.'

'Where am I?'

'Boston General. They brought you here by ambulance.'

Suddenly Alex had a dim recollection of lying on a gurney during a bumpy ride, and a person dressed in a blue uniform yelling questions at her over the sound of sirens as they raced along. 'What happened?' she asked.

'You don't remember?'

Alex shook her head.

'You were stabbed in the back,' said the nurse.

'When?'

'During the night,' she replied.

Alex's brain started to clear. 'Someone was in the house,' she whispered. She remembered hearing Remus, and coming down to the kitchen. Something else…

'Whoever did it left you there to die, but apparently your dog wouldn't stop barking and finally one of the neighbors called the police. By the time they found you, you'd lost an awful lot of blood.'

Remus, she thought. He saved me.

'Doctor Pandava will be in to tell you all about it. I'm going to let him know that you're awake.'

No, Alex wanted to cry out. Stay here. Tell me what happened. But the nurse had disappeared from the room. Does anyone know I'm here? she thought. And… She felt her stomach lurch at the next thought. Who had done this to her?

The door to her room opened and Alex looked up in alarm. 'Who is it?' she asked.

A short, good-looking doctor with tobacco-colored skin approached her bed. 'I am Doctor Pandava,' he said in a lilting accent. 'I was the attending last night when they brought you in, Ms Woods.'

'Thank you,' said Alex, although she didn't exactly know what she was thanking him for.

'No problem.'

'What happened to me?'

'You were stabbed a number of times with some kind of carving knife. You suffered some very large lacerations and several deep wounds in the attack. We sewed you up. It took quite a few stitches. And you lost a great deal of blood. We had to give you a transfusion. As well as medication for the pain, and antibiotics, to avoid the possibility of infection.'

Alex grimaced.

'Luckily and miraculously, none of your vital organs were lacerated in the attack. All in all, you were quite lucky.'

'Lucky,' Alex murmured.

'All in all,' he repeated pleasantly.

'I guess so,' said Alex. 'Is it all right for me to move around? It's pretty painful.'

'The more you move around, the quicker you'll heal,' he said. 'You can be released tomorrow morning. The nurse will give you instructions. You need to take it easy. No strenuous exercise for at least a week. I'll want to see you next week for a check-up. The nurse will give you all the paperwork.'

'Thank you, Doctor,' said Alex humbly.

'No problem,' he repeated, smiling. 'I'll check on you in the morning before you leave.'

Alex nodded as he left. She picked up the glass of water and sipped at it again. It tasted delicious to her. The doctor's matter-of-factness was extremely reassuring. He made it sound as if this pain was just a temporary setback and that she would recover in no time. But she still felt a little disoriented and, admittedly, a bit sorry for herself. There didn't seem to be anyone waiting for her. She wondered if Seth knew what had happened.

Or Louis Orenstein. She suddenly panicked. This would have been her second day on the job. She didn't want to get fired already. She wondered vaguely where her phone was, but there was no reason to think it was here in the hospital. She hadn't exactly had a chance to collect her things before she was carried out of her house.

Just then the door opened again and the nurse came in. 'You up for a little more company?' she asked.

'I guess,' said Alex.

'There are some gentlemen here from the police who want to talk to you.'

'Oh, all right,' she said. 'Um, before they come in, could someone call my work and tell my boss where I am? His name is Louis Orenstein.'

'I'll ask your uncle. He's out in the waiting area. But he probably already took care of it.'

'My uncle's here?' Alex said.

'Been here most of the night. Your neighbor called him when they brought you in.'

'Can I see him?' Alex asked hopefully.

'You'd better talk to the police first. Then you can see your family.' With that the nurse turned and disappeared from the room. In a few moments she was back with the two detectives in tow that Alex had met at the Colsons' apartment. The white detective tilted his head to look at her.

'Ms Woods? Do you remember us? We met at the Colsons. I'm Lieutenant Spagnola. This is Detective Langford. We're cooperating with the Chichester police. We have a few questions for you about the incident at your home last night.'

'OK,' said Alex, although she suddenly felt extremely unsteady. 'I'll try and help.'

Spagnola took a pad and pen out of his coat pocket. 'OK, Ms Woods. First off, do you know who did this to you?'

She hated the fact that Dory's face leapt to mind. 'No,' she said firmly.

'Can you describe the person who attacked you?'

'I didn't see them,' said Alex.

'You live alone in the house?'

Alex thought about explaining, and then decided against it.

'Yes,' she said.

'We heard you haven't got much in the way of security there.'

'It's Chichester,' said Alex wearily. 'It's always been safe.'

'Whoever entered the house came in through the back door. Apparently they opened the lock with a credit card. My colleague in Chichester said that it's a very inadequate lock.' Alex was beginning to feel as if they were blaming her for being stabbed in her own home.

'I'll get it replaced,' she said with a sigh.

'Or perhaps they had a key,' he said. 'Does anyone else have a key to your house?'

Alex felt anxious. 'My neighbor across the street,' she said.

'Mrs Thompson. She's the one who called the police.'

'My Uncle Brian has a key.'

'Oh, yes, we spoke to your uncle. He's out in the waiting room. He told us that your half-sister was staying with you. And, of course, your half-sister is Dory Colson.'

Alex nodded slowly. 'She was staying with me. But, as you know, she went back to her parents yesterday.'

'Is there any reason you can think of for why she might want to hurt you?'

Alex thought about Dory dragging her suitcases out

last night, berating her for her relationship with Seth. She thought of it, but she hesitated to say it. It would take almost nothing for the police to turn their suspicions on Dory.

'Ms Woods?'

'I…don't think so.'

'All right. Tell us what happened. Tell us about the attack.'

Alex drew in a deep breath. 'I was in bed, asleep. I heard Remus barking. He barks a lot so I didn't go down right away. But he kept it up. So I went downstairs. I found him in the kitchen. He seemed to be barking at the pantry door. I thought maybe he heard a mouse in there.'

'And then what?' asked Detective Spagnola.

'Then I…' Alex tried to remember. Suddenly it came back to her. 'I saw something on the floor. I thought it might be what Remus was barking at. You know, a mouse or a rat or something. I tried poking at it, but then I realized it wasn't a living thing. So, I…picked it up.'

'What was it?' the detective asked.

'It was a piece of liver, as far as I could figure out,' said Alex.

'When the ambulance came to get you, they found you lying on top of a piece of raw liver.'

'It was gross,' said Alex, grimacing.

'It was poisoned,' said the detective.

Alex started. 'What? Poisoned? With what?'

Spagnola shook his head. 'We're waiting for the test results. It had a coating of some kind of granulated powder on one side of it. We think it was meant for the dog, to silence him. But for some reason, the dog didn't eat it. When you were stabbed and landed on top of it, your attacker was forced to leave it there and flee.'

'What a sick thing to do,' said Alex.

'We suspect that the dog chased your assailant out of the

house. He may even have bitten the assailant in the course of this struggle. We found some navy-blue fibres snagged on the dog's collar that may have got there when he was struggling with the intruder.'

'Wow,' said Alex. 'He did prove to be a guard dog.'

'Excuse me?' Spagnola asked.

'It's just that when my sister got him, she said he would protect us. Sure enough, he did.'

Spagnola nodded. 'So, as far as we can tell, nothing of value was taken. Of course, the intruder planned to get the dog out of the way with that poisoned liver, but the dog did not cooperate. They left without taking anything, possibly because they had no other choice. They may have intended to come in and to work quickly and quietly and get out. And you might have slept through it all.'

Alex nodded. 'I see.'

Spagnola frowned. 'Now, do you keep anything valuable in the house which might have been targeted by the intruder?'

Alex shook her head slowly. 'Since my parents died the house has sat empty for months. My uncle and I were careful not to leave anything of value there after the funeral because I was heading back out west to school.'

'Strange that they would target the house while you were in it. After it had been sitting empty for months,' mused Spagnola.

'Yes, it is,' said Alex.

'Unfortunately the nature of the attack makes us wonder if perhaps you yourself were the intended victim.' Spagnola smoothed down his mustache and looked over his notes. 'So is there anyone you know of who might have wanted to hurt you? Were you and Dory Colson having any problems…'

Alex shook her head. 'It wasn't my sister,' she said.

'You seem very sure of that.'

'I am,' said Alex. 'Don't get me wrong. It's not that she's so fond of me. But she is an animal lover. I can tell you right now that she would never poison a dog.'

'There's always a first time,' said Spagnola.

Alex shook her head and pains shot through her. 'No. Never. That's just not possible.'

'All right,' said Spagnola. 'Moving on. Anybody else you can think of?'

'I hardly know anybody else around here,' said Alex. 'I've been away at college and grad school. I've lost touch with the people I used to know. Well, except for my neighbors. And my family.'

'What about boyfriends? Lovers? Any nasty break-ups where somebody might be holding a grudge?'

Immediately Alex thought of Seth. He wasn't actually her lover. Not yet. And they were not breaking up, they were just beginning. No, she thought. There was no point in even mentioning Seth. 'Nobody,' she said.

'All right,' said Spagnola, standing up. 'They've got a team going over the house now, collecting fingerprints and footprints, etc. If there's anything to be found, they'll find it. If you think of anything relevant, don't hesitate to call me.' He handed Alex his card. Alex thanked him and set it down on the elevated tray beside her bed.

The two policemen left, encountering Alex's uncle, Brian, coming through the door. He looked tired and unshaven. He rushed over to her bed, ready to hug her, but Alex raised her hands in warning. 'I can't do a hug. Not right at the moment.'

Uncle Brian heeded the warning and pulled a chair up beside her bed. He rubbed the back of her hand with his index finger and smiled at her sadly. 'Alex, I feel like this is all my fault. I should have insisted you stay with us.'

'Don't say that,' she said. 'I was fine until this happened.'

'I should have stopped you,' he said. 'When you went looking for Dory I should have stopped you. She's as crazy as that boy who fathered her. I'll never forgive myself.'

'Uncle Brian, it wasn't Dory who did this.'

'Of course it was. It's the same thing she did to her other sister. Only that one she killed,' he exclaimed.

'No, it wasn't.'

'I don't know how you can say that. It's exactly the same. I told the police all about it. You helped that lunatic to get out of jail, and you took her in. This is the thanks you get.'

'Uncle Brian, will you listen to me?'

Brian shook his head. 'Sorry. I'm exhausted. I've been here most of the night. Since Laney called me.'

'I know,' said Alex. 'I'm very grateful that you came.'

'I just kept going over it in my mind,' he said. 'Wondering why I didn't insist…'

'You didn't insist because you know I'm a grown-up and you can't tell me what to do,' said Alex.

'It was just lucky that you had that dog,' said Brian, shaking his head.

'Dory brought the dog in,' said Alex.

'Yeah, and according to the cops, she tried to poison it so she could get at you without the dog to stop her.'

'That's exactly how I know that it wasn't her,' said Alex. 'She would never poison a dog. She loves animals more than people. She would rather poison herself.'

'You don't know that,' Brian objected. 'What if she's a psychopath, and she doesn't care who she hurts?'

'I just don't think so,' Alex insisted.

'Well, whatever,' he said. 'These cops are going to question her. They'll get to the bottom of it. Meanwhile, we need to get you out of here. They said you can be released tomorrow. So I'm going to head home and help your Aunt Jean get everything ready and I'll be back for you in the morning.'

'What do you mean, get everything ready?' Alex asked.

'At our house,' he said. 'You're coming home with me.'

Alex shook her head. 'Uncle Brian, that is sweet, but no. I'm not.'

'You can't be alone in that house.'

'I won't be alone. Laney is right across the street.'

'Fat lot of good Laney did you when that lunatic was hiding in your pantry!' he cried.

'Obviously we're all going to be a lot more on our guard after this. But I have a job I have to get to. And there's someone I care about—a guy I'm seeing now—who will be back any day…If I call him and tell him, I'm sure he will hurry and get back here.'

Brian held up a hand. 'Hold it,' he said. 'Hold it. Alex, we almost lost you last night. You almost got killed in that house. Now you want to stay there by yourself.'

'I don't want to stay by myself…' Alex admitted.

'Then there's nothing to discuss. You'll come home with me.'

Alex shook her head. 'I can't do that,' she insisted, feigning a confidence which she did not really feel. 'I don't want to run away.'

Brian raised his voice and wagged a finger at her. 'Alex, you listen to me. You are not going to spend a night alone in that house. I won't allow it.'

'She doesn't have to.'

Alex and Brian both looked up.

Dory stood in the doorway to the room, watching them coolly. 'I can stay with her,' she said.

TWENTY-THREE

'EXCUSE ME, BUT who the hell are you?' said Brian.

Alex smiled. 'Unce Brian, this is your niece. Dory Colson.'

Brian struggled to control the expression on his face. 'Really?'

'Dory, this is Brian Reilly. My mother's brother. Your uncle.'

'How do you do?' Dory asked coldly.

Brian looked somewhat chastened. 'Nice to meet you.'

'How did you find me?' Alex asked Dory.

'The cops came around,' Dory said bluntly. 'They were looking to blame me for this mess.'

'I told them it wasn't you,' said Alex.

Dory shrugged. Then a little smile played around her lips. 'I hear that Remus saved you?'

'It's true,' said Alex.

'Told you he was a good dog.'

'You were right.'

'So, if you want, I'll stay in the house with you for a while. I figured you'd be pretty freaked out after this.'

'I don't want you to have to do that,' Alex said.

'I'm not gonna beg,' Dory said irritably.

Brian looked pleadingly at Alex. 'It's nice of you to offer but I think Alex would be better off at our house.'

'Whatever,' said Dory. 'I just came to make sure she was OK.'

Alex smiled at her. 'Dory, if you'd be willing to stay with me for a few days, I'd really be grateful.'

'I said I would,' said Dory.

Brian shook his head. 'Alex, I can't stop you, but I really wish…'

Alex took his hand and squeezed it. 'I know you're concerned about me. And the truth is that I would feel apprehensive to be there alone. But I'll feel safe with Dory in the house. Dory and I will be fine together.' She looked up at Dory. 'Won't we?'

THE NEXT MORNING Dory came to the hospital and picked Alex up in Garth's pick-up truck. 'I'm not that used to driving anymore,' she said.

'It's like riding a bicycle,' said Alex. 'You never forget how.'

'I'm getting the hang of it back,' said Dory. 'I drove my Dad to work this morning and he gave me the truck to use. He said he can take the subway to work for a few days.'

'Doesn't he pick things up in his truck?' Alex asked.

'He's got guys who work for him,' said Dory.

'How does your mom feel about this?' Alex asked as she carefully climbed into the cab of the pick-up and settled herself, gingerly fastening her seat belt over her bandaged torso.

'She feels fine,' said Dory.

Alex nodded. Probably glad you are not in the house, she thought. 'Well, thank you for coming for me.'

'No problem,' said Dory, concentrating on finding the entrance to the highway exit to Chichester.

Alex had to admit to herself, as the truck bounced along on its worn-down shocks, that she was a little more feeble than she had realized. She had been eager to get out of the hospital, but putting on the clothes and boots which Uncle

Brian had brought her had proved to be a challenge. She was exhausted by the time she was dressed. Dory hadn't been impatient, but she also hadn't babied her at all. Instead of bringing the truck around for her, Dory had expected her to walk down to the garage and meet her there. It had taken a little doing, but Alex had managed. It was better that way, Alex told herself. Being self-reliant would help her to recover.

Now, as they pulled into the driveway, Alex felt a positive longing to crawl upstairs and into her bed. Just getting released from the hospital and making this short trip home had worn her out.

'Watch your step,' said Dory as they descended onto the walkway which they had shoveled, but which was still somewhat packed with snow.

Alex took one step and slid. She managed to keep herself upright but the sudden, jerky motion had caused the wound in her back to throb. She took a deep breath and then looked up. Dory extended a hand to her. Alex took it gratefully, and together they made their way up to the house.

ONCE SHE GOT into the house and managed to slowly climb the stairs to her room, Alex fell onto the bed and into a deep sleep. She was awakened by the sound of someone buzzing the front doorbell. She heard Dory answer it and there was a murmur of voices interrupted by barking. Remus was back. She had asked her uncle about the dog and he explained that Laney Thompson had kept Remus at her house while Alex was in the hospital. Laney must have noticed the truck in the driveway and brought the dog over.

Alex wanted to get up, walk to the top of the steps and call down to Laney. She wanted to ask Laney to call Seth and tell him what had happened. She felt oddly shy about doing it herself. She didn't want him to think that she was pleading with him to come right back, but she had a feeling it would sound that way to him.

She felt pretty sure that he didn't know. Who would think to tell him? Nobody knew about the kiss they had shared before he left, except Dory. But as much as she wanted to ask this favor of Laney, she was unable to get off of the bed and to the top of the stairs before she heard the front door closing again. Then she heard Dory talking to the dog as his nails clattered across the hardwood floors through the house. In a few minutes Alex was asleep again.

She awoke when Dory shook her shoulder.

'Hey, wake up. I made you something to eat.'

Alex could smell it. 'Chicken soup.'

'They say it's good for you,' said Dory. 'Do you want me to bring it up here, or can you come down and eat it?'

'I better come down,' said Alex. 'The doctor said I should keep moving around. I'll get my strength back sooner if I push myself a little bit.'

'OK,' said Dory. She walked out of Alex's room and went down the steps.

Alex pulled herself to her feet and followed slowly in her wake.

As soon as he heard Alex coming down the stairs, Remus began to bark. She found the sound oddly comforting now. 'Good boy,' she said.

There were two bowls sitting on the table in the kitchen. Dory was already eating from hers. Alex sat down opposite her and picked up her spoon. She had a few mouthfuls. 'It tastes good. Did you have to go out and buy this?'

Dory shook her head. 'I found a can in the pantry. I just heated it up.'

The thought of the pantry was somewhat troubling to Alex. She glanced over in the direction of the deep closet which had always been her mother's spare food cupboard. She was glad to see that the door was open.

Dory followed her gaze. 'That's where they were?'

Alex nodded.

Dory frowned. 'Do you know who it was?' she said.

Alex shook her head. 'I have no idea.'

'You're lucky Remus was here,' said Dory.

'And that he didn't eat the liver,' Alex said.

'Liver?' Dory asked.

'Whoever did this threw down a piece of poisoned liver for Remus. Hoping to shut him up, obviously. But he didn't eat it.'

Dory summoned Remus to her side. When he sat down obediently beside her she began murmuring to him, calling him a good boy and rubbing him behind his ears.

'Dory, I wanted to ask you something,' said Alex.

Dory looked up at her blankly, still tugging on Remus's ears.

'Were you really mad at me about Seth?'

Dory frowned and her eyes clouded over. 'Why? What do you care?'

'I just want you to know,' said Alex, 'that there was nothing going on between me and Seth. Not until the other night. I had a crush on him but I didn't even know it was mutual.'

'Well, lucky you,' said Dory.

'Dory, I mean it,' said Alex. 'I was not playing any kind of game. I did not mean to make you angry.'

'It's no big deal,' said Dory. 'He's just another guy.'

'OK, well. It's important that we clear this up,' said Alex.

'Why?' Dory asked.

'Well, because I don't want you to have the wrong idea about me.'

'You mean, like I did about Lauren?' Dory asked coolly.

'About Lauren and Rick. Don't worry. I'm not crazy. I still think there was something going on with Rick. But I didn't kill her, and I didn't try to kill you.'

'I know that,' said Alex.

An uneasy silence fell between them.

Finally Alex said, 'Your father told me something about Lauren that might interest you.'

Dory frowned. 'What?'

'He said that Lauren was gay.'

Dory pushed her chair back from the table. 'What?' she cried. 'No way. That's a lie. She had boyfriends.'

'That's what he told me,' Alex insisted.

Dory dismissed this notion with a wave of her hand. 'No. Lauren was gonna get married. To another singer. Some guy named Henley. Walker Henley. He always wears a big white cowboy hat on stage. My parents were all excited about it. My mother was planning the wedding. They were going to have it in Opryland down in Nashville. He lives in Nashville. He came to visit one time when she was home. I remember. He was a pretty nice guy. Too nice for her. But then they broke up.'

'Do you know why they broke up?' Alex asked.

Dory frowned. 'She was too concerned with her precious career. They broke up because Lauren worked too hard.'

'I don't think that was the real reason,' said Alex. 'I think the reason was that Lauren was gay. She kept it secret so it wouldn't destroy her career. They're not real big on gay people in the country music world.'

Dory gave her a withering, sidelong glance. 'Why did he tell you that?'

'I was suggesting to him that maybe you were right to be jealous about Lauren and Rick. That maybe they were going behind your back.'

Dory peered at her. 'You were defending me?'

Alex nodded. 'That's why he told me. Plus, I guess there's no reason to hide it anymore. Since Lauren is dead.'

The expression in Dory's eyes was pained. 'I don't believe this. They tell you, but they don't tell me? Why wouldn't they tell me?'

Alex feigned ignorance. 'Maybe Lauren asked them not to.'

Dory scowled. 'I have to think about this.' She got up abruptly from the table and grabbed her jacket from the utility room.

'Where are you going?' Alex asked.

'I just need to take a walk. Clear my head.'

'You're going out?' Alex cried, and she could hear the anxiety in her own voice.

'I'm not a prisoner here, am I?' Dory asked in a sarcastic tone.

Alex shook her head. 'No,' she whispered.

'I won't go far,' Dory said, more gently. 'Put your phone in your pocket, just in case.'

'I should do that,' said Alex. 'Where is my phone?'

'I saw it in the dining room.' Dory snapped a leash onto Remus's collar. She opened the back door. You're taking Remus too, Alex wanted to protest. But she forced herself not to. It sounded so…weak. Dory looked at her. 'Remus needs to get a walk. We won't be long. You can lock the doors if you're scared. By the way,' she said, 'the locksmith was here while you were sleeping. Nobody can open this back door with a credit card anymore.'

'That's good,' said Alex in a shaky voice.

'It's broad daylight, for God's sake. Go get your phone. I'll wait until you have it.'

Alex obediently rose from her chair and shuffled into the dining room. Her phone was on the sideboard. 'I've got it,' she said. There was a text from Louis Orenstein, saying that he'd heard from Brian, and that Alex should stay at home and stay safe until she felt better. There were twelve missed calls and a text message from Seth.

'OK. We're going now,' said Dory. 'Lock the door.'

Alex shuffled back to the kitchen door and turned the stiff new lock behind Dory as she and Remus lunged out into the snow. You're fine, she told herself. You're perfectly safe. She punched in Seth's number and waited, with dwindling hopes, as it rang and rang. Finally it went to voicemail.

'Hi…Seth,' she said. 'This is…Alex. Sorry I missed your calls. I was…away.' She wanted to tell him everything, but she didn't want to recite it into the phone. She wanted to beg him to drop everything and come home, but she knew better. He needed to tie up all his loose ends while he was out there. And she was fine. Dory was here. 'Everything's fine here. Hope the move is going…OK. I'll speak to you soon.' She paused, not sure how to sign off. "Bye,' she said and ended the call, feeling stupid. She slipped the phone into the pocket of her sweatshirt and went through the house to the front door, to be sure that it too was locked.

TWENTY-FOUR

ALEX WAS SITTING in the worn leather desk chair in her father's first-floor office. It felt like the safest place to be in the house, surrounded by his books and papers, his pipes cold in the ashtray. She was studying the screen of her father's computer when Dory and Remus returned. She felt an undeniable sense of relief when she heard them shambling through the front door.

'How was your walk?' Alex asked.

'Pretty good,' said Dory. 'Cold out there.'

'Feel better?'

Dory stood in the door to the office, slapping her blue jeanclad thigh with the dog's leash. 'It didn't hurt anything. What are you doing there?'

Alex pointed to the chair she had pulled up beside her. 'Come and take a look at this.'

Dory came around and sat down on a Windsor chair beside the desk. She frowned at the screen. 'What is it?'

'It's the Ticketmaster site,' said Alex.

'Ticketmaster? Are you going to a show?' Dory asked.

'I was thinking we'd go together.'

Dory wrinkled her nose in distaste. 'I've never heard of these groups.'

'It's a country music line-up.' Alex sat back in the chair and rubbed her eyes. 'After you left, I started thinking about Lauren and that guy, Walker Henley.'

'Why think about them?' Dory asked in disgust.

'Those cops who came to see me in the hospital? The ones who are reopening Lauren's case?'

'Oh, yeah. Salt and Pepper,' said Dory cynically. 'They look at me like I've got dog-do on my shoe. Even though the DA dropped the charges, those two still want to make a case against me.'

'I was thinking,' said Alex, 'about what happened to Lauren. The only people the cops seem interested in are the people she knew here in Boston. But what about the people she knew in Branson? Or Nashville? Lovers, colleagues, rivals? She was living a secret life in a way. There had to be some people she pissed off.'

Dory sighed. 'I guess so.'

'Well, I Googled this Walker Henley. And among other things I found out that he is on a concert tour right now. He's going to be at this Providence, Rhode Island theater tomorrow night.'

'And?'

'And that's only a couple of hours from here. So I thought maybe we should go down there and try and talk to him. If I can get a message to him, letting him know that you're Lauren's sister, he might be willing to talk with us. Who knows? He'll surely know more about Lauren's private life than we do. He might be able to point us in another direction.'

'We? Us? What makes you think I want to do this?' Dory protested.

Alex looked at her impatiently. 'Look, it's you who's going to have this murder hanging over your head until they find out who really killed Lauren. I should think that would be reason enough.'

Dory shrugged and then peered at her. 'What's in it for you?'

'Somebody tried to kill me here the other night. I feel

like I'm sitting here with a target on my back and I don't
know why. I have a feeling that the attack on me is related
to Lauren's death.'

Dory reared back. 'Why do you think that? What do
you know?'

'I don't know,' said Alex. 'I don't know anything. Let's
just say that I don't believe in coincidences. Call it intu-
ition…'

'There is no such thing,' said Dory flatly.

'Fine. Call it what you want. Are you willing to drive
to Providence?'

'I guess,' said Dory.

'Good.' Alex pressed a button on the computer. 'I just
hit "buy,"' she said.

THE HILLMAN CENTER, the auditorium where Walker Henley was playing on a bill with three other country acts, was
an antiquated facility with a downtown locale and satellite
parking. Dory circled the city block several times, looking
for a place to park in the neighborhood, but finally it began
to look impossible, even though they were several hours
early for the concert.

'I guess I'm going to have to go to the stupid satellite
lot,' said Dory, idling in the vicinity of the double doors at
the front of the Hillman Center. 'You better get out.'

'I'll come with you,' said Alex.

'No, that's too far for you to walk,' said Dory. 'Wait
for me here. I don't know why I let you talk me into this.'

'Are you sure?'

'Just get out,' said Dory.

'OK. Thanks,' said Alex, sliding out of the car and standing on the nearby curb. 'I'll be in the foyer.'

Dory did not reply. She pulled away and disappeared
into the sea of rush-hour taillights in downtown Providence.

Alex slowly climbed the steps and opened the doors to the old-fashioned auditorium. The ornately figured carpets had probably been beautiful when they were installed but they had since been flattened by thousands of pairs of boots and sneakers and high-heeled shoes. The cream-colored walls of the foyer were dingy, and the sconces which flanked the doors had milk-glass shades but were not illuminated. A refreshment and souvenir counter took up the back wall of the foyer. At the moment there was only one person working there, a girl with dyed blonde curls wearing a black vest and tie and a tired-looking white shirt, who was unpacking cartons of candy boxes.

Alex went up to her. 'Excuse me,' she said.

The girl looked faintly surprised to see a customer this early. 'The concession doesn't open for another…' She peered at the roman numerals on the clock above the front doors of the auditorium. 'Half an hour.'

'Actually, I'm trying to find the manager of this place.'

'He's here somewhere,' the girl said vaguely.

'It's very important that I get a message to one of the artists who's playing tonight. Walker Henley? I thought maybe the manager might help me get in to talk to him,' said Alex.

'Have you got a backstage pass?'

'No,' Alex admitted. 'I just took a chance that he would see me.'

The girl made a face. 'They don't let fans backstage.'

'I'm not a fan. It's actually a personal connection. He used to go out with my sister and she…died. I just wanted to talk to him…'

'Deirdre,' an impatient voice demanded from behind Alex. 'What's going on here?'

'This is the manager, Mr Isgro,' said the girl behind the counter.

Alex turned around and saw a very neat, carefully

groomed man in his mid-thirties with narrow eyes and an impatient expression on his face. She stuck out her hand. 'Mr Isgro,' she said. 'I came here looking for you. My name is Alex Woods. I have a personal connection to Walker Henley.'

The man studied her with a glacial glance. Then he turned back to Deirdre. 'How are you getting on back there? Is the counter fully stocked?'

Deirdre nodded. 'Getting there.'

'Hurry it up,' said Isgro.

'Excuse me,' said Alex, digging in her purse and coming up with the note she had written and brought with her. 'I'm sure you think I'm just some kind of crazy fan but I'm not. I wouldn't ask you to let me see Mr Henley. But I would be grateful if you would deliver this message to him from me. He can decide for himself if he wants to see me.'

The manager turned on Alex. 'Do you have a ticket, miss?'

'Yes,' said Alex. 'Well, that is, it's at the box office. I'll have it as soon as your box office opens.'

'Good,' he said. 'Get your ticket and enjoy the show.'

'All I'm asking is that you…'

Isgro invaded her space, putting his face so close to hers that Alex could smell his musky aftershave. 'It's not my job to pester the talent. It's my job to make sure that they are not pestered.' He glanced at the clock over the door. 'Why don't you leave and come back in half an hour when the box office is open.' He turned to the girl behind the counter. 'Deirdre, I want you to flog these T-shirts tonight. Ask every single person who buys so much as a pack of gum if they want to buy a T-shirt. Got it?'

'Yup,' said Deirdre.

'I don't want a lot of excuses at the end of the night. I

want these shirts gone, or you could be looking for another job.'

Without another look at Alex he strode over to a side door in the lobby that appeared to be cut into the plaster friezes on the wall, and disappeared behind it.

'Prick,' Deirdre muttered.

'He must be tough to work for,' said Alex.

'No shit.'

Alex sighed. 'I shouldn't be surprised that he blew me off. I guess people will try anything to get face-to-face with these performers.'

'Usually they say they're journalists,' Deirdre commented.

'I guess it's too late to try that now,' said Alex, smiling ruefully.

Deirdre looked over at the door where Isgro had disappeared. Then she beckoned to Alex with a scarlet-nailed finger. 'My boyfriend is an electrician here. That's how I got this job. Go around to the door beside all the trash cans on Sunnyside Row. It's halfway down the next block. Knock on the door and ask for George. When he comes around, ask George to slip your note to one of Henley's roadies. Tell him I said so.'

'Thank you so much,' said Alex.

'I'm not promising anything,' said Deirdre.

'I understand,' said Alex.

'You better get out. I don't want Isgro seeing me talking to you.'

'Thanks,' said Alex. She pulled her coat tight around her and headed out of the lobby of the auditorium.

DEIRDRE'S GEORGE, a burly guy with a Van Dyke beard, accepted the note with the terse words, 'I'll see.' Then he closed the rear stage door behind him.

'Now what do we do?' Dory asked. 'Wait here?'

'I don't think so,' said Alex. 'Walker Henley's got my number on that piece of paper. I guess we go to the show and wait to hear from him.'

'I don't think this is gonna work,' Dory said.

'Well, what do you suggest we do?' Alex asked as they descended the steps and started down the alleyway back to the main street. Suddenly the end of the street darkened as a pair of black SUVs with tinted windows pulled in and began moving toward them.

Alex and Dory hopped up on the narrow walkway as the SUVs rolled slowly past them and stopped near the stage door. All the car doors began to open and men in boots, cowboy hats and faded jeans descended.

'Is one of them our guy?' Dory asked.

Alex looked anxiously at the men who were mounting the steps to the stage door. 'I'm not sure,' she said.

'I'll go ask,' said Dory.

'Dory, wait,' said Alex as her phone began to buzz. She looked at the caller ID. 'I have to take this.'

Dory headed resolutely toward the SUVs as Alex answered the phone. 'Seth?'

'Alex, finally,' he said.

She felt herself tingling at the sound of his voice. 'How are you? How's it going?'

'Where have you been? I must have called you twenty times.'

She hesitated. She didn't want to alarm him, but she also didn't want to lie. 'I had to go to the hospital unexpectedly. I didn't have my phone.'

'The hospital? What for? Are you all right?'

'I'm fine. I'm OK now.'

'Are you home?'

'Actually, I'm in Providence, Rhode Island at the moment. I'm here with Dory.'

'I guess you are fine. What are you doing there?'

'We're at a concert. Trying to track someone down. It's a long story. I'll tell you when you get home. I can't wait to see you. How did they take it when you told them you were leaving your job?'

'They weren't too happy. But they won't have any trouble replacing me. There's a lot of PhDs out there and not a lot of academic jobs.'

'So you haven't changed your mind,' she said cautiously.

'Never,' he said.

'I can't wait till you get back,' Alex said.

'Me neither. I want to take up exactly where we left off.'

Dory rushed up to Alex, waving her arms. 'Come on,' she said. 'That's him in the white hat and he says he's willing to talk to us.'

Alex looked past the dumpsters and the SUVs at the man in a white cowboy hat, standing at the foot of the steps, peering at them curiously.

'Seth, I have to go…'

'I love you,' he said.

Too taken aback to reply, Alex was silent.

Sounding sorry that he had jumped the gun, Seth quickly said, ''Bye. See you soon.' And ended the call. Alex stared at the phone in her hand, hardly believing what she had heard. He loved her. And she had said nothing.

'Alex,' Dory demanded. 'Hurry up. Let's go. This guy hasn't got all day. He has a show to do.'

Alex hesitated. She wanted to call him back, to say she felt the same and to tell him everything. But Dory was wide-eyed with impatience. 'OK,' said Alex. She slipped the phone into her pocket. Then, she followed her sister down the icy, slippery stones of the dark alley.

TWENTY-FIVE

THE DRESSING ROOMS of the Hillman Center were far from deluxe. They were a series of small, dreary cubicles off a dingy corridor furnished with folding chairs, a mirror, a comb, a brush and a hairdryer. The dressing area was filled with people milling around, joking, eating and drinking. The place was littered with empty soda cans, half-drunk bottles of bourbon and bags of pork rinds.

Walker Henley seemed unfazed by the second-rate accommodations. He invited Dory and Alex into the tiny room and offered them a folding chair. He sat facing a mirror as a girl with multiple piercings and tattoos came into the room with a tool kit full of make-up.

'Better take your hat off,' she said.

Walker did as he was told and, while he faced the mirror, the girl stood beside him and began to daub on make-up. Alex examined his face in the mirror. He was about thirty-five and a good-looking guy in a very clean cut, conservative way. He caught Alex studying him and winked at her.

'Don't blink,' said the make-up girl.

'Sorry. So,' Walker said, 'what's the relationship between you two gals?'

'We're half-sisters,' said Alex.

'Dory, I knew about you, of course. Because of my… friendship with Lauren, I paid a lot of attention to the case. I guess it turned out you did some time for a crime you didn't commit.'

'That's right,' said Dory.

'That's a sin,' said Walker. Alex said nothing.

'Well, what is it you want from me?' Walker asked.

'Um…' Dory looked impatiently at Alex. 'Tell him.'

Alex hoped her voice wasn't shaky. She was still processing that phone call from Seth which had, undeniably, distracted her from her mission. Dory frowned at her, puzzled by her lassitude. They had barged in on Walker Henley, and they owed him an explanation. Alex forced herself to speak. 'Once we…once the charges were dropped against Dory, I started wondering if maybe Lauren's killer wasn't from Boston after all. If maybe it was somebody she knew in the country music world. From Branson. Or Nashville.'

'Don't look at me,' said Walker indignantly. 'I was on tour out west when she was killed.'

'Oh, no, I didn't mean you,' Alex said.

'I remember when it happened. Our manager called me to tell me. I was stunned.'

'Were you two…dating then?' Alex asked carefully.

'No, we'd broken up a few months earlier. But I still cared about Lauren.'

Alex nodded. 'You said "our manager." Did you and Lauren have the same one?'

'We did,' he said. 'That's how we met. Cilla Zander from TAI in Nashville represents us both. She introduced us. When she started out Lauren's mother used to be her manager, but Lauren had to replace her with a pro.'

Alex looked at Dory. 'Did you know that?'

Dory shrugged. 'She was always busy with Lauren's career. That was all she cared about.'

The make-up artist finished her work and patted Walker on the shoulder. 'You can put your hat back on now.'

'Thank you, ma'am,' he said politely. 'Close that door on your way out, would ya? They're raising hell out there,' he said cheerfully.

The girl closed the door and Walker turned his attention back to Alex and Dory. 'So, what was your question again?'

Alex thought about it for a moment. 'You and Lauren were engaged at one time, weren't you?'

A pained look flitted over his even features. 'Well, you know the press. They always exaggerate.'

'You weren't?' asked Alex.

Walker shrugged. 'We dated. Let's just say that. She was always nice and fun to be with, but I don't believe I ever really won her heart. All that girl cared about was her career. In the end I think she did me a favor by being honest.'

'About what?' Alex asked.

'Well, about her ambition. She told me that she'd never love any man the way she loved her music. I think that was probably true.'

'So you never thought it was another man, or something like that,' said Alex.

Walker considered this a minute. Then he shook his head. 'No. Look, I don't want to speak ill of the dead, but your sister was a bit…cold. I mean, she just never could… let herself go. You know what I mean?'

Dory nodded solemnly.

'I was lucky she called it off. I met the right gal last year. We're getting married next summer.'

'Congratulations,' said Dory. 'You were lucky to get away from Lauren.'

Walker frowned and Alex quickly changed the subject. 'Was there anyone you remember that Lauren was close to?' she asked. 'Anyone else we could talk to about her?'

'Besides her mama?' he asked.

'Any friends? Other…relationships? Band members, maybe?'

Walker frowned. 'No. She had no loyalty to the musicians who worked for her. She was always happy to use a house band or a pick-up band. She said to me once, "It's me they come to hear, not the band."'

'That sounds like her,' said Dory.

'What about when she was home? In Branson?'

Walker stretched his legs out in front of him and folded his hands behind his head. 'That was the sad thing. She spent all her time working. She had a nice house out in Branson, but other than the gardener and the housekeeper, she lived alone and kept to herself.'

'What about them?' Alex asked. 'The gardener and the housekeeper? They might know of someone.'

'It's not like we were talking about two particular people. Even they were temporary. They were always quitting on her or getting fired. No one ever lasted long with Lauren.'

The door to the dressing room opened. 'Walker. Fifteen minutes,' said a young man wearing a leather jacket and a headset.

'Ladies, you will have to excuse me,' said Walker Henley, standing up.

'Thank you so much for talking to us,' said Alex.

Walker Henley smiled. 'Enjoy the show.'

THEY STAYED THROUGH Walker's set and then headed out to the car. Alex was tired, and it had been a long day. She navigated as they retraced their route and got onto I-95, heading back to Boston.

They rode along in silence for a while. Then Dory sighed. 'That was a waste of time.'

'He wasn't a lot of help,' Alex admitted. 'Nice guy though.'

'Too nice for my sister,' said Dory.

'I guess we could follow up on this manager, Cilla Zander. Did you ever meet her?'

'No, but I heard about her. My mom was pissed that

she took over Lauren's career. But Lauren was moving to Branson, and my dad wouldn't go.'

'Your mother wanted him to?'

'Of course,' said Dory. 'That was all she cared about.'

'Do you remember when Lauren was dating Walker?'

'She brought him home at one point.'

'I guess at that time your mother didn't know that Lauren was gay.'

'Apparently not. She was planning the wedding,' said Dory ruefully.

'I guess she did it for appearances,' Alex observed. 'It's a high price to pay for success. Living a lie.'

Dory threw her an angry glance. 'Nobody made her do it.'

'Are you sure about that?' Alex asked. 'It sounds like your mother was pretty heavily invested in Lauren's career. She was willing to move to Branson, for heaven's sake.'

'Are you kidding? Lauren was a hog for the spotlight. Pulling out that goddam guitar everywhere. "Do you want to hear ma new song?"' Dory imitated her sister in a sing-song drawl.

'Did she have a Southern accent?' Alex asked.

'She…acquired one,' said Dory bitterly. 'Whatever she had to do.'

Alex was quiet for a moment. 'Was there anything about her that you liked?'

'No,' said Dory.

Alex thought about the song she had listened to, 'Love You Only', and the picture it painted of a woman trying in vain to please her mother, her fans and all the strangers around her. A woman whom no one really knew.

'You think I'm terrible, don't you?' Dory asked. 'You're thinking how you'd be a much better sister than me.'

'No, I'm not,' said Alex, suddenly weary of Dory's automatic habit of taking offense.

'You probably think I was crazy, accusing her of trying to steal Rick Howland away from me. Why would she do that if she was gay? I'll tell you why. Just for the pure meanness of it. She didn't care who she hurt. Look at that Walker guy. He was thinking about marrying her, and she was just using him to make it seem like she went with men.'

Alex felt a headache forming as Dory drove along in the dark, ranting. Suddenly her phone rang.

'Who's that? Seth again?' Dory asked sarcastically. 'Must be nice to be so in demand.'

Alex frowned when she saw the caller ID. It was Detective Langford of the Boston police. She hit the button and answered the phone.

'Ms Woods,' he said. 'How you doing?'

'Much better,' said Alex. 'I'm doing fine.'

'I just wanted to call you,' he said, 'because we got the lab tests back on that piece of liver we found at your house.'

'Oh?' said Alex, wondering why he would call her with that.

'I thought you should know. That wasn't poison on the liver. It was a sedative. A mild sedative for dogs.'

Alex felt a sickening flip in her stomach. 'Why are you telling me this?'

'You ought to be aware that your assailant, whoever he or…she might be, had no intention of poisoning that dog. Only wanted him to take a short nap so she…or he…could carry out their plan.'

Alex understood exactly what he was saying. She did not reply.

'Based on these test results and, in the interests of our own investigation, we have decided to get a search war-

rant for the Colsons' apartment in Boston. We feel that we
need to go over that place again.'

'I see,' said Alex.

Dory was looking at her suspiciously.

'You be on your guard, Ms Woods,' said the detective.

TWENTY-SIX

THE MINUTE THEY walked into the house, Remus rushed to the door to greet them. Dory immediately crouched down and began to tussle with the dog, crooning to him and tugging on his ears. Alex looked on in sickening fascination, thinking about the call from Detective Langford. A canine sedative. A way to quiet the dog without hurting him. Would Dory have done that? Could it have been Dory, after all, who had attacked her? Suddenly Alex felt completely unmoored. She didn't know what to believe. Was it possible that Dory had, in fact, been the one who killed Lauren? It would be difficult to find anyone who hated Lauren more.

'What's the matter with you?' Dory demanded, looking up at Alex.

Alex jumped. 'Nothing. Nothing. I'm going upstairs. I'm worn out.'

'Go ahead,' said Dory.

'G'night,' Alex mumbled as she hurried up the steps to her room, closed the door and locked it. Then, just for good measure, she took her desk chair and tilted it up so that it was wedged beneath the doorknob.

She got into her bed but didn't take off her clothes. She picked up her phone and toyed with it. She was so tempted. Tempted to call Seth and tell him everything. Tell him that she was in the hospital because she had been stabbed. Tell him that now she was locked in her room, and that her possible assailant was just down the hall. But what could Seth do? she chided herself. She would be alarming him when there was no way he could help her. It wasn't fair to put him in that position. She had to handle it herself.

She checked her address book and punched in Laney Thompson's number. The phone rang several times and then went to voicemail. 'Laney, this is Alex across the street. I'm just feeling a little jittery after that incident the other night. Please call me when you get this. I'd feel a lot better knowing you were right there.'

Well, she thought, that was no help. She tilted her head back against the headboard on her bed and tried to think. She couldn't tell Dory that she suspected her of being the one who stabbed her. There was no rational explanation for why she would do that. Surely Dory hadn't become so attached to Seth that she would hate Alex for stealing him away. And want to kill her. A person that did that would be…out of their mind.

Alex shuddered, remembering Dory's rant in the car about Lauren. The force of her anger against her sister. I need to get away from her, Alex thought. No matter what. I have to put distance between us without letting her know of my suspicions. Tomorrow, she thought, I'll tell Dory that I don't need her here after all, that I'm going to stay with Uncle Brian. And this time, Alex thought, I'll actually do it. I'll stay there until Seth gets back, and then I'll be safe.

Alex could feel a tightness in her chest, and her breathing became shallow. Stop it, she thought. Stop getting yourself into such a panic. If Dory had wanted to hurt you, she could have done it yesterday. Last night. Just because the person who attacked her had not tried to poison the dog that didn't mean, ipso facto, that it was Dory. There are lots of dog lovers in this world, she told herself. Lots of people who wouldn't hurt a dog, but wouldn't hesitate to hurt their fellow man. Perhaps, in the end, it was just a burglary gone wrong. She couldn't think of anyone in her life who might want to hurt her. What good would killing Alex Woods do for anyone else? She couldn't think of anyone she had injured to that extent that they would want revenge. And no one stood to gain much if she should die. She didn't even have an heir to leave her property to. She recalled her attorney John Killebrew telling her that she had to make a will and designate an heir, but she hadn't done it yet. It didn't seem necessary. It would probably go to Uncle Brian.

Or…to Dory.

The doorknob to her bedroom suddenly rattled and she cried out in alarm. 'Who is it?'

'Who do you think?' asked Dory.

'What do you want?' Alex demanded.

There was no answer.

'Dory?' She waited. 'Dory?'

She looked anxiously around the room. There was no other way in. From her front windows it was a sheer drop to the ground. Relax, she told herself. You have your phone. You're perfectly safe. But no amount of reassuring herself seemed to work. She sat up in the bed, fully clothed and, try as she might, she could not get to sleep.

DAWN CAME AND went and still Alex sat on her bed. She was not sure if she had dozed off or not but, if she had, it hadn't lasted long. She felt utterly exhausted and nervous at the same time. She realized that Laney Thompson had never called her back. She must have gone away. Well, the night was over, Alex thought. Thank God for that. Suddenly she heard a minor commotion in front of the house. Several cars pulled up, and she heard car doors slamming. Alex jumped off the bed, ran to the window and looked out. A dark sedan was parked in front of the house with a black and white cruiser just behind it. Two men in suits and overcoats were coming up the walk, followed by a pair of uniformed officers. Jiggling the chair out from under the doorknob, Alex left her room and clattered down the steps. She had opened the front door before they even rang the bell.

'Ms Woods,' said Detective Spagnola. 'You look tired.'

'I haven't slept,' said Alex. 'I'm glad to see you.'

'We need to talk to your sister. Is she here?'

'Yes, she's upstairs. I'll call her.' Alex went to the foot of the staircase. 'Dory,' she called out. There was no answer.

Spagnola directed the two young uniformed officers to mount the stairs. They did as they were told, thundering up the steps.

'Last door on the left,' said Alex.

There was silence for a moment, and then one of them shouted down the stairwell, 'No one here.'

At that same moment, Alex realized that there was no sign of Remus. 'Oh, wait. She must have taken the dog out for a walk.'

'Where does she take him?'

'Probably down by the park at the end of the street.'

The detective summoned the uniformed officers to come back downstairs and then directed them to go down to the park at the end of the block to look for Dory and the dog.

Once they were out the door, Alex turned to the detectives. 'Why are you here? What do you want to talk to Dory about?'

'We've just come from the Colsons' home,' said Detective Langford. 'As I told you on the phone, after we found out about the dog we obtained a search warrant and executed it early this morning. There was a knife with traces of blood on it hidden under the mattress in Dory's room. We are testing it against samples of your DNA from the crime scene to confirm whether it is the weapon that was used to stab you.'

Alex felt suddenly light-headed. She sagged against the wall. 'Oh my God.'

At that moment the back door opened and Dory came in with Remus tethered to her on a leash. Her cheeks were pink, and she was wearing a knitted blue cap with ear flaps and long tassels in a Nordic design. She looked as if she had skated in on the Zuider Zee. She bent down to let Remus off the leash and he rushed down the hallway. Dory straightened up and looked at her sister and the two detectives at the end of the hall.

Detective Spagnola turned his back on Dory and began to murmur into a two-way radio which he raised to his mouth.

Dory looked from the police to Alex. 'Why are they here?' she asked.

Alex looked at her coldly. 'They want to talk to you.'

The look on Dory's face shifted from curiosity to anxiety. 'What for?' she asked.

'They want to question you,' said Alex.

Detective Langford raised a hand as if to silence her. 'We'll handle this, Ms Woods,' he said.

'Question me about what?' Dory demanded. She glared at Alex. 'Did you call them?'

'No,' Alex said.

'Based on results of some tests conducted here after the attack on your sister,' said Spagnola, 'we obtained a search warrant and went to your parents' apartment this morning. We found a knife in your room. We believe it is the knife which was used to stab Alex Woods in the attack which occurred in this house the other night.'

'No,' said Dory. 'That's not mine.'

'Come along then, and you can tell us your version of what happened.'

'Come along where?'

'To the police station. We are taking you in for questioning.'

Alex looked on anxiously as Dory pointed an index finger at the detective's face. 'No. I'm not coming. You can't blame this one on me,' she said.

'If you don't come willingly, we'll have to place you under arrest.' With that Detective Langford walked up to her and put a hand under her elbow.

Dory twisted away from him. 'Let go of me.' She turned furiously on Alex. 'Tell them. Tell them I didn't do this. You know I didn't do it.'

Alex felt her face flaming.

'You leave us no choice,' said Spagnola. 'Dorothy Colson, we are placing you under arrest for the attempted murder of Alex Woods.'

'NOOOO…!' Dory shrieked, and her wails echoed through the house.

Detective Langford, aided by Spagnola, lifted her by the arms and started to half-drag, half-carry her down the hallway.

Alex stood back to let them pass. She didn't want to look at Dory as they dragged her by. She was afraid to see the hate, the contempt in Dory's eyes. But as her gaze inadvertently met Dory's, she saw instead the face of a frightened child looking back at her. Confused, defenseless and utterly alone.

TWENTY-SEVEN

MARISOL TORRES WAS sitting in the second-floor lounge of the Justice Initiative, eating yogurt and a PayDay candy bar, and drinking an Orangina while she reviewed a pile of notes spread out before her on the Formica tabletop. Alex hesitated in the doorway of the makeshift lounge. The receptionist, who recognized Alex right away, had sent her up here, but now that she stood in the doorway, watching Marisol multitask, Alex was reluctant to disturb her.

'Can I help you?' asked a curly-headed, owlish-looking young man in shirtsleeves.

'No, I'm fine,' said Alex.

Hearing that familiar voice, Marisol looked up and saw Alex hovering in the doorway. Her serious face broke into a wide smile. 'Alex!'

'I hate to bother you,' Alex said sheepishly.

'I'm glad for the company. Come on in.' She indicated a chair at the table where she was sitting.

Alex sat down across from her.

'No offense,' said Marisol, 'but you're not looking too good.'

'I'm not feeling too good,' Alex admitted.

Marisol looked at her expectantly.

'Dory,' said Alex.

Marisol sighed. 'Well, you can't have your money back,' she said, only half-teasing. Alex had dropped off a generous contribution to the Justice Initiative after the DA decided not to refile the charges against Dory. 'What's going on?'

'Do you know about the incident at my house?'

Marisol winced. 'There was an incident? Oh, no. What?'

'Somebody attacked me with a knife.'

'Oh my God! No. Are you all right?'

'Yes. Thanks to this vicious-looking dog named Remus that Dory got us while she was staying with me. He's not really vicious. He's actually a good boy. He prevented the attack from being much worse.'

'Did they catch the guy?'

'They think they have. This morning, they arrested Dory.'

'Oh, Jesus,' said Marisol, clapping her palm over her heart. 'You're kidding me. Tell me you're kidding.'

Alex shook her head. 'It's the truth.'

'I'm so sorry, Alex. Did you know it was her?'

'I didn't know who it was. I didn't know what to think. The cops arrived this morning. Said they found the knife under her mattress at the Colsons'.'

'Why? Why would she do that? After all this…'

Alex shook her head. 'I'm not sure. She was a little jealous about this guy, Seth, that I'm seeing now.'

'Oh, right. The good-looking guy with the glasses who was at the courthouse. I met him at your house, after the appeal hearing.'

'That's the one. She was attracted to him, apparently. She asked me, and I told her I didn't have a boyfriend, because I didn't at the time. And then things happened between Seth and me and the situation changed. She didn't like it when she found us kissing.'

Marisol shook her head. 'And for that she stabbed you? I'm sorry. Are other people not allowed to have a life when Dory's around? I mean, God forbid you should have a boyfriend. Oh, Alex, there is no help for this girl. Lots of people just can't readjust to life on the outside of prison. It happens all the time. But I had hoped she might give it a little better effort than that. How long she been out? A week?'

'The thing is, Marisol, I'm having trouble believing it. I mean, she seemed a little…miffed at me. But not that angry. Not like that.'

Marisol looked at her with raised eyebrows. 'What is this? Turn the other cheek week?'

'She seemed…more hurt than anything else when they came to get her.'

'Hurt that she got caught,' Marisol fumed.

'Maybe it is that. I don't know. I was just wondering if you could talk to her,' said Alex. 'She really needs the advice of an attorney.'

'I'm not an attorney, as you know.'

'But she trusts you. And she needs someone to advise her. Even as a friend.'

Marisol sighed and shook her head. 'Where's she at now?'

'I'm not sure. Two detectives—the same two that reopened Lauren Colson's case—took her in.'

'Then she's probably at the Back Bay precinct,' said Marisol. 'I'll make some calls and find out. I'll go see her.'

'Can I come with you?' asked Alex.

'No. You can't come with me. You're the victim,' said Marisol.

'Oh. All right,' said Alex. 'I know you think I'm crazy coming here, but if you had seen her…She was so distraught when the police came. She looked completely lost. She insisted that she didn't do it.'

'That's what she said the last time,' Marisol reminded her. 'All right, I'll see what I can do. I'll call you later.'

ALEX WENT HOME, took a shower, lay down on her bed and fell instantly into a deep sleep. She couldn't resist sleep.

She'd been up most of the night. But as she laid her head on the pillow, she had to admit to herself that she felt undeniably safer knowing that Dory had been arrested. There was something fundamentally alarming about her. Maybe it was just the unresolved fear that Dory had escaped her punishment for Lauren's murder because of a judicial technicality.

In any case, Alex slept soundly and awoke at around four in the afternoon feeling refreshed. She began to busy herself with the small chores of the house and the laundry. She had to think about going back to work. She couldn't stay out much longer if she hoped to hold onto her new job. However, as she went about folding her laundry out of the dryer, her good mood seemed to fade. In spite of herself, she kept remembering the look on Dory's face when the detectives arrived to take her away. The look of a frightened child.

Don't do it, she thought. Don't talk yourself into feeling guilty. You did your best. You even got Marisol to help her. The situation was messed up from the beginning. This was not, as Mr Killebrew had said to her from the outset, the sister that your mother had in mind for you. Soon Seth would be back. He would be back, and she would tell him that she felt the same, and they would begin their life together. This interlude with Dory would just be a bad memory.

She decided to go down to the guest room where Dory had stayed and clean it up, almost as if she wanted to remove every trace of Dory from this house. It was over now. She had to put it behind her. She walked into the guest room and looked around. The room was in a chaotic state. The bed was unmade and looked as if wild horses had thrashed around in it. There were pieces of paper in the trash can but also scattered around it, as if Dory had aimed and missed. There were half-empty bottles of water on every surface and food wrappers on the nightstand.

Dory's duffel bag gaped open on the chair with the few clothes she had brought along spilling out of it. Her shoes lay at the foot of the bed. The television was on mute but was still playing. Alex went over to the remote and turned it off. She looked around the messy room with a sigh. She hadn't cleaned it up since Dory first came to stay. She had expected that a grown woman would keep her own room clean. Obviously prison life had not turned Dory into a neatness freak.

Alex began to pick up. She collected all the trash into the trash can and emptied the water bottles into the sink in the guestroom bath. She folded up Dory's clothes and repacked the duffel bag. She put Dory's shoes on top, wondering if she would ever have any need for the clothes and toiletries she had brought along. Not if she ended up with a jail sentence. And this time, Alex thought, I won't be bailing her out. She was almost tempted to take the duffel bag downstairs and put it in the trash. But it seemed as if she would be prematurely sentencing her own sister. She zippered it up and, after a moment's hesitation, placed it on the floor in the closet instead.

Finally she went around to make the bed. She knew she should strip off the sheets and wash them, but it just seemed like more than she was capable of doing at this point. The wounds in her back, though healing, began to ache as she finished the chores. She pulled up the top sheet and tucked it tightly in. Then she pulled up the bedspread and the blankets, smoothed the bedspread and shook out the blanket ready to fold it and replace it at the foot of the bed. But as she shook it, something fell out onto the white counterpane.

It was a dingy stuffed elephant, homemade from a faded flowered fabric. It had been stuffed when it was new, but its body had become flattened with the passage of time. It had large floppy ears made from the same fabric as the body and the trunk, and matching buttons on either side of its head for eyes.

As Alex stared at it her knees began to feel wobbly and she had to sit down on the bed. She knew this elephant. She had had one exactly like this when she was a baby. Different fabric but the same simple pattern sewn together by hand. Her dad had called it her 'guardian elephant.' She kept it for years. It might still be in her toy box in the attic. She knew exactly where it came from. She had heard the story dozens of times. Her mother had made it while she waited for Alex to be born. She told Alex that she had sewn it from a pattern she got when she took home economics in high school. Clearly she had made one while she waited for Dory too. Perhaps she slipped it into the carrier with her when she gave her up to be adopted. Dory probably had no idea where it came from. But for some reason that defied reason, she still secretly carried it around with her and slept with it in her bed.

Alex looked at her watch. Marisol still hadn't called. Clutching the elephant to her chest, she left a message for Marisol to call her as soon as she could. Almost as soon as she hung up, the phone rang. Marisol, she thought.

'Hello,' she said.

'This is Cilla Zander. Is this Alex?'

'Yes.' Alex recognized the name immediately, although she was taken aback to hear from her.

'I'm a talent manager,' said Cilla in a rich, languorous Southern accent. 'I manage Walker Henley and, at one time, I managed Lauren Colson.'

'I know who you are,' said Alex.

'Oh, you do. OK. Well, Walker asked me to call you. He told me about meeting you and your sister last night in Providence.'

Was that only last night? Alex thought. It seemed a

lifetime ago. 'Yes,' she said. 'It was very nice of him to talk to…us.'

'Well, he's a very nice guy. And he thought I might be able to help you.'

'Really?' said Alex cautiously.

'You live in Boston?'

'Just outside of…'

Cilla Zander, for all the honeyed civility in her voice, wasn't interested in specifics. 'Listen, Ms Woods, I'm going to be flying into Portsmouth, New Hampshire tomorrow. They're trying to set up a kind of Bonaroo North for the summer, and they want three of my clients to appear. I need to check out the venue. I know that Portsmouth's not too far from Boston. About an hour's drive, I think.'

'Yes,' said Alex. 'That seems right.'

'If you want to talk about Lauren, you can meet me up there tomorrow. I'll text you the location.'

Alex didn't want to go to Portsmouth, New Hampshire. She had to get back to work. Besides, what was left to discuss? Dory was in jail for trying to kill her. Obviously it was exactly what she had done to Lauren. What difference did it make what Lauren's life had been like? The police had been right in the first place. Right all along.

'Ms Woods, are you there?'

'Yes,' said Alex. She looked down at the elephant tucked under her arm.

'Shall I send these directions? Do you want to meet with me?'

'Yes,' said Alex. 'I do.'

TWENTY-EIGHT

THE TRIP TO Portsmouth was short and relatively smooth once she got past the highway congestion in Boston. When she arrived in New Hampshire she only had to travel a few miles until she exited the road in Portsmouth. She followed Cilla's directions to downtown center on the waterfront. Portsmouth was clearly a town rich in history and lovingly refurbished by its citizens since the early days of its founding. It retained many of its original buildings and all of its early American flavor. The town square was anchored by a red-brick, white-steepled church. It was easy to imagine those snowy, cobblestone streets when they were peopled by women in mobcaps and bewigged men in greatcoats. She found a parking space quite easily on Main Street and got out of the car.

Cilla Zander was meeting the young organizers of the music festival at a restaurant called Lucky Toast. Even though it was in the next block, it was easy for Alex to spot it. There was a black limousine parked outside and still running. A man in a driver's uniform, complete with gloves and hat, was leaning against the side of the shiny town car, looking extremely out of place. Alex walked down to the restaurant and nodded to him as she pulled open the door.

Inside, the decor of the restaurant was a genial explosion of kitsch. Kitchen tables with Formica tops in primary colors and matching chair seats stood side by side with tables covered by white cotton cloths bright with apple or cherry prints. Each table had a lamp on it, some with Hawaiian hula dancers, others with bucking bronco riders as a base. There were hordes of old posters framed on the walls and lots of warm wood surfaces. The overall impression was homey and easygoing.

Seated in the middle of the room was a table of patrons as mismatched as the décor. Three young people with long hair, North Face parkas and hiking boots were sharing the table with a heavyset woman wearing ropes of pearls and a fur coat. Her hair was shiny black and swung in an expert cut around her creamy-skinned, double-chinned face. She seemed to perch on the very edge of the kitchen chair, her posture perfect, her blue-eyed gaze looking coolly at the younger people at the table.

Alex hesitated and then approached the table. 'Excuse me, I'm looking for Cilla Zander?'

The woman in furs looked up at her hopefully. 'Ms Woods?'

Alex nodded. Cilla Zander gathered her expensive handbag and her furs around her and abruptly stood up. 'My friends, I hate to leave you, but I have another meeting. I would ask y'all to get me those specs that we talked about ASAP if you have any hope of my performers considering your festival.'

'We'll do that, Miss Zander.' The best-looking of the three young people at the table stood up and offered her his hand. He had pale skin, fine eyes and matted dreadlocks falling over the collar of his parka.

Cilla Zander looked at his extended hand as if there were a spider in his palm. She did not offer her hand in return. 'I hope you know,' she said in a Southern accent that sounded like molasses over steel, 'that you have taken me far out of my way, when you were not actually prepared for this meeting.'

'And we will make up for that,' the young man insisted,

still holding out his hand to her. 'We really regret that we didn't have all the answers to your questions, but the planning is still a little preliminary. We will get those answers for you. I promise.'

Cilla extended one pudgy, beautifully manicured hand and basically tapped the young man's hand with her own. 'See that you do. I do not appreciate having my time wasted.'

'Yes, ma'am,' he said, frowning.

Cilla took Alex's arm by the elbow and began to propel her to the door. 'Let's get out of here,' she said. 'They do not serve alcohol at this establishment. What kind of a business meeting takes place at a restaurant with no alcohol on the menu? That name is very deceiving.' As she talked she led the way up the street to a fern bar on the next corner. Alex followed her in and Cilla flopped down onto a banquette at a table near the door. Alex sat down opposite her in a chair. Cilla immediately began to scan the room for the nearest available waitress. Once she had her attention and had ordered a drink, she sat back against the banquette with a sigh.

'I'll tell you something. There are going to be some heads rolling in my New York office. They set this meeting up without even making sure that we were dealing with bona fide promoters. This is completely unacceptable.'

The waitress, sensing the urgency of her customer's thirst, appeared quickly with the glass of Makers Mark neat, and set it down in front of Cilla. Cilla lifted it, took a soothing sip and closed her eyes in sensual delight. Then she set the glass down carefully on the table in front of her and smoothed out the napkin underneath.

'Now then, Alex.'

Alex nodded.

'Tell me again how you are related to Lauren.'

Alex explained about Dory and made sure to keep her explanation brief and to the point. 'It was really good of you to see me.'

Cilla rolled the whisky around on her tongue as she listened. Finally she looked Alex in the eye. 'Walker called and said you were wondering about Lauren's personal life.'

'Yes,' said Alex. 'The Boston police have reopened the investigation into her murder. They are questioning the same people who were on the scene when the murder occurred. I was thinking about the fact that they never considered anyone as a suspect who was part of Lauren's life outside of Boston. Like in Branson or Nashville. I began to wonder if there might be such a person. Lauren's father told me she was gay, but she was busy passing for straight. That can lead to a lot of hard feelings.'

'Her parents knew she was gay?' Cilla asked, her eyebrows raised in surprise.

Alex nodded.

'Hmmm. I guess Lauren finally broke down and told them. Elaine certainly didn't know about it when Lauren was first keeping company with Walker. Elaine was always calling me, telling me what a storybook wedding it would be for country music if they got married. It was all I could do to hold my tongue.

'I won't lie to you, Ms Woods. The only reason I was willing to see you is because I am trying to protect my own investment here. After all, I was the one who set Lauren up with Walker. At the time he didn't have a gal, and I knew about Lauren. I knew she wasn't going to be dating any men. But it's just not good for an entertainer's image to look like they don't have any love in their lives. I mean, fans have that problem in their own lives. They want to believe that their idols are gettin' more ass than a toilet seat.'

Alex laughed in surprise. The expression seemed so

alien coming out of this expensively dressed, proper-looking woman. 'Did you tell Walker that she was gay?' Alex asked.

Cilla grimaced in disbelief. 'No. Of course not. That's the point. He would be furious even now if he found out what I did. He would never have agreed to it. Even at the time I didn't make a big deal out of it. I just introduced them, said how I was hoping to raise their public profiles, and that nothing did that better than when two stars start dating. I said they should just start seeing one another out in public, even as friends.'

'Her father said she had to keep it quiet for her career,' Alex observed.

'Do you know anything about country music? There is no such thing as gay in country music. On that point, I would have to agree with her father.'

'So, Lauren was gay, but she didn't act on it?'

'Oh, honey, I'm sure she acted on it. She was a grown woman.'

'Did you know any of her girlfriends?' Alex asked.

Cilla shook her head and finished off her drink. 'No, I did not. And I did not want to. It was none of my business.'

Alex felt deflated. 'So you don't know any of the women she was involved with? She didn't live with anyone or anything like that?'

'Well, she didn't live with anyone in the eyes of the world. It was just Lauren all by her lonesome. Of course she did have help in the house.'

Alex frowned at her. 'What does that mean?'

'It means that if you have a live-in housekeeper, nobody suspects anything.'

'You mean, even if they're not actually a housekeeper,' Alex said slowly.

Cilla gazed at her coolly. 'They always had chores to

do. Shopping. Cooking. That sort of thing. Probably ran a vacuum once in a while. But they weren't housekeepers.'

'Did she have a "housekeeper" around the time she was killed?'

'She did. A young, pretty one from Alabama. I had to pay her off not to sell her story to the tabloids. But don't get any ideas. I know exactly where she was when Lauren was killed.'

'Where?'

'In Nashville. In rehab. I paid for it.'

'Oh,' said Alex, discouraged.

'There was only one she really cared about, I think,' said Cilla. 'It was years before she died. Only lasted about six months but it broke her heart in two. Lauren couldn't hold on to her. She was a beauty though. Older than Lauren. She had long dark hair and a pretty little mole beside her mouth. Showed up in Branson one day and moved in with Lauren. Lauren was head over heels. It was tough to keep her from telling the world about it. In fact, she wrote some songs about the break-up that had to be rewritten so that you couldn't tell she was talking about a girl. I believe her name was… Joy. Joy. Ironic, isn't it? Should have been Sorrow.'

TWENTY-NINE

ALEX'S BRAIN SEEMED to be seething as she drove back to Boston. She went directly to the South End and parked nearby the Colsons' apartment. Maybe it was a coincidence, but Alex didn't believe that. It was exactly the sort of connection she had been looking for. She knew it didn't mean that Joy had killed Lauren. Why would she? But there was a secret between them. That was obvious. And it might have proved to be an explosive secret. Alex needed more information.

She knocked on the Colsons' front door. Elaine answered.

'You're home,' said Alex. 'Thank goodness.'

'It's a Catholic feast day. The office is closed.'

'I wanted to talk to you,' said Alex.

'Look, don't blame me. I warned you about Dory,' said Elaine wearily. 'I wish I could say I was surprised when they showed up here with that warrant and found the knife. But honestly, I wasn't. I'm sorry that she hurt you, but I told you she would.'

'This isn't about Dory,' said Alex, amazed yet again at Elaine's dislike for her own daughter, which seemed to be permanently frozen in place. 'Not directly, anyway. Can I come in? I really need to talk to you.'

Elaine shrugged and stood back from the door. Alex followed her down the hall and then the steps into the great room. There was a smell of burnt sugar in the air. Elaine had obviously been working in the kitchen when Alex arrived. There were measuring cups and baking ingredients on the counter, and a fruit pie cooling on a rack by the stove. The smell of smoke was heavy in the kitchen, and the back-garden door had been opened to let it out. Elaine returned to the flour-covered counter and resumed her mixing and measuring.

'What happened?' Alex asked.

'I was making a pineapple upside-down cake for Father Finnegan's retirement dinner and it overflowed the pan. What a mess. I don't know how that could have happened. I've made that recipe a million times. Anyway, I have to start all over again. I wouldn't bother, but the dinner is tomorrow night and my pineapple upside-down cake is his favorite.'

'That's nice,' said Alex. Looking around the cozy, great room, the kitchen full of wonderful smells in spite of the smoke, the pie cooling on the counter, Alex thought that it was the image of a happy home. When Dory was adopted it must have seemed to the Catholic Foundlings Agency that this was the perfect setting to raise a child. Except that Dory's mother seemed to be unable to love her without reservation which was, in the end, more important than the cozy house and all the baked goods in the world.

'Have a seat,' said Elaine, pointing to a tall stool by the center island in the kitchen.

Alex sat down.

'I don't really know how I can help you,' she went on. 'I don't know what possessed her to do it.'

'Actually, I'm not here to talk about Dory. I'm here about something else,' said Alex.

Elaine turned and looked at her in surprise. 'What else could you and I have to talk about?'

'Lauren,' Alex said.

'Lauren? What about Lauren?'

'Elaine, Garth told me that Lauren was gay.'

Elaine, who was scrubbing out the burnt-on batter from the pineapple upside-down cake mold, stopped for a moment, and Alex could see her jaw working, as if she were grinding her teeth. Then she shook her head. 'There's nothing to talk about. That has nothing to do with you.'

Alex was not about to be put off by Elaine's chilly reception. 'I was just wondering how you knew that. Did Lauren tell you?'

'Of course she told us,' said Elaine in exasperation. 'Did you think he was making it up?'

'No, not at all,' said Alex. 'It's just one of those things people often keep to themselves. You know, it's difficult to say something like that to your mother, I imagine. It can come as a shock. Or did you always kind of suspect?'

Elaine shook the water droplets off the pan and began to dry it carefully with a kitchen towel. 'No, of course not. I never would have suspected any such thing,' she said. She looked at the door of the refrigerator. 'You've seen her pictures. She was a beautiful girl. Very feminine.' Elaine shook her head. 'I still don't understand it.'

'So, if you don't mind my asking, how did she tell you? What prompted her to tell you that?'

Elaine sighed. 'What business is this of yours? This is a private, family matter. How dare you come in here and ask me about the most personal things in my life?'

Alex almost had to admire Elaine's forbidding manner. She doubted that anybody ever got to Father Finnegan without the approval of Elaine. 'Look, I'm asking because of the reopened investigation into Lauren's murder. Dory was cleared, but until they arrest someone for that murder...'

'Oh, I don't believe you,' said Elaine. 'You still take her side in this? After what she did to you? Right there was proof of what the police had said all along. Dory's jealousy is murderous.'

'I don't think the police ever looked any farther than Dory,' said Alex stubbornly. 'And I'm beginning to have my doubts. Just humor me, if you would. When did you find about Lauren's homosexuality?'

Elaine shuddered. 'I hate that word.' Then she sighed. 'When? Well, I didn't have any hint of it while she lived at home. I guess it didn't really come up until that business with Walker Henley. They'd been dating for a while. I was getting impatient. They were both of age. I couldn't see what they were waiting for. I wanted to start planning the wedding. And Lauren kept stalling. The more I pressed her on it, the more she made excuses. So finally, one day we had it out. That's when she told me. She said she was only going out with Walker Henley to keep up appearances. She said that she was a lesbian. I wanted to die...'

'Was it that bad?'

'You wait until you have children,' said Elaine tartly.

'Obviously it was a big shock,' said Alex.

'For most people, tolerance is just a political term. It's a whole different ballgame when it's in your own family. Hey, why are you asking me this anyway? What has this got to do with anything?'

Alex mulled over what she wanted to say. 'I had occasion to talk to Cilla Zander today.'

'Cilla Zander,' Elaine exclaimed. 'Awful woman. Well, I shouldn't say that. She was good for Lauren's career. I didn't like her personally. It was her attitude.'

'She told me she was the one who kind of pushed Walker and Lauren together,' said Alex. 'They were both her clients. They both needed publicity.'

'Maybe she did. I wouldn't know,' said Elaine dismissively.

'Did Lauren ever have any...relationships with girls around here?'

'No. I told you that. Lauren did not have time for re-
lationships. She was home-schooled, and she had lots of
music lessons and auditions going on. She was focused on
the future. On her career.'

'But she must have been close to someone as a teenager.
Some friend or someone.'

'She didn't need friends. She had me. We were as close
as a mother and daughter could be,' said Elaine.

'What about the Ennis family? Chris and Joy…'

'They're our neighbors. We share a house. Of course
she was close to them. When she was in high school Joy
already had Therese. Lauren used to go upstairs and help
her sometimes. Just for a change of scene. But I wouldn't
say they were friends.'

'And then Lauren moved to Branson.'

Elaine sighed again. 'Her career was taking off. She was
starting to get noticed. She hired that awful woman to manage her career, and she moved out west.'

Alex nodded. 'That must have been tough.'

'It wasn't easy,' said Elaine. 'I adjusted.'

'You still had Dory,' said Alex.

'There was no getting rid of Dory,' said Elaine with a
sigh.

'Didn't you tell me that Joy left her family for a while?'
Alex asked.

'I didn't tell you that,' Elaine contradicted her angrily.

'It must have been Dory who told me,' said Alex. 'Are
you saying it's not true?'

'Oh, it was true all right. When Therese was about seven
or eight years old, Joy decided that she had to find herself.
She went to some Yoga ashram out in California. She was
gone for six months. It was terribly hard on Therese. And
on Chris. I stepped in and tried to help out with Therese as

much as possible. She couldn't understand how her mother could just leave her like that. Well, I couldn't either, to be honest with you. Anyway, this has been like Therese's second home ever since.'

'She was lucky to have you,' said Alex. But her mind was turning over these facts and re-examining them. Joy left her family and went out west. She said she was in California, but maybe she actually went to Missouri.

'Why are you asking about Joy? What business is it of yours if Joy went to a yoga retreat eight years ago?'

Alex looked at Elaine coolly. 'I'm just wondering if that's where Joy really went,' she said.

'Where else would she have gone?'

'She might have gone to be with Lauren.'

'That's ridiculous,' said Elaine.

'Is it?' asked Alex.

'Yes. Of course. Joy's not a lesbian. She's married.'

Alex nodded as she caught a glimpse of uncertainty in Elaine's eyes. Even she knew that it was not impossible. In spite of herself, Elaine was suddenly curious. 'Cilla Zander told me that Lauren lived briefly with a woman named Joy out in Branson,' said Alex. 'A dark-haired woman with dimples and a beauty mark by her lips.'

Elaine thought that over for a minute and then shook her head. 'That's not possible. I would have known if that were true.'

'Why would Cilla Zander lie about it?' Alex asked.

Elaine dusted the flour off her hands and placed them on her hips. 'I don't know. But you know what? I don't appreciate this. You are speculating about the most private business of a woman you didn't even know.'

'I'm not just speculating,' said Alex. 'I'm asking myself

who, besides Dory, might have been angry with Lauren. Angry enough to kill her.'

Suddenly there was the unmistakable thud of a door closing.

'What was that?' said Alex.

Elaine looked at her, frazzled. 'The garden door probably blew shut. Where in the world did you get these ideas?'

'I start from the premise that my sister might be innocent,' said Alex.

Elaine raised her floury hands as if to say STOP. 'I don't want to hear another word. Take all your sick accusations and get out of my house.'

Alex got up from the stool. 'All right. If that's what you want.'

Elaine walked into the living area and pulled open one of the French doors to the garden, which were now shut. 'You can go out this way. Take those steps to the street. Please don't come back.'

Alex walked past her, crossed the patio and climbed the outside stairs to the street without looking back. Elaine didn't want to know about Lauren and Joy, even if it was the truth. She didn't want to think of the two of them in that way. But Alex couldn't help thinking that this was a secret that had the potential to lead to trouble.

She just wasn't sure how to find out if it had.

As she got into her car and began to pull out of the parking space, her phone began to ring. She stopped halfway in the parking space and frowned at the unfamiliar number. Then she answered it.

'Alex, it's me. It's Dory.' Her voice was flat.

'What's the matter?' Alex said warily.

'I'm at the Suffolk County Jail. Can you come over here?'

'I'm not sure if I'm allowed to,' said Alex.

'Please, Alex, I wasn't the one who stabbed you. I wouldn't do that to you. I want you to know that.'

'They did find the knife that stabbed me under your mattress,' Alex reminded her.

'I did not put it there,' said Dory listlessly, like a child reciting a memorized answer, 'because I never had it. Look, I can have visitors from three-thirty to five. Will you come? There's some things I need to say in person.'

'Yes, I'll come,' said Alex. She ended the call but she knew that it was not really over. She looked up the address for the jail on her iPhone. Nashua Street, she thought. I know where that is. She thought about it for a minute, and then pulled out of her parking space.

THIRTY

THE SUFFOLK COUNTY Jail was a recently built facility, situated right in downtown Boston near the waterfront. Alex presented herself at the visitors' entrance and followed all the procedures. I'm getting to be a veteran at this, she thought. She went into the visitors' room and waited for Dory.

In a few minutes Dory came shuffling in. Alex could hardly suppress the alarm she felt at the sight of her. Dory's pale, freckled complexion was ashen, her shoulders hunched, her gray eyes dull and hopeless. She sat down opposite Alex without even acknowledging her.

'Dory, are you OK?' asked Alex.

'OK? Do you see where I am?' Dory asked. She looked up and around the noisy room at the green cinder-block walls, the small windows near the ceiling letting in only the narrowest shafts of light. 'What do you think?'

'I know,' said Alex. 'It's terrible. What did Marisol tell you?'

Dory shrugged. 'To keep quiet. Not to tell them anything they might use against me.'

Alex studied her. 'Do you have anything they could use?'

Dory was not even indignant. 'No,' she said softly. 'I didn't do anything to you. My mother thinks I did, though. She never believes me.'

'I know that's hard to take,' said Alex.

'But do you believe me?' Dory asked, and then she waved a hand limply. 'Never mind. It doesn't matter.'

'It does matter,' said Alex. 'For what it's worth, Dory, I don't think you were the one who attacked me. But somehow, that knife got under your mattress.'

'It doesn't matter what I say,' Dory lamented, as if she had not even heard Alex's words. 'They blame me.'

'Look, you just need to do what Marisol tells you,' said Alex. 'You'll get through this.'

Dory shook her head. 'No. Whatever I do, this is how I end up. Alone. A prisoner. I don't feel like fighting this anymore. It's just my…destiny.'

'That's not true,' said Alex. 'It's not your destiny.'

'You don't know,' said Dory.

'Don't know what?' said Alex.

'Nothing. Never mind.'

'Tell me,' said Alex. 'What are you thinking?'

Dory looked at her, and her eyes were haunted. 'I'm not wanted,' she said. 'Nobody wants me.'

'Dory, you can't…'

'That's who I am,' Dory insisted. 'Someone who is not wanted. Starting with your mother. Starting from the day I was born.'

Alex wanted to protest on her mother's behalf, but suddenly she realized that she could not. She knew that it wasn't like that for her mother, but that wasn't really the issue. Being unwanted was Dory's reality and there were no words to reassure her. It would only be a further insult to tell Dory that her reality was not true.

Alex felt a nagging sense of déjà vu and could hardly bear to look in her sister's eyes. 'Dory, when you asked me to come over, it sounded like there was something specific you wanted to tell me.'

Dory frowned and then seemed to be struggling to remember. Finally she said, 'I wanted to tell you that I'm sorry. I'm sorry you got hurt. And I'm sorry we didn't have a chance to get to know each other.'

'That's not your fault,' said Alex. 'We met under some pretty…difficult conditions.'

Dory nodded but her eyes remained downcast, her body slumped over. 'Still. It was kind of like a second chance that didn't work out…' Her voice trailed away.

'It's not too late,' said Alex.

'Yes, it is.' Dory shook her head hopelessly, and the expression in her eyes reminded Alex, with a jolt, of herself, and of how she had felt the day she learned about her parents' accident. That day, when she got the news, she'd had the sense that life was a cruel joke, and she couldn't figure out a reason to keep going.

'You seem terribly…down,' she said.

Dory did not protest. In fact, she didn't even reply.

'Dory, are they giving you any medication? Anything for depression?'

'I'm not depressed,' Dory insisted.

'No one would blame you if you were,' said Alex.

'I'm not,' Dory insisted. 'I'm accepting it. I need to be more accepting.'

'No, you don't,' said Alex. 'You need to have hope. You're going to get out of here. I feel sure of it. You just need to hang on, and don't give up hope.'

'The real reason I asked you here was in case I don't see you again,' said Dory. 'I wanted to say goodbye.'

'Don't say that,' Alex insisted.

Dory said softly, 'I'm just saying "in case."'

'And I'm just saying that you mustn't give up. This is not over. OK?'

Dory shook her head. Then she stood up and reached out a hand, pressing the back of Alex's hand with her fingertips. 'OK,' she said dully. Then she turned away. Alex watched her go with a feeling of dread in the pit of her stomach. She knew how it felt to be depressed. She had suffered a pretty terrible bout of depression this last year. But somewhere inside her, even during the worst of it, she knew that her suffering would lessen, that she would be happy again. She did not think Dory had that same bed-rock sense of well-being. How could she, when she felt as if her own mother had forsaken her?

The guard in the visitors' room came over to her, point-ing to his watch. Alex got up and walked out into the main receiving area. There were two guards at the front desk. She approached them, studying the two men as she waited her turn in line. One of the guards was an enormous black man with a mustache and a forbidding expression. His badge and picture read: S. Robinson. The other guard was pale and overweight, with a crew cut and rheumy eyes. His badge read: B. Witkowski.

Finally she reached the front of the line.

The pale, sweaty guard looked at her with disinterest. 'Yes?'

'My name is Alex Woods. I've just been here to visit my sister, Dory Colson. She seems very depressed.'

'Everybody in here is depressed, lady,' Witkowski said dismissively.

'I think she might need to be seen by someone.'

'Like who?' he asked sarcastically.

'Like a shrink. I think she needs medication. I'm wor-ried that she might…try to harm herself.'

'She can't,' said the guard. 'We keep an eye on them.'

'She was telling me goodbye,' Alex insisted. 'As if she was considering it.'

'Shrink comes in once a week,' said Witkowski. 'She can see him next Tuesday.'

'We can't afford to wait. It might be too late by next

Tuesday,' Alex said angrily. Suddenly she realized why her conversation with Dory had given her a sense of déjà vu. She thought of that story she had heard from Uncle Brian about Dory's father, Neil Parafin, despairing at being abandoned before he shot himself in the driveway of her mother's house. 'There's a history of suicide in her family,' she said bluntly.

'Lady, this isn't a spa. We do things on a schedule here.'

'No matter what,' said Alex grimly.

'We've got rules,' he said.

Alex realized that nothing she could say was going to impress this guard. He had his mind made up about the people in this facility and he wasn't about to start being sympathetic. To be fair, sympathy for all these inmates was a road with no end. But it was not reassuring to Alex. She looked up imploringly at the other guard. He had listened to the whole exchange but hadn't spoken.

'Please. Her name is Dory Colson. Couldn't you find a doctor to take a look at her? I know all these inmates are depressed, but she seems dangerously so.'

'What are you looking at him for?' Witkowski asked irritably.

Robinson ignored his fellow guard. 'What's her name?' he asked.

'Dory Colson. And my name is Alex Woods. This is my information.' Alex took out a piece of paper and wrote it down. She handed it to Robinson.

Robinson looked it over thoroughly. Then he looked up at Alex. 'I'll give it to the doc when he comes in Tuesday,' he said.

Witkowski laughed.

Alex could feel herself trembling with rage. 'She's a human being. Even if she's in jail, she deserves to be treated fairly. I promise you, if anything happens to my sister, I'm going to hold you both responsible.'

Witkowski's lizard-like eyes widened and then narrowed again. 'Don't you threaten me, ma'am.'

Alex did not back down. 'Don't you ignore my sister,' she said.

ALEX WENT OUT to her car and sat down in the driver's seat, still fuming from her encounter with the guards. Maybe, she thought, if she called the detectives who were working on Lauren's murder, she could tell them about Joy and ask them to intercede on Dory's behalf at the same time. It was worth a try.

She looked up Langford's number on her cell and rang it. The phone went directly to voicemail. 'Detective Langford,' she said. 'I'm…uh…this is Alex Woods. I just came from seeing my sister in jail and she is dangerously depressed. No one seems willing to get her treatment, and I wondered if you could help. Also, I may know something about Lauren's murder. A possibility to explore, anyway. Please call me back as soon as you get this.'

Alex ended the call and sat, lost in thought, in the front seat of her car. Then she made one more call. This time, she was successful.

'Alex?'

'Hey, Seth,' she said.

'You sound terrible. What's the matter?'

'How much time have you got?' she asked ruefully.

'All the time in the world for you,' he said.

Alex sighed. 'I just came from the Suffolk County Jail.'

'What were you doing there?'

'Visiting Dory.'

'Dory's back in jail?' he exclaimed. 'What happened?'

'They think she was the one who stabbed me.'

'Stabbed you? Jesus, Alex. What is going on? Are you all right?'

'Yes, I'm fine,' she said. 'I needed some stitches, but I'm OK.'

'Why did Dory stab you?' he cried.

'I'm not sure she did,' Alex said.

'I can't believe you didn't tell me this before.'

Alex shook her head. 'I didn't want you to race home. I know you have a lot of loose ends to tie up out there.'

'None more important than this,' he said, with a hint of annoyance. 'I can always come back here and do the rest. If something…happened to you, none of it would matter anyway.'

Alex smiled. 'Thanks.'

'You have to tell me what's going on with you.'

'I know,' she said wearily.

'I'm not yelling at you,' he said. 'But it makes me feel so helpless. Hearing that you were stabbed. Where did this happen?'

'At home.'

'And Dory did it.'

'They think so.'

'You don't?' he asked.

'I don't…know. I don't really think so.'

'You didn't see the person.'

'No,' she said.

'And now you're visiting Dory in jail?' he asked, incredulous.

'She's very depressed, Seth. And no one at the jail gives a damn. I'm worried.'

'She should be depressed,' he said shortly.

Alex was silent in response. She had the sense that she could feel him trying to adjust his perspective at the other end of the line.

'OK, look,' he said. 'I'm going to leave here tonight. It's better to drive at night anyway. When I get back I'll go with you to the jail, and we'll make sure that they get her treatment or something.'

'OK,' she said. 'I'm in the car. I better go.'

'Try not to worry,' he said.

'I'm worried about you,' she said. 'Driving at night.'

'I'll be fine. I'll be with you tomorrow.'

'I can't wait,' she said. 'I feel better just thinking about it.'

'OK. Till tomorrow then.' She noticed that he hadn't repeated his 'I love you,' but then again, she hadn't yet said it in return. Tomorrow, she thought.

'Safe journey home,' she said, and ended the call.

THE LIGHT OF the winter day was fading as she pulled into the driveway. Along the tree line she could see the brilliant oranges, purples and grays of a winter sunset. She was glad to be home.

Wearily, she got out of the car and walked up to the house. She opened the front door and, as she walked in, relished the quiet. And then realized that it was wrong.

'Remus?' she said.

There was no barking, no excited sliding down the hall, no panting as he crowded her, eager to be petted. Her heart suddenly turned cold. 'Where are you, boy?' she asked.

There was no response.

Could he possibly be sleeping? she wondered. She knew better. Even if he were asleep, his keen young ears would hear the car stopping in the driveway, her tread on the front porch, the door opening. 'Remus,' she whispered. She began to walk through the house, hesitating before glancing in each room. When he wasn't there, she felt a little bit hopeful, until she arrived at the doorway of the next room

and turned on the light. Every step she took she felt a terrible dread that she would find him lying on the floor, his
life gone or ebbing away from him.

Don't think like that, she told herself. He's fine. He's
just a pup. Maybe he got out when the mailman opened
the door to drop the mail on the floor. Maybe Laney came
over and let him out by accident. Maybe he's off running
somewhere. But she knew in her heart that no one would
see Remus bounding out of the house and just calmly walk
away. There had to be another explanation. You automatically think he's dead, she admonished herself. Always the
worst-case scenario. It was no wonder she thought that way
after what had happened to her parents. She allowed herself that. But still…

Room by room she went through the first floor, calling
for him. But he did not respond. She reached the back of
the house, opened the door to the porch and stepped out,
shivering in the dim twilight. Even though darkness was
descending on the yard, and Remus was dark himself, it
only took a moment to discern his shape prone on the porch
floor—still, but not sleeping. No movement, no sound.

'Remus!' she cried. She fell to her knees beside him and
reached out her hand, laying it on his shiny, smooth coat.
He was rigid.

'Remus,' she wailed.

And then she was hit on the head from behind. She
crumpled to the floor beside her dog.

THIRTY-ONE

WHEN SHE WOKE UP she was in the kitchen, tied to one of the cheerfully painted wooden kitchen chairs. Her hands and feet were bound. Joy Ennis stood in front of her, watching her come around.

Alex's head was pounding. 'Joy. What the hell?' Alex blinked at her, trying to clear her vision. Her eyes struggled to focus on details. The beauty mark nestled between Joy's lips and the dimple in her cheek. Her chin-length hair, streaked with gray, but still a mass of fetching, unruly curls. Her liquid brown eyes were sorrowful. The remains of a devastating beauty.

'I'm sorry,' said Joy.

'You're sorry? Seriously? Let me go,' Alex insisted.

Joy shook her head regretfully and picked up a gun from the counter beside her, holding it with both hands and pointing it at Alex.

Alex gasped.

'I had to use this on Remus,' Joy said apologetically. 'I had to get him out of the way. Last time he made things difficult.'

'Last time,' Alex said in an unsteady, ragged voice.

'All that barking drawing attention. Not to mention this,' Joy said, revealing a bite wound on her forearm.

'Jesus. How could you?'

Joy shrugged. 'I had to.'

Alex felt angry tears pricking her eyelids. 'How could you kill a dog? It's like killing a child.'

'Oh, no,' said Joy hurriedly. 'I wouldn't do that. Of course not.'

Alex looked up at her, confusion mixed with her relief. 'But you just said…' She stared at the gun in Joy's hand.

'Oh, this. It isn't a real gun. It's a tranquilizer gun. It's made out of hard plastic. It shoots tranquilizer darts. You can buy them on the Internet. I just used it to drug the dog. Knock him out. After I knocked you out, I dragged the dog out to the utility shed at the edge of the backyard and locked him in. Hopefully he won't wake up for a while.'

'You knocked me out with a plastic gun?' Alex asked weakly.

'Oh, no. I used that,' said Joy, pointing to a cast-iron frying pan sitting on one of the stove's burners.

'Why?' Alex asked, trying to keep from weeping. 'Why Remus? Why me?'

'I'm sorry,' said Joy. 'I had to. That dog was ready to tear me apart the other night when I was in the pantry.'

Alex's heart thudded in her chest. 'It was you in the pantry.'

'That seems pretty obvious,' said Joy.

'Wasn't that enough? Why are you doing this? What did I ever do to you?'

Alex's phone began to ring.

Joy set down the stun gun on the counter, rummaged in Alex's pocket for the phone and looked at the caller ID. She grimaced, hesitating, and then held the phone to Alex's ear. 'Answer it,' she said. 'Sound normal. Be careful what you say.' She pulled the frying pan off the range top and brandished it to remind Alex that she would knock her out again if she had to.

Alex answered the phone. 'Hello?'

'Hello? This is Detective Spagnola. You called a little while ago? Ms Woods?'

'Yes. I called,' said Alex.

'I got your message. I was a little surprised to hear that you were worried about Dory. Since we've arrested her for attacking you.'

It wasn't Dory, she wanted to say. It was this maniac, who is holding me captive right now. Alex found that she could not form a reply. She was acutely conscious of Joy, standing beside her, holding the phone to her ear, and the cast-iron pan over her head. Joy smelled like a frightened animal.

'Ms Woods? Is something wrong?'

'Dory,' she choked out, 'needs to see a shrink. She needs medication.'

'That's not really our call,' said Spagnola. 'I'll see what I can do, but that's the jurisdiction of the corrections department. You mentioned something else. Something important?'

Alex could see the skillet in Joy's hand, trembling beside her ear. 'I can't talk now,' said Alex. She could hear the frantic note in her own voice. Joy abruptly ended the call, threw the phone down on the floor and stomped on it.

Why didn't I say her name? Alex thought miserably. But there was no use in second-guessing herself. Her head was still foggy from the blow, and she had no doubt that Joy would hit her again if she had to.

'OK,' said Alex. 'OK. Whatever you want.'

'You should never have gotten involved in this,' said Joy. She lowered the skillet and went over to the stove. She turned her back to Alex and began to fiddle with something on the burners.

Alex looked around the kitchen where she had spent so many happy times after school, talking to her mother, eating a snack. Or having a cup of tea with her father. The safest of places. Long ago. Nevermore.

'I know why you stabbed me,' said Alex. 'You wanted Dory to be blamed.'

Joy sighed and turned back around. 'You're right. As long as she was convicted of Lauren's murder, I was safe. Once she got out, I had to throw suspicion back on her. I had to end that probe into Lauren's death.'

'Because you were afraid the police would find out you were Lauren's lover,' said Alex. 'And realize that you were the one who killed her.'

'I didn't kill her,' said Joy wearily.

'It's kind of stupid to deny it to me,' said Alex.

Joy shook her head and, to Alex's amazement, tears sprang to her eyes. 'I didn't kill her. Therese killed her.'

'Therese?' Alex was genuinely shocked. 'Your daughter, Therese?'

Joy nodded and hung her head.

'Delicate little Therese?'

'She's stronger than she looks. Especially when she's upset.'

'But she was only a kid when Lauren died.'

'She was fourteen.'

'What happened?'

Joy wiped away her tears. 'You may as well know. She was coming by to see Elaine. She was coming in the garden doors like she always did. Just like she was yesterday, when she heard you talking about me. That day—the day Lauren died—she heard Lauren pleading with me to go back to Branson with her. Lauren was talking about how wonderful it used to be between us, and how it could be that way again. She began reminding me of details, kissing me.

'You know, there was something about Lauren I could never resist. Even when she was a teenager and began to visit me upstairs, I could feel her intensity. She was so lonely and desperate. Elaine wouldn't even give her room to breathe. I knew it was crazy to get involved with her, but Lauren was such a seductive creature. When she moved to Branson I was almost relieved. But she kept pleading with me to come to her—and finally, I gave in. I love Chris. I do. And I was always straight. But desire can be a kind of madness.

'Anyway, that day, when she started kissing me, I found myself kind of falling into her again. I think we both got a little bit carried away. I wasn't really going back to her. It was too hard on Therese the last time. But I may have been agreeing with Lauren, saying that maybe I would go back with her. I didn't really mean it. It was just in the passion of the moment.

'Therese saw it all and just flipped. She ran in and grabbed a knife. She started stabbing Lauren. I was so shocked. I know how frail she looks, but she was out of control. It was like a frenzy. I just froze. Lauren couldn't get away. She was hobbled by the surgery. She never had a chance.

'It was my fault, really. Therese hadn't known about my affair with Lauren. But my leaving had put her through so much pain. She thought it was going to begin all over again.'

'Holy shit,' said Alex. 'That poor kid.'

'I had no idea she was capable of such a thing. I'm sure she didn't know either.'

'What did you do?' Alex asked.

'I hurried her out of there. Back upstairs. I cleaned her up and we left the building. Didn't come back till late.'

'And you let Dory take the blame,' said Alex.

'I was only thinking about Therese. I didn't know that Dory was going to be arrested,' said Joy. 'Don't bother trying to make me feel worse than I already do.'

Suddenly Alex realized what Joy had been doing at

the stove. She smelled gas. 'Joy, for God's sake. Turn the gas off.'

Joy shook her head. 'I have to do this. To protect Therese. Everything has just spun out of control. I have got to put a stop to it. You have to be prevented from spreading this story around about my affair with Lauren. Sooner or later, someone will believe it and it will lead them, inevitably, to Therese. She doesn't deserve that. This was all my fault anyway. I was playing with fire. I just kept thinking I wouldn't get caught and I never did, until it was too late.'

'Doesn't Chris know?'

'No, actually, he doesn't. He was always an innocent. I have to protect him too. He still thinks I was on a yoga retreat all those years ago. Of course, he assumed I was involved with an instructor or something. But when I came to my senses and left Lauren, he took me back without any question.'

The smell of the gas was beginning to seep into the corners of the room and make Alex's stomach churn. It would not be long before the slightest spark would cause an explosion. Just then, Joy took a lighter from her pocket and held it up. She placed it in the palm of her hand and stared at it.

'You'll be killed too if you strike that thing!' Alex cried.

'That's the idea,' said Joy flatly.

Alex's stomach swooped down. 'You're going to kill us both?'

'It will end all the questions, for once and for all. I owe Therese that much. I left a note, confessing to Lauren's murder. No one will be able to blame Therese.'

'Why do I have to die for your crimes?' Alex protested.

'Because it's your fault all of this came out in the first place. If you had minded your own business and not come barging into our lives, none of this would have happened. Dory would probably still be in prison…But no, you had to find your sister. And then you had to start digging up the past. Therese is not going to pay the price for your idle curiosity. You know what they say—curiosity killed the cat,' said Joy.

Alex felt her heart thud again. There was no reasoning with someone who thought this way. But she had to try. 'You know, you're not doing Therese any favors. She'll always have to live with the guilt of what she did,' she said.

'Sometimes I think she doesn't even remember what she did. But, no matter what, she won't have to rot in prison for it,' said Joy. 'At least she'll have a shot at a good life. And look on the bright side. They'll know that Dory didn't hurt you. And she will be free.'

Just then there was a knock at the front door.

Joy froze. 'Who is it?'

'I don't know,' Alex said truthfully.

'They'll go away.'

'I doubt it,' said Alex. 'They can see my car in the driveway.'

Joy sighed. 'All right. I'll get rid of them.' She reached into the kitchen drawer of dishtowels and pulled out a clean dishrag. 'Open up,' she said.

Alex tried to keep her mouth clamped shut.

'I said, open up!' Joy cried, whacking Alex on the side of the head with the bottom of the skillet.

Alex's mouth opened in a cry and Joy stuffed the wadded dishrag inside. Then she ran down the hall to the front door. Alex could hear her open the door.

'Ms Woods,' said a low, rumbling voice. 'Alex Woods.'

'I'm Alex Woods,' said Joy.

There was a moment's silence. Then the man said, 'No, you ain't.'

Joy murmured something but the man persisted. ''Less there's two of you.'

Joy faked an airy laugh. It came out sounding tragic.
'I'm kidding. We're cousins,' she said.

'I smell gas,' he said.

THIRTY-TWO

'I DON'T SMELL ANYTHING,' Joy said.

Yes, it's gas. Help. Alex tried to cry out through the gag in her mouth. All that emerged were grunting noises. She tried to dislodge the dishrag with her tongue to no avail.

'It sure smells like gas to me,' the man at the door said.

'Well, I can't help that,' Joy said impatiently. 'Is that all, officer?'

Officer? Alex thought. Was it Detective Langford, she wondered, her heart leaping up in hope. The man's voice sounded as if he might be black.

'Don't go closing that door on me,' said the man. 'Answer my question, please. Where is Alex Woods? This is her house, isn't it?'

'She's not here,' said Joy. 'Look, I really have to go.'

'Ma'am, that is gas that I smell. You better get out of this house. I can call the gas company for you from out here.'

'No, don't!' Joy cried. 'Just go away. It's fine.'

'Fine? The house could blow up.'

'I'm sure it's nothing. Maybe the flame went out on one of the burners. I'll go have a look.'

'And Ms Woods?' the man said stubbornly.

'Do you have her number?' Joy asked.

'Yeah, I do.'

'You should call her.'

'I need to talk to her face-to-face,' the man insisted.

'Can't help you with that,' said Joy. 'Now, if you don't mind…'

Alex could not hear what the man said in reply. She heard the murmur of his deep voice and then silence. She was praying that he would insist on coming in. That he would not acquiesce. After a minute, she heard Joy mutter, 'Finally.' The front door slammed shut.

Alex's heart sank. Between the smell of the gas and the rag in her mouth, she felt like she was on the verge of suffocation. And now the man at the door had given up and departed. He may have been unconvinced, but he probably wasn't about to force his way into a house where the lone occupant appeared to be a young woman. She didn't blame him. That was lawsuit territory. It could be the end of his career. But she felt as if she had lost her only hope for escape.

Maybe he'll call the gas company, she thought. And then she felt a renewed sense of futility. The gas company never responded promptly. Everybody knew that. Joy will have set off the explosion by then. At that moment Joy walked back into the kitchen.

Alex looked up at her balefully.

'That was close,' Joy said. 'For a minute I thought he was going to insist on coming in here. He doesn't realize how lucky he is. One flick of this lighter…' She had taken it from her pocket and was looking down at it as if mesmerized.

Alex's stomach churned. Was it coming now? No, she thought. Shit. I don't want to die. I'm not ready.

'Don't worry,' said Joy, picking up the tranquilizer gun from the counter and tucking it into her waistband. 'I'll knock you out before I set it off. You won't even feel it.'

Joy's phone rang, and she pulled it from another pocket.

The desperate look in her eyes softened. 'It's Therese,' she said. 'I have to take this.' She walked out of the kitchen, and, from the next room, Alex could hear the sound of her voice rising and falling. She must be saying her goodbyes,

Alex thought. How nice for her. What about my goodbyes? She thought of Seth, arriving tomorrow. A day late. She thought of the life she would never have with him, and it made her heart ache. Tears seeped out from under her closed eyelids.

All of this had happened because she had decided to search for her sister. Her mother could never have imagined that her letter, revealing Alex's long-lost sister, would lead to this. You couldn't have known, Alex thought, addressing her mother in her heart.

Suddenly Alex heard a faint tapping sound. Her eyes widened. She turned her head and looked in the direction of the porch door. Darkness had fallen over the yard outside and darkness was all she could see. That, and the reflection on the glass panes in the door of the lights from the house. And then, with a start, and a cry muffled by her gag, she realized that she was looking into a pair of eyes in the darkness. They were frowning at her. Peering past the reflections in the glass, she made out the contours of a face.

It was a black man, looking in. He was wearing something dark, and was rendered almost invisible in the night. But his electric gaze was sweeping the room. He looked straight into Alex's eyes again and pressed a finger to his lips.

Alex stared back at him. She looked in the direction of the dining room. She could still hear Joy talking on the phone, her voice strained and anxious.

The man frowned and reached down for the doorknob. He turned it, but it didn't open. Joy had locked it. And thanks to the recent visit from the locksmith, the lock was not about to disengage easily.

Alex looked at him helplessly. From his place out on the porch, he was studying the kitchen, searching for something. Alex glanced back toward the murmuring voice in the other room.

The man outside the door fastened his gaze on a waist-high, rolling wooden cart beside Alex. Alex followed his gaze. The open cart had always served as a makeshift bar for her parents. There were several bottles of alcohol on it, the liquid inside them at varying heights. There was also a pair of shot glasses, some wine glasses and two brandy snifters.

The man at the door gestured to Alex. She did not understand what he was trying to convey. She shook her head. He pointed to the glass pane in the door nearest the doorknob. Then he pantomimed breaking the glass and reaching inside. At last, Alex understood what he was saying. He was going to break the pane, reach through and unlock the door from the inside. She watched him, hope and fear mixed in her gaze.

Then he pointed to Alex and from her, to the whiskey cart beside her. He jerked his body as if to show her what to do. It took her a minute to read his signals. He wanted her to knock into the cart. For a moment she couldn't comprehend why he would want her to do this. She looked at him helplessly, shaking her head. The man stood still for a moment, thinking. Then he pretended to lift a glass to his lips. He used his large fingers in a dainty fashion to indicate that it was a glass with a stem. A wine glass. She frowned as he pretended to hurl the glass to the ground. As Alex watched him closely, he pointed from his invisible broken glass to the top of the rolling bar cart. Then it came to her. There were glasses on the cart. He wanted her to knock the glasses off the cart so they would break on the tiled floor. Why? she wondered. She felt confused, the oppressive smell of the gas making it difficult to think.

The man seemed to sense her confusion. He patiently

pointed to glasses on the cart and then to himself, pantomiming once again, the act of breaking the glass pane in the door. Suddenly Alex got it. Aha! she thought. She understood. When the glasses fell, their breaking would cover the sound of the door pane breaking. Alex sagged with relief that she finally knew what he meant. When Joy heard the glass break, she would rush into the kitchen. If her attention weren't diverted, Joy would instantly see Alex's rescuer opening the door. This diversion of breaking the glasses on the bar cart might give the man a short but necessary window of time to enter the house.

Alex got it. She nodded and shifted her chair slightly. Alex didn't dare scrape it too far along the floor. If Joy heard that she would be in here in a flash, her lighter at the ready. She just moved a few inches closer to the cart so that she would be in position to knock the glasses off it.

The man raised three fingers. Alex understood. On the count of three. She nodded again. The man grimly mimed a fist bump. Then he raised one finger. Two. Three. On three, Alex used her shoulder, her side and even the back of the chair to crash into the cart.

There was the sound of smashing glass.

Joy came running in, still holding the phone in her hand. 'What was that?'

Alex looked sheepishly at the broken snifters on the floor.

'What did you do that for?' Joy asked.

Alex looked down at the broken glass.

'You think you're going to cut yourself loose? Use them as a weapon maybe? Forget it, Alex. You can't stop me. This is the end for us. Use your time to say your prayers.' Joy turned her back on Alex and put the phone back to her ear.

'All right, sweetie,' Joy said. 'I have to go now. But I want you to remember how much I love you. Don't ever forget.'

The man on the porch reached through the door pane and unlocked the door. Alex made as loud a gargling sound as possible in her throat to cover the click of the lock.

The next moments seemed to pass in slow motion. The man pushed the door open as Joy turned and suddenly realized what was happening. Alex saw, as if from underwater, the door banging open. The man, who was wearing a midnight-blue uniform, lunged across the room and tackled Joy before she could react. Her phone skittered across the tiles, landing near Alex.

'No,' Joy wailed. 'Let me go. I have to do this.'

But Mr S. Robinson, for Alex recognized him at last, was huge and strong, and in no mood to be blown sky-high. 'Sorry, lady. Not gonna happen today.' He pressed Joy's face to the floor, straddled her and, with one hand, took his handcuffs off his belt and fastened them around her wrists. Then he stood up, dragging Joy to her feet, and hauled her out onto the porch where he shoved her roughly into a chair. She began to weep, crying out in frustration.

He came back inside, rushed to the stove and turned off the gas. He ran to the windows and threw them open. Finally he picked up Alex, chair and all, and half-dragged, half-carried her out onto the porch, leaving the door wide open. He removed her gag.

Alex gasped and drank in the air. Her lungs ached, but her heart rose up like a balloon. 'Thank you,' she gasped.

Joy slid from the chair to the floor, on her knees, wailing.

'She has a tranquilizer gun. And a lighter,' Alex said.

Robinson crouched down and patted Joy's pockets. He tucked the gun into his own waistband and pulled out the lighter. He slipped it into his own pocket. 'Not anymore she don't,' he said.

'I was so afraid you were going to leave,' Alex said.

The man shook his head as he untied her. 'No. But I

could tell that, for some reason, she didn't care if she ended up in an explosion. I had to be careful.'

'You're right. She was planning to blow us both up.'

The man exhaled. 'Whew. What's she got against you?'

'It's a long story,' said Alex.

'I'm gonna call for some help here,' he said.

Alex nodded as the man opened the door to the porch and went out on the steps. He fished his phone from the pocket of his jacket and punched in 911. Alex shook out her arms and legs and looked in amazement at Joy, who had tumbled all the way over onto the porch floor, her hands cuffed behind her. Her face was streaked and puffy with tears.

'What have I done to my baby?' Joy cried.

'Stop it,' Alex said. 'At least you're still alive. She still has you.'

'Her life will be ruined. I can't stand to watch it.'

'You think that Therese would be better off living her life with that terrible secret? She's already suffering. Stop feeling so sorry for yourself.'

'FUCK YOU!' Joy screamed.

'Scream all you want,' said Alex. 'It's over.'

Mr Robinson ended his call and came back to the porch.

Alex rubbed her liberated wrists and studied his face. 'I recognize you,' she said. 'You're the guard from the county jail.'

'Yes, ma'am,' he said.

'How did you find me?' Alex asked.

Robinson sighed. 'You gave me all your information at the jail,' he said. 'Remember?'

'That's right,' said Alex. 'That's right. God, I'm so lucky that you showed up here.' And then Alex was struck with an alarming thought. 'Wait a minute. Why did you show up here?' she asked.

Officer Robinson grimaced. 'I need to talk to you about your sister,' he said.

'Dory? What about her?' Alex asked.

'Well, when you visited her earlier, you made such a fuss about her being depressed. You said that if we didn't watch out for her you'd be all over us. I'm ashamed that we kind of blew off your concern. 'Cause you were right. I figured I had better come over here and tell you what happened in person.'

Alex stared at him, hardly daring to ask. She was trembling from head to toe. 'Right about what?' she asked.

'I'm sorry, Ms Woods. You weren't gone half an hour when your sister hanged herself in her cell.'

THIRTY-THREE

'No!' ALEX CRIED. 'No. She's dead?'

'She's not dead,' said Robinson. 'Thanks to you, she's not dead. After you came around raising hell like that, Witkowski decided to go and make an unscheduled check on her cell. He found her just in time. She'd used her bedsheet to make a noose. She's in the hospital though.'

'Oh my God. Is she gonna live?' Alex asked.

Robinson nodded. 'Luckily she didn't snap her neck. And didn't have time to asphyxiate herself. The doctor said she's gonna be all right. I swear, it was just luck that you came by and raised hell about that. It turns out you were right on the money.'

'Oh, Lord,' said Alex. 'Oh, Dory.' She turned on Joy who was still on the floor, sniffling. 'This is your fault,' she said. 'You framed her. Both times. Did you hide that knife so it would look like Dory was the one who attacked me?'

Joy nodded, her body shuddering with quiet sobs. 'I had to,' she said.

Alex glared at her. 'You have not done Therese any favors. Although you're probably more likely to go to jail than she is.'

Joy stared ahead blankly and did not reply.

Alex turned to Officer Robinson. 'Look, I shouldn't ask you for another thing, but I don't think I can drive. I'm too shaken up. Could I ask you to take me to the hospital where Dory is?'

'Sure. That's one reason I came by. I figured you might

need someone to take you there. It seems like the least I could do. But we have to stay here a little longer until the police arrive. They're going to want to question you.'

'How long will that take?' Alex asked.

'Not too long, I hope,' he said. 'Try calling the hospital.'

'Which one? I don't even know where she is.'

Officer Robinson took her phone and began to punch numbers into it. He handed the phone to Alex. 'At least you can check on her condition.'

There were sirens approaching and it sounded as if the noise was going to engulf the house. Alex put a finger in her ear and waited while the phone rang.

'Boston General,' said a pleasant voice.

'Hi,' said Alex. 'I'm calling to check on my sister's condition. She was brought in to emergency this evening.'

While Alex sat on hold, listening to a classical music quartet, a phalanx of policemen entered the house, led by Officer Robinson who had greeted them at the door. Robinson pointed out Joy, who was curled up on the porch floor, seemingly oblivious to the cold night air.

'This woman was planning to blow up this house and everything in it. Including herself and this young woman over here on the phone. I found this one gagged and tied to a chair.'

Alex's call had reached the nurse's station. 'I'm calling about my sister, Dory Colson. They brought her in earlier.'

The nurse hesitated. 'This the one they brought in from the prison?'

'That's the one,' said Alex.

'She's stable. But she's not leaving. She's under observation in the psych wing.'

'Thank you,' said Alex. At least she's stable. That was some consolation, she thought. Before she gave the phone back to Officer Robinson, she made one more call. The phone rang and a woman picked up.

'Elaine,' said Alex.

'Yes?'

'This is Alex. I'm calling about Dory. She attempted suicide at the jail this evening.'

There was a silence from Elaine's end of the phone.

'She tried to hang herself but luckily they found her in time. She's at Boston General. She's stable. She'll survive.'

'Why are you telling me this?' asked Elaine in a confrontational tone, although her voice was shaky.

'You're her mother. I thought you would want to know,' said Alex. 'I thought you also might want to know that Joy tried to blow up my house this evening. With me in it.'

'Joy? Our Joy?'

Our Joy? Alex thought. What about our Dory? 'Yes, your Joy. She tried to kill me. She's about to be arrested for that. Also for stabbing me in the back last week and hiding the knife in Dory's room,' said Alex. It was undeniably gratifying, relating all this to Elaine.

'I don't understand,' said Elaine weakly.

'Well, it's a long story, which will all come out in due time. But I'll tell you right now. Dory had nothing to do with Lauren's death. That's for sure.'

'How do you know that?' Elaine demanded.

'Because now I know who her killer was.'

'Who?' Elaine demanded anxiously. 'You have to tell me what you know.'

Alex looked up at the detective in charge, who was waiting to talk to her. She liked the idea of Elaine having to wait. How long had she made Dory wait? 'I can't talk now. I have to go,' Alex said. 'I have to go get my dog free. She locked him in the shed out back. I just called to let you know about Dory.'

IT WAS ALMOST an hour before the police were finished with Alex and Joy had been taken away, under arrest for attempted murder. Alex looked regretfully at Officer Robinson. 'It's late. You probably want to get home,' she said. 'You'll miss dinner.'

Officer Robinson shook his head. 'I promised I'd take you to the hospital,' he said.

'I can get a cab,' Alex demurred.

'You can get a cab home,' he said. 'Once you get over there, they may try to tell you that it's too late for you to see her. I can smooth the way with that.'

Alex thanked him profusely and, in a few minutes, she was in the car and on her way to Boston General.

As Robinson had predicted, the nurses on duty told Alex she was too late and couldn't visit at this hour. They immediately deferred, however, to the oversized corrections officer who insisted that Alex be allowed in to Dory's room. As Alex reached the doorway, Officer Robinson greeted the uniformed corrections officer who was standing guard there. 'Hey,' he said, 'I am going to head home now. Hannity here will help you. Whatever you need.'

Alex held out a hand to Robinson and he shook it. 'I can never thank you enough,' she said. 'I owe you my life, for heaven's sake.'

'Buy me a hero sandwich one of these days,' he said, 'and we'll call it even.'

'You're on,' she said.

He waved as he disappeared down the hall and around the corner to the elevators. Alex waved for as long as she could see him and then, giving Hannity a shaky smile, she took a deep breath and tiptoed into Dory's room.

Dory had been looking out into the darkness but she turned her head when Alex came in and fixed her with a vacant stare.

'Dory,' Alex exclaimed. She rushed to the side of Dory's bed and peered down at her. She put a gentle hand on Dory's shoulder. There was an abrasion on Dory's neck that was turning purple. 'Oh my God, Dory. I'm so glad they found you in time.'

'How did you know I was here?' Dory asked dully.

'Somebody from the jail told me. It doesn't matter. I'll tell you all that when you're better. There's just one thing that I have to tell you right now: you're not going back to jail. These charges against you are going to be dropped, just like the other ones were. You're going to walk out of this hospital free and clear.'

Dory looked at her blankly.

'I mean it, Dory,' said Alex. 'Joy has been arrested for attacking me and for hiding the knife in your room. The police know it was her. They may have dropped the charges already.'

'Joy?' Dory asked. 'Joy Ennis?'

Alex looked at the door and then back at the frail woman on the bed. 'It's all going to come out. She told me what happened. It was Therese who killed your sister. She killed Lauren. Everything Joy did was to cover up for what Therese had done.'

Alex expected to see surprise. Relief. She did not know what form it would take—smiles or tears—but she certainly expected one or the other. What she did not expect was the grave, unchanging look of hopelessness in Dory's eyes.

Dory frowned and turned her head to the window. The view from her room was a blur of lights on the expressway below. Dory looked out at the moving traffic under the inky sky without speaking.

Alex pulled up a chair and sat down beside her sister. She wondered if perhaps Dory had sustained some kind of cognitive impairment from the lack of oxygen she suffered before they found her, hanging in her cell. 'Dory. Do you understand what I'm saying to you?'

'Yes. I think so,' said Dory. 'Therese. Why? Why would Therese hurt Lauren? Lauren was her idol.'

'Well, it turns out that Joy and your sister were secretly lovers. When everyone thought Joy left her family to go to a yoga retreat, she was actually living with Lauren. The day that Lauren died she was trying to convince Joy to come back to her, to move back to Branson with her. Therese overheard it and flipped out.'

'Wow,' said Dory thoughtfully.

'Joy just reacted. She thought she was protecting Therese. And she didn't care who got hurt.'

'Meaning me,' said Dory dully.

'Yes. She sacrificed you for her daughter. And when you were set free from prison, she attacked me to try to blame you. To have you sent back. She didn't care what happened to anybody but her daughter.'

'That's what mothers do, right?' said Dory bleakly.

'But it's all going to come out now. At least now we know who really killed Lauren.'

'That's good,' said Dory.

'Thank God you didn't succeed with this,' said Alex, putting her hand over her own throat. 'You are cleared, once and for all.'

'I wonder if my mother will believe it,' Dory said, a rueful note in her voice.

'She'll have to believe it. She won't have any choice,' said Alex impatiently.

'I guess not,' said Dory in a dull, scratchy voice.

Alex nodded. 'Well, I guess it will take a little while for all this to sink in. It's got to be a little bewildering.'

'I hope it won't upset her too much. She loves Therese

like a grandchild. I don't know how she'll take this news,' Dory murmured.

'Therese is not her child,' said Alex with a trace of bitterness.

Dory nodded slightly. 'No one believed me,' she said.

'I know,' said Alex, blushing. 'You're right. I'm so sorry about that.'

'Doesn't matter,' said Dory.

Alex reached over and covered Dory's hand with her own. Dory's was icy cold. 'Everyone will believe you now,' she said.

Dory sighed. 'Maybe.'

'Look, Dory. When you get out of here,' said Alex, 'I want you to come back home with me. You can stay there as long as you like. Remus keeps looking for you.' Alex didn't actually know that to be true, but she felt as if Dory needed something to hold on to. Something to give her the will to recover. Alex wasn't about to tell her that Joy had tranquilized Remus and locked him up. There would be time to explain all the details another day.

Dory's faint smile came and went, like a fleeting ray of sun on a cloudy day. 'He's a good dog,' she said.

'He really is,' said Alex.

An awkward silence fell between them. Dory seemed to have no further interest in all that had happened. No more questions about the events which had led to her exoneration.

Finally Dory sighed. 'Well, you better get going. Remus will need walking.'

'You're right about that,' Alex said.

There was a rustling noise near the door of Dory's room and voices in the hallway. Dory glanced past Alex in the direction of the door, and suddenly there was a stunning change of expression on her face. Her eyes widened in surprise, and then a smile began to break across her face like the dawn.

Garth and Elaine had entered the room. Garth was holding his hat and steering Elaine by the elbow. His eyes were fastened onto the pale figure in the bed. Elaine hung back, looking frightened.

'Hey, darlin',' Garth breathed. He came over to the bedside, leaned down and scooped Dory carefully up in his arms. 'Wow, I'm glad you're OK.'

While her father embraced her, Dory stared past his shoulder at Elaine.

Garth reluctantly loosened his grip and let Dory back down onto the pillow.

'Dory has company, Garth,' said Elaine, nodding toward Alex.

'It doesn't matter,' said Dory hastily.

Alex tried not to take offense. She stood up. 'Well, I need to be going anyway.' She stepped away from the chair and offered it to Elaine.

Elaine sat down. Immediately Dory reached out a hand to her. 'Mom. You're here,' she whispered.

Elaine hesitated and then took the proffered hand. 'You're like ice,' Elaine observed. But she continued to let her hand rest in Dory's.

'OK. I'm gonna go. I'll be back to see you tomorrow,' said Alex to Dory. 'Remember what I said about staying with me.'

Dory nodded but did not reply. She was oblivious to everything but those intertwined hands on the bedsheet. Elaine frowned and shifted uneasily in her chair. But she did not let go.

EPILOGUE

'Do you know when Dory will be back?' Alex asked.

Elaine glanced at the clock and shook her head.

'She should be here now. Maybe something happened with one of the dogs.'

Alex nodded and nibbled at the cookie which Garth had offered when they arrived. She glanced at Seth, who looked relaxed in the other corner of the sofa, eating his third cookie.

'These are great, Elaine,' he said.

'Thank you.'

'So,' said Garth, rubbing his jeans with his open palms. 'I hear you two are planning on making it official.'

'That's right,' said Seth.

'Well, I wish you all the best,' said Garth.

'Thanks,' said Seth.

Alex said nothing. After Dory got out of the hospital, she moved directly back into the Colsons' apartment, explaining to Alex that she wanted to revive her pet-sitting business and it was easier to do it right there, in the South End. At first, Alex saw Dory regularly. They would have lunch while she was working at the gallery, or Dory would come out to Chichester for dinner. Dory's depression seemed to have lifted, and she reported that she was feeling good and making plans for her future. But lately she seemed glum and evasive, and no matter how often Alex had invited her to come to dinner Dory always had an excuse. She had to get up too early the next day, or she couldn't get the truck from her dad, or she wasn't feeling well. Finally, with her upcoming wedding to Seth, Alex had the perfect reason to pay Dory a visit. She asked Seth to come along, partly for moral support, and partly because she had come to trust his impressions of people.

'Right, Elaine?' said Garth. 'We're happy for these two.'

'Of course,' said Elaine.

'I'm kind of glad that Dory's not here,' said Alex. 'I wanted to talk to the two of you. How do you think she is doing?' she asked. 'Do you think she's gotten over the trauma of all that happened?'

Garth glanced uneasily at Elaine, but Elaine stared straight back at Alex. 'She's fine,' said Elaine. 'She's perfectly fine. There's nothing for you to be concerned about.'

'Now, honey,' said Garth, 'you and I were talking about her moodiness just the other day. I'm sure Alex is worried about her the way any sister would be.' He looked earnestly at Alex. 'I think it's nice of you to care.'

'There's no question that these days life is very different around here. With the changes in our building,' Elaine said in a faintly accusatory tone.

'Dory told me that Chris Ennis moved out to be near the prison where Joy is waiting for her trial, and the group home where Therese has been placed,' said Alex.

'Yes,' said Elaine tartly. 'We have some very noisy students upstairs now.'

'That's too bad,' said Seth. 'Although, after what happened, I can't imagine you all living in the same building any longer.'

'No, of course not,' said Elaine.

'I imagine you miss Therese though,' said Alex.

Elaine looked at her indignantly. 'Miss Therese? After what she did to Lauren? I hardly think so.'

'I know, but after all those years of treating her like a granddaughter...'

Garth's face seemed to lose all its color and he quickly, furtively wiped his eyes with the heel of his hand.

'Therese is dead to me now,' said Elaine angrily. 'I never think about her.'

Just then the front door opened and slammed shut again, and the heavy thud of boots being kicked off could be heard upstairs.

'I'm home!' Dory cried out. She appeared at the top of the steps in her stocking feet. Her strawberry-blonde hair was pinned up in a messy knot, and she could have passed, from a distance, for a teenager. She was wearing an old, shapeless sweater and jeans, the colors of which were dulled by a gossamer layer of animal fur. She was carrying a bouquet of flowers. 'Mom, I brought you...' She stopped short when she saw Alex and Seth sitting with her parents in the great room.

Alex was actually surprised at how happy she was to see her. 'Dory,' she said. She stood up and reached out to embrace her.

Dory looked anxiously at her mother, and then back at Alex. 'Oh, no,' she said, pulling away. 'I'm covered with dog hair.'

'So am I,' said Alex, insisting on a hug. 'Remus is missing you.'

Dory's smile was painful. 'That's good,' she said. 'I mean, good that he still thinks of me.'

'Regina called me the other day. She said she's got a beauty of a pup and she's hoping for someone to adopt him.'

'Are you going to take him?' Dory asked.

'Not me. I meant you.'

'No. Not in this house,' Elaine said immediately.

'I thought the only reason you couldn't have pets was because of Lauren,' said Alex.

'I'm not adopting anyone else's problems,' said Elaine. 'Thank you very much.' If Elaine was sorry for how cruel her remark sounded, given Dory's origins, she gave no indication of it.

Dory's gaze was blank. 'I don't need a dog,' she said.

'Maybe when you get your own place,' said Garth encouragingly.

'Are you moving?' Alex asked.

Dory looked taken aback. 'No,' she said.

Alex nodded. 'Oh. Well, never mind.'

'Mom, I brought you these flowers,' said Dory. 'Down by the Back Bay station.'

Elaine looked at the flowers without expression. 'There's a vase under the sink, Dory. Put them in water or they'll die.'

Dory obediently went to the sink and rummaged around for the vase. Alex walked over to her. Seth, understanding his mission, began to talk to Garth about an old church which was being demolished in Dorchester.

'Hey,' said Alex. 'How are you doing?'

'Good,' said Dory, nodding. She took out two vases and compared them, holding the bouquet against each one.

'I haven't seen you in so long,' said Alex.

'I know,' said Dory. 'Which one do you think?'

'This one,' said Alex.

Dory put the other vase away and began to fill Alex's choice with water. 'So, you just decided to drop by? My mother always says to call first.'

'Your mother's right. I should have,' said Alex. 'But there was something I wanted to ask you. Seth and I have set a date for the wedding.'

Dory nodded, unsmiling. 'Congratulations.'

'Thanks. It's only going to be a small affair, but I still need a maid of honor. I was wondering if you might want to do it. Be my maid of honor.'

Dory looked surprised, and then a smile broke slowly in her eyes. 'Really? You want me to do it?'

'Yes,' said Alex. 'You're my sister.'

Dory glanced over at Elaine, who was watching her. 'Wow. That's really nice of you,' she said.

'Will you do it?'

Dory sighed, and then squared her shoulders. 'Sure. I'll do it.'

'You may have to go shopping with me. Try on dresses.'

'I guess I can do that,' said Dory.

Alex embraced her once again, and Dory endured it stiffly.

Elaine came over and took the vase of flowers from the side of the sink. 'These are lovely,' she said.

Dory beamed. 'You like them?'

'Of course I like them,' said Elaine. 'What's going on over here?'

'Alex asked me to be in her wedding.'

'How nice. What did you say?' Elaine asked.

'I said…OK. Probably,' said Dory.

Elaine nodded. Her expression was placid. Alex could see no sign of judgment in it. She took the vase of flowers and carefully placed them in the center of the table.

Dory looked at Alex apologetically. 'I'm not positive. Can I call you about it?'

Alex looked at Elaine. She felt as if Elaine had emitted some warning signal to Dory that was undetectable outside of Elaine's sphere of influence. Dory suddenly looked miserable. Elaine returned Alex's gaze with a mixture of triumph and disgust in her eyes.

Alex closed her eyes for a moment and then turned to
Seth. 'OK. We'd better be going,' she said.

As soon as they left the apartment and began to walk, arm
in arm, toward the car, Alex began to sputter. 'I'm telling
you,' she said, 'it's like she's a prisoner there. She was all
set to agree. She was happy to be asked, and then one sidelong glance from Elaine…'

'She's thirty-two years old, Alex,' he said. 'If she wants
to leave, I'm sure no one would stop her.'

'It's as if nothing has changed. Even though they now
know that Dory was not to blame for Lauren's death, they
treat her as if she is still…not to be trusted.'

Seth shrugged. 'You always thought Elaine treated her
that way because of Lauren's death. I suspect that she has
always treated her the same way.'

'It's not fair!' Alex cried. 'She needs to get away from
that woman. I mean, Garth's nice enough. Ineffectual, but
nice enough. Elaine though…'

'She doesn't want to get away from Elaine,' said Seth.
'That's her life's work. Trying to get Elaine to love her.'

'Do you really think that?' she asked.

'Yes,' he said. 'I do.'

'It's never gonna happen, is it?' said Alex.

Seth tightened his arm around her and shook his head.
'Nope.'

'That's so sad,' said Alex.

They walked on in silence for a little ways. Then Alex
said, 'Should I just leave her alone? Maybe Elaine is making Dory's life more miserable when she sees me. I think
Elaine believes that my meddling in Dory's life brought
about this whole collapse of their world. Now Therese is
gone and she has Dory at home again, and there is no way

that she is happy about it. I think Elaine was happier when Dory was in prison and she could blame it all on her.'

'It does seem that way,' he said.

'Maybe that's why Dory has been so scarce lately.'

'I wouldn't be surprised,' he said. 'She probably has to pay a price for spending time with you.'

Alex sighed. 'I don't want to make her life worse.'

'You're not, Alex,' he said. 'You're trying to be a sister to her. And she needs you, whether she knows it or not. Someday she may come to her senses and realize how futile it is to try and please that woman. If it's ever gonna happen, somebody has to be on her side.'

'But you just said that it would never happen.'

'Well, I'm trying to be realistic. That sick relationship with Elaine is pretty strong. But that doesn't mean I think you should give up. Elaine would like to keep you out of Dory's life. Isolate her. It's easier to torment her that way, with no one to object. But if you're not in Dory's life, who will be there for her?'

'You're right. I have to try,' said Alex.

Seth nodded. 'We'll keep trying.'

'We?' she asked.

'We're in this together,' he said. 'Right?'

'Right,' she said.

Alex thought about her mother's letter, offering her a sister she didn't know she had. She had wanted Alex to have a sister to depend on. The sister Alex had found had turned out to be something much more complicated. But still, Alex felt there was a connection between them that defied explanation. She knew that her mother had worried that Alex would not have a family to rely on, to lean on, to celebrate with. Alex glanced at Seth's profile. I have you, she thought, full of gratitude. You are my family now.

She huddled closer to him as they walked through the

cold in the darkening twilight. We are a family, Mom, she thought. Seth and I. And children some day, and a home. A life together. This is the family you wanted me to have. And as for the sister you wanted me to have? As for Dory?

Dory has us both.

* * * * *

REQUEST YOUR FREE BOOKS!

2 FREE NOVELS
PLUS 2 FREE GIFTS!

WORLDWIDE LIBRARY®
Your Partner in Crime

WWL13R

REQUEST YOUR FREE BOOKS!
2 FREE NOVELS PLUS 2 FREE GIFTS!

HARLEQUIN®

INTRIGUE®

BREATHTAKING ROMANTIC SUSPENSE

YES! Please send me 2 FREE Harlequin Intrigue® novels and my 2 FREE gifts (gifts are worth about $10). After receiving them, if I don't wish to receive any more books, I can return the shipping statement marked "cancel." If I don't cancel, I will receive 6 brand-new novels every month and be billed just $4.74 per book in the U.S. or $5.24 per book in Canada. That's a savings of at least 14% off the cover price! It's quite a bargain! Shipping and handling is just 50¢ per book in the U.S. and 75¢ per book in Canada.* I understand that accepting the 2 free books and gifts places me under no obligation to buy anything. I can always return a shipment and cancel at any time. Even if I never buy another book, the two free books and gifts are mine to keep forever.

182/382 HDN F43C

Name	(PLEASE PRINT)
Address	Apt. #
City	State/Prov.	Zip/Postal Code

Signature (if under 18, a parent or guardian must sign)

Mail to the **Harlequin® Reader Service:**
IN U.S.A.: P.O. Box 1867, Buffalo, NY 14240-1867
IN CANADA: P.O. Box 609, Fort Erie, Ontario L2A 5X3

**Are you a subscriber to Harlequin Intrigue books
and want to receive the larger-print edition?
Call 1-800-873-8635 or visit www.ReaderService.com.**

* Terms and prices subject to change without notice. Prices do not include applicable taxes. Sales tax applicable in N.Y. Canadian residents will be charged applicable taxes. Offer not valid in Quebec. This offer is limited to one order per household. Not valid for current subscribers to Harlequin Intrigue books. All orders subject to credit approval. Credit or debit balances in a customer's account(s) may be offset by any other outstanding balance owed by or to the customer. Please allow 4 to 6 weeks for delivery. Offer available while quantities last.

Your Privacy—The Harlequin® Reader Service is committed to protecting your privacy. Our Privacy Policy is available online at www.ReaderService.com or upon request from the Harlequin Reader Service.

We make a portion of our mailing list available to reputable third parties that offer products we believe may interest you. If you prefer that we not exchange your name with third parties, or if you wish to clarify or modify your communication preferences, please visit us at www.ReaderService.com/consumerchoice or write to us at Harlequin Reader Service Preference Service, P.O. Box 9062, Buffalo, NY 14269. Include your complete name and address.

ReaderService.com

Manage your account online!

- Review your order history
- Manage your payments
- Update your address

---

*We've designed
the Harlequin® Reader Service
website just for you.*

Enjoy all the features!

- Reader excerpts from any series
- Respond to mailings and
  special monthly offers
- Discover new series available to you
- Browse the Bonus Bucks catalog
- Share your feedback

Visit us at:

ReaderService.com